I0660824

Heinrich Zschokke, M.A. Faber

The Princess of Brunswick-Wolfenbüttel

And other tales

Heinrich Zschokke, M.A. Faber

The Princess of Brunswick-Wolfenbüttel
And other tales

ISBN/EAN: 9783337070823

Printed in Europe, USA, Canada, Australia, Japan

Cover: Foto ©Andreas Hilbeck / pixelio.de

More available books at **www.hansebooks.com**

THE PRINCESS

OF

BRUNSWICK-WOLFENBÜTTEL

AND OTHER TALES

BY

HEINRICH ZSCHOKKE.

FROM THE GERMAN
BY
M. A. FABER.

LEIPZIG 1867
BERNHARD TAUCHNITZ.

LONDON: SAMPSON LOW, MARSTON, LOW & SEARLE.
CROWN BUILDINGS, 188, FLEET STREET.
PARIS: C. REINWALD & Cⁱᵉ, 15, RUE DES SAINTS PÈRES.

THE PRINCESS

OF

BRUNSWICK-WOLFENBÜTTEL.

THE subject-matter of this tale is no longer unknown. Travellers and historians have mentioned the extraordinary occurrences narrated in these pages. The world was first made acquainted with them, together with many additional details, by an unknown author in "Pièces interessantes et peu connues, pour servir à l'Histoire," &c. &c. The Chevalier le Bossu relates them in almost the same terms in his "Nouveaux voyages d'Amerique septentrionale." Yet to him they seemed to border on the fabulous. "Je vous avoue," he says at page 48, "que quoique je tienne tous ces faits d'un *assez grand nombre* de personnes *dignes de foi*, je ne voudrais cependant pas en garantir l'authenticité."

Russian historians conceal the facts, or narrate them only as they were officially made public. Peter Henry Bruce even relates the death of the Grand Duchess with a minuteness that scarcely allows one to doubt its truth.

In the Magazine entitled "Flora," dedicated to the daughters of Germany (in May of the year 1797), is also to be found, under the title, "The German Princess," an abridgment of the story, together with some added particulars respecting the last residence of the Princess in Europe.

1*

' BOOK THE FIRST.

———

THE CHEVALIER D'AUBANT TO LAURENCE BELLISLE.

Petersburg, 13th August 1714.

AT last, dear Bellisle, at last my wishes are gratified! I shall soon return to your arms, to spend some months with you upon your property in the bosom of the country and of nature. Oh! how impatiently I long for the moment of our first embrace! How many hundred miles is it not from hence — from the gloomy north, to the blooming fields of France!

Six months have already passed since I applied for my discharge. It was only a few days ago that I received it; and indeed, in the most gracious terms, from His Majesty the great Czar himself. I was borne on the strength of the Russian army during those memorable days at Aland, when nearly the entire Swedish fleet was captured. Fortune was propitious. I fought in the same ship with, and by the side of, the Czar, who on this occasion commanded the vanguard under Admiral Aprarin. The Swedish Vice-Admiral Ehrenschild, almost equal to us in force, opened the attack, whilst he ordered a frigate to the front to note our strength and movements. Soon the conflict became general; soon a thousand guns from the ships thundered death and destruction against each other. The Czar, in the midst of fire, smoke, and

death, was as cool—I might say gay—as though (like
the Salamander in the fire) he were moving in his
native element. He was by turns now sailor, now
general, now helmsman, now soldier. The fearful
combat lasted for two hours. Corpses and pieces of
wreck danced on the wild waves; whilst, to increase the
terrible misery, the cannons still boomed unceasingly.
By a bold turn we succeeded in getting the weather-
gage of the enemy's fleet, in disuniting it, in surrounding one portion of it among rocks, and in bringing it into the harbour of Abo.·

The Czar was more delighted at this victory than
I had ever seen him. Several of the officers of highest rank came from the other ships to congratulate
him. "Who would have thought twenty years ago,"
cried the Czar, "that we Russians should this day
fight and conquer in the Baltic with ships of our own
building!"

After he had given the necessary orders for setting
sail towards the island of Aland in order to take possession of it, he ordered me to be summoned to his
presence. He signed some orders, drank off a large
glass of brandy at a draught, rose, embraced me, and
said: "Young man, you have borne yourself bravely!
What is your name?"

"Chevalier d'Aubant, your Majesty."

"Good! You shall be promoted to be colonel.
Go to your post, and serve me in the future as well
as you have done to-day."

The goodness of the Czar affected me deeply.
But I took advantage of this favourable moment to
ask for my discharge. I told him the most essential
points of my connexion with France, of the death of

my father, and of the necessity for my return home
in order to arrange the pecuniary affairs of my family,
which were in confusion. The monarch listened to
me in silence, then pressed my hand, and said: "I
am unwilling to lose brave men; but go, I will not
forbid it."

Soon afterwards, immediately on our arrival in
Petersburg, my discharge was sent to me; together
with an invitation to take part in all the banquets and
festivities at court, so long as I should remain in
Petersburg. One does not willingly decline such an
invitation, and I the less, because I was compelled to
wait for a portion of my property which had been left
behind in Moscow. Meanwhile I occupied myself in
watching the new works which the Emperor multiplies
with each day; and truly one would require years
merely to run one's eye over the whole of what this
wonderful man has created in this short period. Oh!
how miserably paltry is the life of thousands of kings
in comparison with that of this single sovereign, whose
almost every hour gives birth to some gigantic undertaking!

The battle-field of Pultowa, where Peter conquered
his formidable rival, Charles XII., and shattered the
power of Sweden, has placed him in the rank of the
first generals of his age; in the waters of Aland he
has won fame as a naval commander; and has received,
from his own hand, the rank of Vice-Admiral. Eleven
years ago, in the swamps of the Neva, he laid the
foundations of a new city; he was himself surveyor
and architect — now the vast city of Petersburg extends for miles. Yet works are always going on in
it; more than forty thousand Russians, and a countless

number of Swedish prisoners of war, are daily engaged in building.

And all this, one-half of which would suffice to render any prince immortal, can only be reckoned among his less important acts. He is at the same time the legislator and reformer of his people. He is leading this barbarous northern nation into the world of civilization; he has curbed the tyrannical priests of fanaticism and superstition, has broken their power, has abolished the title of patriarch; he is himself head of the Church. He has created a new people, formed an army, built a capital for the empire, established a navy in his seas, and has erected altars to the Arts and Muses of Rome and Greece amid the forests of the Muscovite territory. Posterity can erect no monument to this man; for such could only be a worthless trifle, and a proof of the narrow mind of him who should attempt it. His own colossal monument, raised by his own hand for eternity, stands firm. Europe and Asia form its basis; its name is — Russia.

But whither am I wandering? Forgive me, dear Bellisle, if instead of a letter you receive a eulogium on the great man who, for so long as the history of the world has been written, can find no rival among all the thousand princes of the thousand nations who have existed.

Romulus and Numa did great things when they formed a well-ordered state out of a horde of robbers; but what was their petty labour by the side of the Russian Colossus, surrounded by states of a dissimilar policy? Charles the Great might perhaps enter the lists with Peter for fame, but also without hope of victory.

I am returning to France; but the recollection of all that I have beheld that is great will accompany me thither; and, beneath the gigantic standard with which I shall in future measure the merits of our ministers, generals, and princes, all that I once held worthy of admiration will dwindle into miserable insignificance. As a courtier at least I am thoroughly spoiled.

Oh! Bellisle, how great that little prince deems himself who blows the dust off the mechanism of a state already set in motion, so that it shall not stop! How a general is puffed up, thinking when he has won a few battles that in future no one can be compared with him! What dreams has not a minister or a senator of his own talent, if when he introduces a bill he finds it attended with happy results! Vanity and prejudice are the unfailing marks of a narrow mind. The stream flows on in calm majesty when it bears along the richly-freighted bark.

The Czar, however, meets the fate of all mortals who, like apparitions from a better world, move about from time to time on our earth to enlighten, ennoble, and elevate it. That which men ought to honor in him, they hate. His work has not been easy to him. He has had to battle with dangers of a thousand kinds. The priests curse him secretly: the peasantry utter imprecations at him: the Boyards calumniate him; the life-guards would gladly murder him; in a word all the mob, rich and poor, the idle clods of all ranks whose authority, position, rule, privileges, prejudices, superstitions, whims, and caprices, are touched; this moral wolf-herd, who ignorant of all but their own vain, selfish notions of importance, and unconcerned as to the good sense of the offered improvement, are only conscious of feeling comfortable in their old native mire: all these join in idle, dastardly slanders against this grand man.   At their head is the Czar's own son — the Grand-duke Alexis.

This young man, far from weeping, like Alexander of old, over the great deeds of his father because they will leave nothing for him to do, plays the sage, and shrugs his shoulders at the lofty character which ought to form his ideal. He avoids the court, and associates with ignorant Russians who flatter his vanity, and vie with him in brandy-drinking. Instead of being surrounded by learned men, lovers of art, generals, and statesmen, when he is in Moscow or Petersburg, he is seen in the company of low priests who bless him as an honorable, brave, orthodox Russian that loves the old holy paths, and hates the new ways, in which they cannot themselves appear to advantage, because they have neither soul, education, nor virtue, sufficient. The Grand-duke Alexis is at present at the baths at Carlsbad; whither he has, I believe, taken with him his mistress Euphrosyne, a girl from the lowest class of the people, and a Finn. The Czar, his father, is very angry at this; especially as the Grand-duke's wife gave birth to a Princess only a short time ago, and under circumstances of considerable danger. But no more about this scamp, of whom all the Muscovites are hoping that he will be the restorer of their long beards, and of their extraordinary national costume.

More to-morrow! To-day the ball takes place at the Peterhof.

14th August.

You must not indeed imagine, dear Bellisle, that the far-famed capital of the Russian Empire, which has scarcely existed ten years, can vie with our Paris in splendour and beauty. You would seek in vain for Louvres, Tuileries, Notre Dames, Boulevards, and Quais. Most of the houses here are still of wood, laid beam on beam; these are only worked on the inner side, almost like the huts in the villages of the Swiss Alps. They are roofed with shingles, or sometimes merely with boards; and in order to keep out the rain the better, the inner side of the roof is again overlaid with the bark of the birch-tree; or the outer side with green sods, which, when looked down upon in the summer time, appear like fragments of a meadow broken up by an earthquake. Up to the present time there are but very few houses in Petersburg built of stone. The residence of the Czar, the most powerful sovereign of Europe and Asia, rises from the banks of the Neva: it is two stories in height, and is built of brick. It possesses the single advantage that from it one can overlook the fort and the greater portion of the city. By order of the Czar, all the nobles are compelled to build their houses of solid materials: one may everywhere see carts, stone-cutters, lime-burners, masons, and carpenters. The mighty Petersburg affords a miniature type of the movement and progress of the whole empire which has likewise been newly-modelled from its foundations. In the city all is still so new that I cannot describe to you where I live: for even the smallest streets have universally newly-imported names. One is obliged to be guided by well-informed people to escape wandering the day long about this vast labyrinth.

The country around is not attractive: on the contrary, it is dreary, abounding in water, swamps, barren fields, and moorland. All these still wait for some arranging and beautifying hand of later days. The plough has only here and there made sparing efforts to break up this ungenial soil. Everything is expensive, because all the necessaries of life have to be brought many hundred miles from distant parts. Not so much as household vegetables will grow round here; the solitary eatable product that the soil yields freely is the mushroom. Forests still reign unmolested; yet they mostly present a dull and gloomy appearance. Instead of the smiling foliage of the beech and oak, one sees only the sombre green of the pine and fir, or perhaps some birches, elms, aspens, or alders. The oak had to be brought from Kasan. It was a happy thought of the Czar's that suggested the order desiring every householder to plant linden-trees before his door.

In order to give you in a few words some idea of this capital of the greatest empire in Europe, I need only say that, even during last winter, wolves and bears were hunted from its very gates; that we have here a winter nearly eight months long; that during the shortest days the sun is visible barely for three hours, whilst during the longest days it is scarcely three hours below the horizon, and the summer-nights are really only composed of evening and morning twilight.

26th August.

You will readily believe that I am not ambitious enough to resolve on spending my life in this desert, no matter what prize might be held before me. Just as little would I wish to redeem from memory the rough days which I spent amid the tumult of war, and in danger of all kinds. We live our day once for all! and he is a fool who does not make as soft a bed for himself as he can. I now long for quiet, and to be again beneath the shade of my native groves. I have reached the middle point of my earthly career; and desire to pass the second half of my days in sweet repose, since I have spent the first half in the whirl of ceaseless occupation. I sometimes think of the world as a gigantic ants' nest, and compare mankind with the active, restless, little insects. How petty mortals and their doings then appear to me! they build one day, the next destroys their labour. Is then the being who has collected a store of luxuries, and who revels in his fancied wealth, is he richer or more happy than the other ant who has always only just what he needs? That which he *could* enjoy does not belong to a man; only that which he has enjoyed, or is enjoying. A breath! and what was his becomes the property of another. Therefore a thirst for riches does not fret me; he who can satisfy his wants is rich; — he who possesses more is but the owner of dead dust. And if the ant issue his commands to thousands who wander to and fro around him, and the thousands obey; is he therefore more than a weak, perishing creature? Is it otherwise with the dignity of man? No solid good; but a poor, petty game of his own flattering imagination. I admire the little insect that puts out his life to usury; goes everywhere, sees everything, enjoys everything, and does not amuse himself with empty dreams: he pleases me. The world is my Fatherland. I have all but crossed it; I have sat at table with beggars and princes; I have entered into brotherhood with Catholics, Jews, Greeks, and Lutherans. I have taken part in the strifes of men; and have learnt by experience for a longer or shorter time how they live in nearly every rank of society.

———

This has made me a philosopher; yet I am only half one. So many of the nursery tales and notions of my childhood still cling to me. I will throw them off, as one throws away the burr that sticks to one whilst gathering wild flowers. We no longer believe in ghosts and witchcraft; but we still believe in many other and more injurious things which cripple our spirit, and have power to embitter our whole existence. The art of education is indeed still in its infancy, despite all the noted men who have fancied they had .brought it to perfection, and despite all the libraries they have written amongst them.

You do not comprehend me, dear Bellisle, and I can easily believe it. If you will have patience with me, I will give you an explanation in this letter. You might lay this sheet before a thousand of your fellow citizens; they might read it, and read it over again, and yet they would not understand it. He who would be initiated into my mysteries must first have viewed the world from all points as I have done, and must have learned that appearance is not reality, nor reality appearance.

I had the dvantage of the best of educations; such as is now considered the best; and have been completely ruined by the multitude of prejudices which I imbibed from my infancy. That is not a healthy body whose cheeks are made rosy with carmine, whose lost teeth are replaced with ivory, whose deformed limbs are concealed by padding and splints.

But look around you, and search amid the millions who encircle you for one healthy mind! Seek for one vigorous, uncrippled man who is at one with nature! The jest of the lantern of Diogenes is not yet understood by the greater portion of either narrators or listeners.

It is true that senseless ghost stories are no longer told us in our childhood: but our sensitive souls are poisoned with superstitions of a different kind. We are taught to place great value on riches, to esteem millionaires highly; the possession of a ton of gold is lauded as a lofty object for man's attainment. Awful folly! Thus are children early inoculated with an insatiable greed for gold, and a ceaseless discontent with that which they possess. Instead of the beauties of nature, people praise fine clothes to us; we must needs begin early to bow down before a lace frock; we learn to find happiness in the use of equipages, and in the attendance of servants. Hence proceed a host of frivolities that follow us throughout life. We are no longer satisfied to dress ourselves in plain, clean garments: we must shine in grander weeds. We allow the prejudice to take root that judges a man by his dress, and esteems him the more highly on account of his fine linen. The thirst for honor and applause cannot be excited too soon in childhood; this thirst remains unquenchable even to the grave. We accustom ourselves to look upon a man of note as a superior man; a man in office as something extraordinary. Our unfortunate tendencies lead in this direction; and if at last we win some post of honor or gain a name, then we fancy ourselves greater men than the rest of our fellow-creatures. It is quite sufficient to wear a star fastened on the coat, a silk frog at the buttonhole, a chamberlain's key (just as among those people whom we term savages, they wear an ivory bracelet) for us to fancy ourselves worshipped. Childish self-deception! And this is universal amongst us who believe ourselves to be exalted far above the savages of the Orinoco, yet resemble them within a hair's breadth; only that we have multiplied our wants, and increased our follies, to a degree of which the savage has no idea.

The consequences of this plan of early education are twofold. We worship the clay, and overlook the soul: our better self is lost in the whirlpool of unreality, vain emotions, and frivolities. We live, not for what we are, but for what is not worth a breath. If circumstances, or a want of talent, prevent us from attaining the goal we have set before us, then we endeavour to make the world believe that we no longer desire it. We accustom ourselves to appear to be in all things what we would like really to be. We become players, and represent other characters which have no similarity with our own.

Oh, Bellisle! look around you; and, from the royal audience chamber to the workshop of the mechanic, you will find but masks instead of real men. Each is deceived by all, and therefore each would deceive all. There is no real nature: all is imagination and emptiness. We desire, not the gold, but the glitter. We do not dread real dangers, but die of anxiety and despair in the presence of phantoms. It is but another phase of fear of ghosts, or superstitious digging for treasure; and our education is to blame for the whole.

You have not received a letter from me for a long time, dear Bellisle; you have not seen me for a long time.   For this reason it is well that you should learn something of my inner self, that I should write to you as I think.   You can, it is true, read moral disquisitions in books if you are so inclined: but I do not know that you will find in them exactly the same train of thought that runs through this letter.   I have not told you of my adventure, only of its results.

After midnight.

Morning will soon dawn.   All are asleep: I am unable to rest.   The blood in my veins has turned to flame: my breathings are so many sobs; my spirit reels in the heaven and hell of frenzy.   I am no longer myself.   I know it.   In the midst of the delirium of fever, I seize my pen: it will write nonsense; I know this beforehand.   But I will read this again when I recover, in order to see how I have borne myself in this state of transformation.   That I can still think of this, convinces me of the superiority of my spirit, which can soar over the storm of turbid feeling as the eagle soars over the storms of earth and ocean.   Pride gives this superiority: but it is still sweeter when arising from such delicious infatuation.   I will again sink into the floods; I will be myself no longer: first I must awake again.

Oh, Bellisle! that even at this moment I can think of you, that in the midst of this bewilderment I can write your name, is the greatest proof of love that I have ever given you.   But no more words; to my story! I curse the tardiness of my pen, over whose lazy strokes millions of thoughts sweep every second like lightning flashes; and only the poorest of them are caught upon my paper, soulless corpses. But no, in one word I can express all my rapture, my grief; all, all, of heaven and hell-like that dwells both above and beneath the stars. And I will! Christina, Christina is the word: I tremble as I write it, and my whole being sinks as though consumed, dissolved, burnt to ashes, by an ardent flame.

No, I am not in love; oh, Bellisle, decidedly not. I know well what love is: I have already loved. No, it is madness which glows in my veins; a wonderfully sweet madness, intoxication, ecstasy, what shall I call it? Metamorphosis, destruction, all this; since I have beheld Christina. When Semele would behold Jupiter, the god of gods, in the plenitude of his majesty, and in the splendour of his godlike existence, the poor mortal! and he appeared in his incomprehensible, unveiled, godlike nature, illuming all around, shedding lightning beams over all things, then (like me) she knew no longer admiration, rapture, love, but annihilation.

And this is my position. Do not deceive yourself, Bellisle, when you read these confused lines: it is not love: Christina is further removed from me than the sun from our earth. Through an eternity I could never traverse the endless abyss between her and me. Besides I do not desire it, would not, — I am leaving Petersburg, Russia, all. I am going to France without the shadow of a wish to remain. Christina is married; Alexis, the son of the Czar Peter the Great is her husband, the German empress is her sister. Perhaps Fate has destined the present Grand-duchess to be the future ruler of the North, of Russia.

No, Bellisle! I will not weary you with rhapsodies. I will narrate to you the story of this day without further interruption; I will impose assumed patience on myself, until I shall have related the pretty romance, and have poured forth to you the full outburst of my feelings.

This evening the ball at the Peterhof took place. The Czar's palace is not yet completed; but to-day it looked as though it were to undergo the ceremony of consecration. All was done in honor of the lovely Grand-duchess Christina, who, deserving of the happiest lot, honored by the Czar, worshipped by all the Russians, idolized even by the hoary Boyards, is married to a fiend who prefers the love of a common girl from Finland to the heaven of Christina's heart. Set the kingly crown on the head of a wild boar, and he will wallow in the mire with it, just as he did before.

The Grand-duchess has quitted her room. On the 23d of July she presented her husband with a princess, who received at her baptism the name of Natalie. The unfeeling barbarian Alexis remained with his Finn mistress in Carlsbad; paternal joy could not recall him. Meantime his father, the great Czar, has almost exhausted himself in his endeavours to make his daughter-in-law forget the dissipation and unkindness of his ill-advised son.

He has surrounded her with a brilliant court: festivities of every kind are numerous as the days of the year.

And I saw her on that of this day. Nine days ago her twentieth birthday was celebrated.

Ah, Bellisle! do you remember a miniature that I

allowed you to look at some years ago in Calais? At
that time you did not believe that it was the work of
my brush and of my imagination. I remember well
how you looked at it with a quiet smile of approval,
gazed at the sky, and exclaimed: "No such angelic
being dwells beneath thy blue vault; I would willingly die to-morrow, if I could find such an one
above!" You saw me blush, you saw my eyes glisten
with a hidden tear. You asked my secret; ah! how
willingly would I have concealed it, even from myself.

I reel through a garden full of wonders. My life
has become a magic labyrinth; I understand nothing;
visions appear and disappear, fling a spell over my
soul, and draw it down into the tide of events. It
will never be free from the spell, even in death.

Whilst I was mixing in the festive crowd at the
assembly at the Peterhof — as I was being presented
to the Czar — folding doors opened, and she entered,
leaning on the arm of the Countess von Königsmark.
Oh, Bellisle! how shall I describe her to you? If my
imagination could penetrate to the innermost heaven,
never could it find there among the beatified such a
form as hers. It was herself again.

But no, not a word more. I am terrified at my
own words; they reflect my frenzy as the mirror the
figure before it. Already the waters of the Neva are
ruddy in the morning light. I must go to rest, and
allow my fever to subside a little before I take up my
pen again.

THE GRAND-DUCHESS CHRISTINA TO THE
COUNTESS JULIA VON B***.

Petersburg, 2d September 1714.

How touching is the utterance of your love, my
Julia! When I read your letter, even look at the
lines your hand has traced, then, dreaming, I forget
where I am; then the soft airs of Germany breathe on
me again; then I see once more the shady walks and
bowers in the. garden of my father's castle, where, as
children, we danced in happy innocence amid a thousand flowers; then, in this northern desert whither
fate has banished me, I behold once more the silvery
blossoms of the fruit-trees beneath whose shade we used
to wreath our garlands.

Cold and wild are man and nature alike in the
neighbourhood of the North Pole. For nearly three
years I have been living far from my dear ones at
home, and still I am living among strangers. No one
understands my language, and the gentle tones of my
heart die away, finding no echo in any responsive
breast. So little do our modes of thought and our
views of things agree, that, but for the Countess of
Königsmark I might believe myself already dead, or
banished by the Creator to some desolate planet where
for a long eternity I was doomed to expiate my sins.
My health is once more restored. Thanks for that to
the renovating powers of youth. Now I will write
oftener to you. Conversing with you will occupy my
brightest morning hours. Your picture hangs before
me; representative of the dreams of the past, it fills
my mind with illusions. Do not, I entreat you, believe that in this abode of eternal winter my heart can

ever become chilled.   No, Julia, you are dear to me
as a gem that I have brought from a better world; as
a sister whose loving heart has been indissolubly bound
to mine by the hand of sweet nature herself.   And,
Julia, if I have not returned your gentle confidence,
if for years I have been silent to your thousand questions, believe me I wished that you should think me
happy.   I wished to deceive you that I might know
you without anxiety on my account.   Am I more
happy, or more consoled, now that you weep for me?

You say the whole of Europe is aware of my sad
position, the whole of Europe knows the bitterness of
my lot, and accords me compassion: yet I wished to
conceal from you my undeserved misery.

But now.   You shall know it: the Grand-duke,
my husband, is naturally of a morose disposition.   I
have not, — oh, Julia, how hard it is for me to write
it! — the good fortune to please him.   I was not the
wife of his choice, and hence springs his indifference.
For three long years I in vain sought his favour.
People say indeed that we women can work wonders
with a smile, a tear; that nothing is impossible to us.
Alas! nature seems to have denied to me the blessed
talent.   Every art was lost on the temper of my Alexis.
He appears, so far as I am concerned, to have drunk
of that magic spring from which Ariosto's Rinaldo imbibed his unconquerable hatred for Angelica.

I have at last — and three years is a long school-
ing-time — accustomed myself, to the aversion of my
husband; perhaps also he has accustomed himself to
the love that I accord him.   We shall see in the end
who will win the prize.

Yes, beloved Julia, since now you know the secret

of my fate, you may know everything. I have suffered inexpressibly for three years, and hidden grief has consumed my strength to the very dregs.

Formerly I was the darling of my princely parents. Love cradled me till I grew up; joyousness educated me. Wherever I turned I met kindly hearts. I knew no strangers in the world; knew no cares but those of seeking to give and receive pleasure: no tears but those which gentle sympathy drew from my eyes in seeing suffering, in reading a poem, or in listening to strains of melancholy music. Every morning I awoke to a little feast-day; every night I fell asleep amid bright expectations. One day was like another; each greeted me with smiles like a friendly genius, each bade me adieu with smiles.

Then I was betrothed to the son of the greatest of monarchs. Alas! with prophetic grief I beheld little Wolfenbüttel vanish, like an Eden of which I had been pronounced unworthy. The first sight of him to whom my hand was destined, filled me with heavy forebodings. Not that Alexis is a man who might not expect to prepossess one by his exterior. The Grand-duke is tall, slight in figure, and of manly bearing. Black hair and eyes, a pleasing gravity in the expression of his features, a certain undefinable something which pronounces him, let him do or be what he will, the heir of the greatest empire in the world, give interest to his person. He speaks German fluently. He can be very loveable when he chooses to be so — but — he never does choose.

His education was neglected. Whilst the Czar, his noble father, journeyed throughout Europe with the object of engrafting the arts and sciences of more genial climates upon his northern snows; whilst he gave fleets to shipless seas, civilized customs to a tribe of wild barbarians, towns to untraversed forests — he forgot to render this new creation, the heir to his throne, worthy of it.   The prince, surrounded by discontented Boyards and superstitious priests, imbibed from boyhood all the prejudices of his nation, and hatred for all the improvements of his talented father. The fate of his mother, Eudoxia, whom the Czar sent into a convent and compelled to take the veil, poured additional bitterness into his heart.   A gloomy pride became peculiar to him.   Whatever his father originated, he hated: whatever vexed his father, pleased him.   He adopted the superstitions of the stupid priests, the rough manners of the Boyards;   and took delight in becoming the idol of the lowest class of the people.   Thus he degenerated.   His deportment is rough, his clothes are untidy and uncleanly, his companions are a crowd of monks and of ruined profligates.

And, Julia! this is my husband!

On the day of our wedding the Czar drew me to him towards a window of the large assembly-hall at which the prince was standing.   "See," he said to his son, "you cannot forget the old customs, and long beards still turn your head.   You do not follow my example.   But I hope everything from the sway of a pretty, clever, and virtuous lady over your heart.   If you come out of her school unimproved, then indeed you will be lost to the world."

I cast down my eyes, and felt my cheeks burn. This speech which so deeply touched my every tender feeling, filled the prince with suspicion of me, and vexation with me. Already, from the first day, I had observed by a thousand little traits that Alexis was elevating me to the rank of his wife, not from his own free choice, but from obedience to the command of his father. And when, with timid embarrassment, I cast my glance on my bridegroom, oh Julia! I read in the gloomy knitting of his brow, in the gleam of his darkening eye, an oath of endless aversion, and the sentence of my dreadful fate.

Thus it was — thus has remained.

Be silent, and love me.

THE GRAND-DUCHESS TO THE SAME.

I HAD scarcely, dear Julia, sent off my last letter when I received yours. How enchanting is the family picture as you send it to me, in which you are your-self the worshipped idol!

I can see you at your castle in the country, under the shade of the majestic chesnuts and oaks, at your feet the smiling garden over which even autumn is strewing a hundred blossoms; in the background the cheerful village whose inhabitants reverence you as their guardian angel. I see you, happy mother! your lovely babe in your arms; how he playfully stretches out his little hand to your drooping ringlets; and the husband of your heart, how he stands by, enchanted with the lovely group, now with a father's fondness kissing the wingless cupid on your lap, now pressing his glowing lips to yours with all the tenderness of a bridegroom.

Oh! in what have I sinned that I must give up these joys! How would they gladden my heart!

what a poor indemnity does the glitter of my mournful rank afford me!

Daughters of princes, among all women of earth the most deserving of pity, envy the daughter of your poorest subject! For she dares to love; she dares to bestow her hand on the man she prefers, to dream away her life on his heart, on his heart to die in calm happiness. We, decked out like eastern slaves, are given to such powerful beings as demand us: state policy signs the contract, and our broken hearts are turned into merchandize.

People call us the deities of the earth, but take away our heaven. We are human, but we are robbed of the holy rights of free will; we have a heart, but dare not acknowledge it: Nature is our mother, and we must disown her. We look down with tears from our thrones upon the domestic joys of poverty which are denied to us. With all our jewels and treasures we cannot purchase the happiness which dwells under the straw thatch of the country-man. We adorn our bodies with precious metals and stones; we clothe ourselves in splendid materials, the dainties of foreign climes and seas deck our tables; but we leave the chief good of life to those who are of lower rank; our jewels do not warm our hearts, our crowns are not friends; and, alas! although millions may bow the knee before us, and the people of the earth may admire us, all this hollow splendor is not worth the living love and truth of one solitary heart.

Barbarous decree, which, poisoned by the insanity of ambition, gave to the meanest of mortals all that life has of most attractive, and condemned us to golden fetters!

Forgive me, Julia, if for a moment, I sink under the misery of my princely position. My laments will not change the course of the world; the prejudices of rank and birth will still maintain their supremacy so long as nations are not freed from barbarism. Thousands of secret, bitter, tears have already bedewed the purple of princes, and will bedew it yet for ages to come. Alas! no one understands me but you; I complain to no one but you.

I live, — accept, as a companion to yours, a family picture from me, — I live the lonely life of a widow, notwithstanding the brilliant retinue with which the kindness of the Czar has surrounded me; and notwithstanding the series of festal days which he interweaves throughout my life in Russia, in order to distract my grief.

I stand in these festive assemblies, at these merrymakings and amusements, like a stranger-spectator: my eyes wander inquiringly through the brilliant crowd, my heart remains unsatisfied, and a yearning for something better alone stirs me.

Sometimes I see the Czar and his wife, the Empress Catharina Alexiewna. All goes well with me whilst I am with this noble pair: but their cares for this vast empire seldom permit them to have a leisure moment.

Much is said in Europe about this wonderful man to whom I am bound, as to a second father, by ties of childlike love; and in the thousand tales told, his character is often very much misrepresented. I will insert in my letter an anecdote which is still so new as to be unknown to you, and which is very characteristic of both him and the Empress.

It is about a year ago that the Czar was dining at the house of a foreign merchant who has some property here. He saw this man's daughter, who indeed well deserves to be called a beauty, fell in love with her, and exhausted all his arts of persuasion to induce her to break her faith to her husband. But, with courageous nobility, she withstood his proposals. She trembled at the consequences of such a passion in a prince all-powerful in his empire, took some money, and vanished on the self-same day without allowing even her family to know whither. She fled to a village where her nurse was living, the wife of a charcoal burner, bade them conduct her to the forest in which the latter worked, and there she made him build a hut for her. In this she lived, concealed from all the world. The faithful nurse daily brought her her necessary food.

The day after her flight the Czar returned to the house of the merchant. He wished to see the daughter. The father related tremblingly how she had gone away. The Czar, glowing with anger, ordered the whole house, and the houses of all her relations to be searched; but found all his efforts fruitless.

A year passed away. Nothing more was heard of the beautiful and virtuous fugitive. She was supposed to have died, as her husband had during this time. By accident, a colonel who was hunting in this same forest discovered her hut. He succeeded in putting her at ease respecting the plots of the Czar, and in bringing her back to the house of her parents. He informed the Empress of his discovery. She conducted him herself to the Czar; and there he had to narrate all that the virtuous wife had suffered during her disappearance. The Czar, moved to tears, loaded himself

with reproaches. He vowed to atone for his injustice.
The young widow became the wife of the Colonel.
The Czar made the most handsome presents to the
happy pair, and secured a pension of three thousand
roubles to the former object of his love.

Thus kindness of heart, and harshness, respect for
virtue, and rude passion, alternate continually in his
actions. He is the wild child of nature, and she endows
him, stormy, beneficent, and lofty as herself, with unrestrained longings and fearful powers.

The Countess von Ostfriesland and the Countess
von Königsmark are my daily companions. It is impossible to me to form a close and confidential friendship with the former. Breathing only in a court
atmosphere, paying homage only to etiquette, ignorant
of all noble sentiments, she only sees in me the future
Empress of Russia, not a suffering woman. The ever
amiable Königsmark is more interesting, notwithstanding her thoughtlessness. She attends with untiring
interest to each of my wishes, to each of my complaints. She is one of those gentle, pleasing creatures
(the very opposite of starched independence) who enter
fully into the turn of thought of others; and, involuntarily, she makes the moods and the feelings of
others her own. Among the merry, she is the merriest;
among the grave, she is the philosopher, among the
unhappy, the most dejected: she moulds herself to be
all things to all men, and is therefore only a tender
echo, an amiable chameleon.

You know old Herbert? Do you still recollect
him, how he used to draw us about, when children, in
the castle garden, and called himself our little horse? —
sometimes went with us over fences and ditches, was

sometimes our boatman, sometimes our builder? This faithful domestic is still with me; still the same; and his temperament cheerful as ever. He has become indispensable to me. If I were to lose him, I should be inconsolable.

Now you know the principal people who surround me. All beside, glide about like shadows on the wall; I see them and forget them. Each moves in his own sphere, pays court to me in .order to show off his own glitter, and troubles himself less about me than about his gaming, or dinner, table.

The sole joy that is granted me — you are a mother, my Julia, and guess it beforehand — is my little Natalie. How charming my little angel is! How much I pity her already, that she is the daughter of a prince, that she must one day endure the fate of her mother!

Whilst I close this letter Herbert has come in, and announced the arrival of the Grand-duke Alexis, of my husband. Oh, Julia! I trace these lines with a trembling hand. Herbert, in order to save me alarm, prepared me some time ago for this news, and not in vain. My misery is now renewed. Alas! that I should greet him with fear and trembling to whose heart I ought to fly in delight at meeting him again.

Farewell, and weep for me!

CHEVALIER D'AUBANT TO LAURENCE BELLISLE.

My letters are still dated from the capital of the Russian Empire. I am bound to this wild land as if by a spell. Whilst in France all the leaves are still green, and hundreds of flowers look bright, and the song of the vintager resounds on the hills, here the foggy days are already becoming short, the leaves are falling withered from the trees, and owing to the cold of the nights the hoar frost sparkles on the dark firs, and announces the approaching snow.

Yet at this moment in which I am quitting it — this pitiless region of the world has charms for me. Even it has its beauties and its wonders. The sun when it breaks with its red light through the grey fog, and sheds a melancholy gleam over the dark forests, over the barren plains and miserable huts, possesses a charm such as it scarcely displays when it beams in the fulness of its glory over the luxuriant fields of Champagne. The wooden houses have in their appearance something invitingly homelike. The delicious warmth of the rooms invites one to confidential intercourse.

Laugh on, Bellisle, but everywhere the world is neither perfectly hideous nor perfectly beautiful: it is a colourless picture that we must ourselves paint from our own hearts. As soon as we bring life and feeling into it we see, not it, but ourselves in it. To the Siberian wanderer his village amid the snowy wastes is as attractive as splendid Rome is to the Parisian artist. Habit makes all things endurable: but the voice within our heart owns the spell which changes the sandy steppe into a fairy garden.

I still owe to you the tale of my presentation to the Grand-duchess Christina, and the explanation of the hidden picture. I will forget myself, and relate the fable-like story, as simply as though it were a nursery tale.

During my journey through Germany I once

roamed into the Hartz mountains. I sent the horses and carriage on to the next town that I might wander through this country on foot. You know how fond I am of mountain scenery.

One day, the noontide sun was burning fiercely and I quitted the great road. I think it was near a place called Blankenburg: I chose a foot-path which, amid the shade of a wood, seemed to run close to the coach road, and in the same direction. The country people who were working in the fields assured me that I could not lose my way by taking it. I penetrated more and more deeply into the wilds of the forest. The path beneath my feet had vanished imperceptibly. I turned back, found a road, followed it, soon discovered that it was leading me quite away from my destination, left it again, sought the first; and at last, lost myself so completely that I no longer knew whence I had come, nor whither I should go.

Evening came on, still I was in the horrid forest thicket; the further I went, the more endless it seemed. I had already prepared myself for making my couch on the damp moss, and for an adventure with wolves or bears. Meanwhile I had pressed on through the hateful underwood into a little meadow surrounded on all sides by the forest. The grass stood high. I resolved to cross it in the hope of discovering a beaten track.

I was still standing undecided in which direction to bend my steps when, on the opposite side of the meadow, two ladies emerged from the darkness of the wood, like a pair of friendly fairies. They perceived me: they shouted and beckoned. Delighted at the glad sight, I flew forwards. Their simple, yet costly and tasteful dress led me to suppose that they were of good family; from their distress and perplexity, I saw that something unpleasant had befallen them.

Oh, Bellisle! when I approached more closely, when the younger addressed me: "Do guide us back to the hunting lodge! We have lost our way; we cannot now be more than half a mile distant from it!" — then I believed that the old wonders of the fairy world had come to life again in this forest. The imagination of the most favoured poet never, during the creative hours of his muse, beheld such an ideal of high-born beauty as was here, with inexpressible grace, requesting my assistance.

I, myself, lost in this enchanted forest, forgot that I entered the unexplored region for the first time. The impossible appeared to me to become possible. I accompanied the young ladies back in the direction in which they seemed to have come. They were exhausted. They rested by the way. They inquired my name, my rank, my country. I replied.

"What!" exclaimed the younger of the graces, laughing; "you are a stranger here yourself, and lost; and you would guide us!"

I answered her with such re-assuring confidence that at last she believed me. We continued our way. Tired, they both leaned on my arm. Yes, Bellisle, I was the happiest of mortals during those priceless moments in which the unknown being, who will now for ever be the idol of my dreams and aspirations, moved by my side. Ah! how sweet, how never-to-be-forgotten, was each moment, each word, each little care that I bestowed on this wondrous and angelic being. Sometimes I must free her dress from a thorn, sometimes must break a path for her through the overgrown brushwood; how on each occasion did she laugh her thanks so kindly, and with a glance that shed the pure light of heaven over my soul!

Suddenly we were in the open country, on a coach road which ran near the forest. Not far from us a handsome carriage was waiting. It drove up. The young ladies thanked me, got into it, and vanished.

Like one in a dream, like one intoxicated, I gazed for a long time after the carriage whose track the clouds of dust betrayed to me. It seemed as though my soul itself were torn from me. I followed the road taken by the unknown ladies. Yet once more I would see her. —

But no, I will tell you my story in plain words. Well then, with deep emotion I pursued my way, thinking only of her. It was dark. The stars shone in the heavens. I was not tired; I walked from road to road, Heaven knows whither, till towards midnight I reached a village. My inquiries for the carriage and the two ladies were all fruitless. No one could give me any information. Probably I had again missed my way some ten times, and had rather taken myself further from those I sought than nearer to them.

Enough; I saw the enchantress of the forest no more; neither learned her name, nor her place of residence; and returned to my own country with a hopeless yearning.

In my solitary hours I sought to paint from memory the lovely angel-face so full of childlike innocence and true dignity. You saw the picture.

The whole adventure was simple: but it influenced

the course of my life. It often happens that the decline of an empire is replete with less of interest than the history of a moment. I loved what I lost — a dream, an ideal — but enough, my soul clung to it with unchanging tenacity. No hero of romance could be more deserving of ridicule, than I myself — but I loved.

I did not venture to breathe a syllable to any of my friends lest I should be make a joke of; but all the more the secret filled my whole soul with an undying fervour of love.

And now I am in Russia — into this most distant zone the enchanting image has followed me. It sped before me amid the terrors of battle, went with me into the gaudy saloons of the great, smiled over my sick bed like a consoling seraph, brought heaven to my fevered dreams.

Oh, Bellisle! and she who entered the festive assembly at the Peterhof on the arm of the Countess of Königsmark, — she was the lovely fairy of the forest again — the long lost — now the wife of the Grandduke Alexis, heir to the Russian throne.

Do not ask, dear Bellisle, how I felt. I distrusted all that I saw, even the reality of life itself. And whilst I exclaimed to myself a thousand times, "You are becoming delirious, poor d'Aubant! do not fancy this! you do not see her! it is a wild delusion!" I moved about in a state of ecstasy and devotion.

Foreigners were presented to her according to their rank. I, then, must approach her. It seemed to me as if I were entering within the sphere of some supernatural being.

She observed my embarrassment; but, to spare me, appeared not to perceive it.

The chamberlain told her my name. "What!" said she, "Chevalier d'Aubant!" and looked at me more attentively, and added doubtfully; "I have a dim recollection of this name; and also of you, that I have seen you before. Perhaps in Germany." As she thus spoke, a faint blush overspread her lovely face like a reflection from the morning sky.

I trembled. The answer died on my lips. At last I stammered out a falsehood. I pretended never to have seen her whose image had never left me for years. I did not know what I said and did.

"Surely," said she after a short pause, "it was you who once guided my friend and myself out of a forest in which we had lost ourselves. You see that gratitude, at least, has a faithful memory."

How gladly now did I confess that that day was the brightest, the most impossible to be forgotten, of my life! With a smile that was worth an empire, she called herself my debtor, and then turned towards the other foreigners.

Now, Bellisle, you know my position! And though the lawyers at home swallow up all the residue of my little property, and though I become a beggar — I cannot yet quit Petersburg. Do not ask what I wish, what I hope — do not blame my emotion — do not call me a fool! No, you are wrong! I do *not* love the Grand-duchess; that would be insanity! But I worship her with the reverence with which we worship an exalted being whose very proximity to us elevates us above our common selves.

To die in the service of this princess, Bellisle, is my fondest wish.

THE GRAND-DUCHESS TO JULIA.

THE Grand-duke, my lord and husband, is in truth, come back with his whole suite. On the second day after his arrival he first honored me with a visit. What can I tell you, my Julia, of this visit? He fulfilled none of the hopes with which I had so willingly flattered myself, although I knew the morose disposition of the Czarovitch.

After a long absence Alexis returned to meet his wife who had in the meantime been at the gates of death. Alas! why did not those gates open to receive me!

I was prepared for his arrival. I hoped this time to appear more loveable in his eyes than formerly, for I was now a mother. I dressed in my handsomest jewels — with Natalie in my arms I went to meet him. This bright, attractive, little creature would surely, with her innocent smiles, win the heart of her father for her mother.

Alexis, as though he had foreseen my design, as though he had feared to be overcome by the powerful voice of nature, had armed himself with all the coldness possible; and, in order to avoid any confidential intercourse, brought with him as companion the artful flatterer, General Glebow. What could a husband and wife say to each other in the presence of such a third person? And yet as soon as Alexis entered, I forgot the hateful Glebow. I hastened towards him with smiles. I presented his child to him; I said to him all that love and constancy could say. Alas! a stranger from the most distant corner of the world would have said more in reply than did Alexis. No embrace rewarded his wife: no father's kiss blessed his child. He could not extort from himself one kindly smile. He inquired in common-place terms after my health, and about my employments, looked at my new pictures, and permitted Glebow to torment me with dull flatteries. Then in half an hour he left me again; and when he disappeared, I wept in my loneliness bitter tears over my forsaken child, unloved by her own father.

Alexis treats me with contempt. He appears at none of the balls, none of the banquets, which the kindness of the Czar gives for me. He always has some pretext for avoiding them: sometimes he is indisposed, sometimes a hunting expedition falls on that day, sometimes other engagements detain him. And whilst I grieve secretly over my sorrow, would you believe it, Alexis feels himself very happy in the rough companionship he chooses, and gets drunk to excess with his Russian friends in their gay revels.

The more his father, the Czar, reproaches him for this behaviour, the more reason he believes he has for hating me. Ah! if he only knew how often I have entreated the Emperor with tears to forbear! If he only knew how unceasingly I make excuses for him!

And now I am so lonely, though every day fills my halls with gay company: I am a mourning widow, and yet my husband lives within the walls of the same city as myself; I am so poor, yet the wife of the heir to a throne, and sister of an empress.

No one understands me; no one speaks to my

heart. It is cold, locked up; it lies within my breast as in a coffin; the heavenly strains of music alone sometimes reach its grave and speak intelligibly to its inmost feelings.

Julia, you have loved; you are beloved; you know a happiness whose extent is a secret from me; you know the extent of your own happiness, you know therefore my misery.

What avail all the splendours of life, all the glitter, all the grandeur, if our nobler feelings are starving? Can the dead either rejoice or grieve over the crowns and standards, the statues and ornaments, that surround their ashes? I was a woman before I was a princess. What a sad degeneracy is there in the human race! From the cradle to the grave we torment ourselves with what is contrary to nature; millions bewail their wretched life with tears, and curse a world which is in itself perfect, and in which, by their own fault, they are the imperfections. Each stone, each plant, each beast, surpasses us in the glories of perfection; for each is what, according to its nature, it ought to be; and is neither more nor less than this. We, human beings, alone, endowed with high gifts, mutilate ourselves, and become and remain pitiful cripples, hideous caricatures.

Julia, Julia! My knees tremble; my heart is broken! — Oh! how wretched I am!

It was a bright, sunny day, an unusual thing in this country. I heard that my husband was walking in the new garden of the castle. I wrapped myself up warmly, and flew thither without any attendants, to see him, to talk to him, to win him by affectionate conversation.

Oh, Julia! am I then so ugly? Even if my own self-love and my mirror deceive me, do not the tongues of those who do not care for me, confess that I am at least no object for aversion? Did not I once know how to please thousands? Did not all once treat me as their pet? Has not my mind obtained some attractive qualities from the tender nurture of my parents? Have I not been virtuous both in word and deed; or has my conscience only been forgetful?

And yet I am sunk so low that a creature of the meanest class, and of the worst conduct, a creature who can make no pretence to beauty or wit; a common girl, scarcely good enough to captivate the vulgar wicked, brought up in the school of vice, triumphs over me, and has won the heart of my husband!

I went with shy impatience through the garden. I sought Alexis, and yet feared to find him. I had a great deal to tell him and to say to him, and yet was puzzled how I should address him.

And as I turned down a shrubbery, there I saw him at a little distance, sitting beside his mistress, their hands confidingly clasped in each other. The girl set up a shrill laugh, and put her hand before his mouth, as though refusing to listen to his endearments or jests.

I stood still, as if struck by lightning, breathless, annihilated. The girl perceived me, sprang up, and wished to go away. He detained her, looked at me, and laughed almost as noisily as she had done before. Meantime she freed herself from him, and ran down the path. He laughed as before, and cried several

times, "Euphrosyne! Euphrosyne! do not be a fool!"
then followed her with hasty steps.

About me, who stood there degraded, perplexed,
stunned with distress; about me, who would willingly
have followed him as she fled from him; about me,
his wife; about me, Alexis did not trouble himself.

Then now I will shut myself up with my blighted
hopes, and with my ceaseless yearnings. Alas! why
am I still so young: why are my powers still so vigorous — why does not Death find out me — he who
carries away so many of the blessed ones from the
midst of their happiness?

CHEVALIER D'AUBANT TO LAURENCE BELLISLE.

Breslau, 3d May 1715.

You will not expect, dear Bellisle, to hear that I
am so soon journeying towards France! — I, who filled
only my last letter with vehement protestations of
living and dying in Petersburg — I, who entreated you
to set in order for me all my domestic affairs in my
own country. Spare yourself the trouble now; I am
coming myself. You say that the larger part of my
property is lost; you would console me! Truly, the
intelligence has troubled me very little. I can bear
poverty. I do but lose some means which I might
have employed for the good of others; for I should not
have needed all myself.

I am a fugitive, have left the greater portion of
my properties at Petersburg; and beside a little money,
have saved nothing but my life. This then, and the
rank of captain, is the whole result of the weary years
I have spent in the Russian service. Others did less

than I, and flew from step to step; others knew less, and they are bragging with importance and wealth. People praised my talents, made use of them, and forgot me; they loaded me with flattery on account of my many virtues: every one wished to be my friend, but none was really so. Men all love themselves, and no one but themselves. He who sacrifices himself for them, they call a useful fool.

But do not think that what now fills my whole soul is any little vexation on the score of neglect and disappointment. No, I should be ashamed of that, and should conceal it from you as a mean defect. I have always hoped rather to become successful through some freak of fortune, some fortunate combination of favouring circumstances, than through the integrity and kindness of men. The hopes of that man can never be disappointed who estimates the citizens of this strange world not at what they should be, but at what they are. Many are their called ones, but few their chosen. Every man loves the common good in so far as it does not interfere with his own, and this is called patriotism; every one loves and serves others when he expects service in return; this, in the language of life, is called friendship. Only one exists among millions who, without regard to his own wishes and interest, without regard to the opinion of the prudent multitude, decides and acts as he ought to do, even if disgrace or death be the result. Holy enthusiasm of virtue! the vulgar herd may for ever miscall thee, thee whom a thousand poets, a thousand priests, a thousand philosophers laud, albeit not one of them all has courage to take thee home to his own breast, — I laud thee from my heart! I may lose my position; but, con-

scious of rectitude, let the world condemn me if it
will.

But to the point. You can see, dear Bellisle, that
I am deeply moved; the torrent roars, but you do not
yet know its source.

I lived quietly and happily at Petersburg. My
luggage had arrived from Moscow; yet I did not meditate departure. I wished — but my wishes are no
secret to you.

I was only waiting some favourable opportunity
that should enable me to approach my adored princess,
to venture to tell her that I should esteem it my highest privilege to live in her service. But she had forgotten me. In vain, with dawn of each morning, did
I hope this might be the herald of the happy day on
which I should receive an invitation to the palace of
the Grand-Duke.

Thus weeks and months passed away. My inac-
tivity became a burden to me. I was ashamed to ask
for service again with the Czar, as he had ordered my
discharge to be given to me. And yet this was the
only way in which I could obtain admission into that
society which, by Christina's presence, had become the
most attractive in the whole wide world to me.

I had at last, after a long struggle with myself,
resolved at the next public audience (at which every
petitioner has the right of approaching the Czar direct),
to ask the monarch to admit me again to his service,
when the most untoward event in the world banished
me once and for ever from Russia.

I was one evening at a dinner-party at the house
of Colonel Larine in company with several other
officers. After the dinner was removed, drinking

began in the true Russian fashion. Every one said what he liked, and much joking went on. Among other subjects, conversation turned upon the Grand-duke Alexis who returned from the baths some little time ago. They spoke pretty freely of the differences existing between him and his wife. They took sides. Some defended the Czarovitch, some the virtuous Christina. One rough young Russian, an officer and a near relation of Marshal Scheremetoff, defended the conduct of the Grand-duke, and cast the greatest opprobrium upon Christina's virtue. The others laughed at his foolish ideas; this gave him courage, and he became ten times more bold in his speeches against the Princess. As a relation of Scheremetoff, no one contradicted him; and if any one wished so to do, he was afraid of drunken jeers.

When a miserable wretch without heart or intellect stands up, and scoffs with his small understanding at the talented man whom he is incapable of comprehending; when an ignorant fool censures the deeds and projects of a wise man; then I can join in the laugh, and shrug my shoulders at the poor fellow who exposes himself thus. But when a wretched creature dares, with shameless countenance, to rail at that which is noble and good; when he would slander virtue and detract from great deeds; then it becomes no longer weakness of understanding which may serve to raise a laugh, it is a wickedness which stirs our heart. He who can laugh when a malicious person slanders virtue, he who can laugh when a mean fellow turns a suffering fellow-creature into an object of ridicule, he is akin to the scoffer, and a mean fellow himself.

I approached the Russian, and entreated him,

quietly and courteously, to restrain himself; not to forget that Christina was the daughter of a noble German prince, the sister of an empress, and the daughter-in-law of our revered monarch.

The Russian, apparently one of the followers of Alexis, who thought by his hatred against foreigners to insinuate himself into favor, imagined he had found an opportunity of proving himself worthy of his master. He looked askance at me with a scornful glance, and replied with a rudeness that could only be pardoned in one of the mob. The others filled their glasses, and laughed heartily at the uncourteous retort. This excited him to fresh slanders. I entreated him to be quiet; I threatened. All in vain. He continued to abuse her even more shamelessly; and the others laughed more loudly. What could I do among these drunkards? I seized my hat and sword, intending to leave. The miserable wretch, proud of his victory, followed me to the door; and cried, as he gave me a kick: "In like manner all foreigners, fortune-hunters, and adventurers ought to be driven from the country!"

I turned round, gave the shameless fellow a tingling box on the ear; and when he would have closed with me, I felled the enraged man to the ground with my fist, so that it took the wind out of him.

I walked slowly towards home. But I had scarcely taken two hundred steps, when the Russian sprang after me with his sabre drawn; and, with a hundred abusive terms, demanded that I should stop. I prepared myself for defence. The moon shone brightly. Several others of our party stood at a distance to watch the course of things. I promised to give the Russian satisfaction on the following day, and begged him to sleep off his excitement. Vain effort! He attacked me in a rage; I could scarcely guard myself from his sabre-cuts. Scarcely two minutes passed before he lay lifeless at my feet. I bent over him. He sighed but once, and died. I called up the others. They carried him back. I hastened to my home, packed up what was really necessary, and disappeared from Petersburg at break of day, that I might not be compelled to go off to Siberia.

Now, dear Bellisle, you know all. I hope to be with you in a few weeks. My lot is a hard one, and yet perhaps one day I shall bless it. I have accustomed myself to believe that every evil is the well-spring of a good; and every joy the mother of a pang. Separated from the only being whom of all that dwell under Heaven I most revere, my heart will again attain complete composure. She will perhaps hear of what I have done, and of my flight; and my name will at least be so blessed as to be once more listened to by her.

Farewell, Bellisle; we shall soon see each other again. Ah! I have still much to tell you; but it disgusts me to paint pen-pictures. I am disappointed — embittered against man and fate — I should like to fling myself into some wild, distracting occupation in which, as in a foaming torrent, I could forget all — everything — even my own self. My miserable, wretched self who, deeply injured by force of prejudice and education, persists in seeking happiness in outward objects, not within itself: and persists in loading reproaches on others, never on itself even though alone deserving of them.

Farewell!

THE GRAND-DUCHESS TO THE COUNTESS JULIA.

YES, Julia, I will endure my fate, and will follow your advice, although I cannot see in the distance of the future the alluring hopes that you would mirror to me. Vain is it to expect that I should tame the wild spirit of my husband. He hates, he scorns me; he is incapable of understanding me; he is incapable of loving me. His character is now so formed; he cannot change his nature.

And I also, Julia, can no longer love him. He himself has erected a barrier between us that can never be destroyed. I should receive it as the greatest boon from Heaven if death were to free me from my sorrowful condition; or if the Grand-duke, attaining the supreme power, were to immure me somewhere in a lonely cloister.

That he perfers the Finlander, Euphrosyne, to me — that I could bear. I am conscious of my own worth, and should only pity the deluded man. But — oh! that I should write it, Julia — I am a prince's daughter, I am used to courteous treatment; Julia, he ill-uses me in such a manner as a barbarian master would scarcely ill-use his slave.

Yesterday he came into my boudoir, more sullen than usual. I approached him with caresses. I had intended to induce him to intercede with the Emperor, his father, for the Chevalier d'Aubant. This d'Aubant, an infantry captain, is the same young man whom we once met in the forest at Blankenburg when we had lost ourselves, and who guided us back into the road. Perhaps you do not remember him. Since then, he has been in the Russian service; some days ago, he got into a quarrel with a young Russian who has some powerful relations in Petersburg, and killed him in a duel. People maintain that I was the innocent cause of the quarrel: that the Russian had spoken evil of me at some drinking party, and that d'Aubant had taken my part with too great warmth. Suffice it to say, that d'Aubant has become invisible for some days. It is affirmed that he has concealed himself in Petersburg; he is sought for everywhere; and should the unfortunate man be caught, his banishment to Siberia will be inevitable.

I had scarcely uttered the name of the unhappy d'Aubant when the Grand-duke cast a fearful look at me, and ordered me to be silent. I obeyed in trembling. I had never seen him look so: never had any one spoken thus to me.

I was going away. "Where are you going?" he cried, seized me by the arm, and flung me back into the middle of the room. "Doubtless to the Emperor again, in order to blacken me to him, that I may hear his reproaches wherever I go, and before all the world. But, Madam, I am weary of these cabals; and, once and for all, I beg that you will not trouble yourself any further to increase the Emperor's dislike to me."

I could not answer. I sobbed, and stretched my arms towards him. He paid no attention, but continued to threaten me. "Woe betide you," cried he, "if you gratify yourself any more by complaining of me to the Emperor. I swear to you I will then speak somewhat differently to you."

"But who," replied I, "who has been wicked enough to calumniate me thus to my husband? If I had the greatest cause for complaint, yet not a word disparaging to my husband should ever cross my lips."

"Oh," he exclaimed, "I know everything! You cannot pass yourself off for innocent. I still have more friends than the Emperor and his newly-found foreigners suppose. Mark this. New times will come some day. Patience!"

"I only request one single favor," I replied, "that you will give me the names of those who assert that I have complained of you to His Majesty. If I am guilty, then I deserve your hatred: if I am innocent, oh! do not then spurn the love of your wife! Permit me at least to clear myself to you from all such suspicion."

He again ordered me to be silent, and repeated his threats with even harsher expressions, if I should again complain to the Emperor. Tears choked my utterance. I could do nothing, but silently extend my arms towards him. I would have thrown myself on his breast, and have sought in his heart a refuge from all slanderers. He thrust me away with such violence and vehemence that I should have been thrown to the ground, had not a chair that was standing near prevented it. But I struck my forehead against the wall so that it swelled up with the hurt. The Grand-duke paid no attention to me; but left the room, banging the door angrily after him.

I lay for a long time in the arm-chair, stunned; all my senses were in a state of dulled activity, as in a fever. Little by little all began to clear, and I realized the fearfulness of my position. A flood of tears relieved my overburdened heart. I tried to recover myself that I might be able to conceal my pain from strange eyes. I walked about the room, but my knees sank under me. Then, prostrating myself on the carpeted floor, I stretched out my hands to heaven and prayed to a merciful God for rescue, or for strength to bear my fate bravely.

Oh, Julia! how great, how blessed, is the power of prayer! What happiness indeed is there in ever thinking of our God! When far around all have forsaken us, when men shut their hearts to our sorrows, when every hope is blasted by the thunder-storms of life, when we stand alone with our suffering in the midst of creation; then, Julia, one look to Him who understands all our woes, and we are already receiving help.

He it was who called us into existence: He it is in whom the afflicted soul can find refuge.

I arose strengthened, and more courageous and better than before. All passion had now died away, and all resentment at the outrage I had endured. To my God I bemoaned it; you I tell of it. But do not try to console me, Julia; for I am already comforted! I summoned my ladies in waiting. They came. I remarked that they were alarmed at my appearance. I spoke of the injury to my forehead as the result of my own thoughtlessness, ordered all visitors to be denied, and only received — what was not agreeable to me — the visit of the physician.

You see, Julia, how I am now circumstanced — far from you, from my parents, in a foreign country, unloved by the Russians, disliked and ill-used by my husband, without any one in whom I can venture to confide, without any hope of better days.

Write to me soon. Describe your own happiness

to me. My soul revives again at the pictures of your joys: I forget my grief then, and live in your paradise. Oh, how willingly would I change places with the poorest peasant woman in your village, so that I might but live in Germany, in your neighbourhood, under your protection.

THE CHEVALIER D'AUBANT TO LAURENCE BELLISLE.

Villiers, 25th July 1715.

Not lose courage! Oh, my Bellisle, how do you judge of your d'Aubant! Timid in the lap of Fortune, but brave when endurance and death lie in the field before us! This is my motto.

Even so! my fortune is — clean gone; or perhaps I never had any. I have settled with my father's creditors, have paid everything. Property, cattle, river-rights, all are sold. The residue left me of the lordly domains and properties of my ancestors stands in thirty six thousand livres net, and not a sou more or less. If all goes well with me, I shall put out my little capital at five per cent, and have three hundred thalers yearly income: the poorest village-priest has more for his masses.

I see clearly, there is nothing figurative in it — I shall literally prove the knight of the mournful visage. I shall live conformably to my position; I cannot drive any trade, cannot do carpenter's work, cannot sell goods — to beg I am ashamed.

Meantime I have not been so cheerful for a long while as I am now. I can live in my paternal house for four weeks yet, then it passes over formally to the new owner. He has already everywhere begun to improve, to repair, to clean', to make a noise in every corner. This new owner is a large, stout, good-hearted man, of the name of Maillard who, by speculation as a merchant, has collected a round sum of money; and seems to have no fault but this, that he knows he is rich and would like to play the part of benefactor, protector, and patron. In a very kind manner, he offered to me a home at his house when he should have taken possession; but I, although I do not yet know where I shall lay my head, naturally declined. To be poor, Bellisle, does not make one unhappy; but the patronizing manner of a wealthy fellow on whom Providence has showered down the loved gold in his sleep, the patronizing airs of a wealthy man who has no virtue under the sun but his well-filled coffers — oh, Bellisle, these do pain one.

Yes, Bellisle, I would rather, if any accident were to deprive me of my two thousand livres and my sturdy limbs, beg my bread from house to house with our peasants than take a pension from people with these patronizing airs.

What is it but this? I am poor, but all is well with me. That which I am, I became without any fault of my own: that which I shall become, shall be the proof of my strength — my own creating.

Poverty is not only what it falls to the greater portion of mankind to bear; but is also the unsatisfied desire of the ambitious. They would soar into higher spheres. Bread and water do not taste so badly; but to be surprised whilst partaking of them, that *is* bitter to most people.

Poverty is the element of great minds, the mother of wisdom, the instructor of mankind, the inventor

of all art and science, the bold guide over oceans
and mountains, the priestess of a better life.   Wealth
enervates body and soul, checks the soaring of the
spirit, chokes and kills it with the pleasures of sense,
makes nations degenerate, produces unheard-of diseases,
unheard-of desires, unheard-of vices.

The poor man is rich in hopes, in projects; his
life flies on amid thoughts and aspirations that the
rich man knows not.   The muses themselves fail to
fret him.   Every flower, every fruit, every kindly
glance, is for him a new pleasure.   The spare, self-
earned meal is a revel for him; his sweet sleep is
full of golden dreams.   Poverty leads us back to the
breast of nature; riches lead us to what is contrary to
nature — to fightings for rank, to indolence, to dissipation.

Do you see, Bellisle, that without having intended
it, I have written a eulogium on poverty.   But I
have done so in all seriousness.   The rich man only
feels what he *has;* but the poor man, what he *is.*
Thus I, for the first time, feel keenly what I am;
and this feeling makes me proud and cheerful.   That
which in the fashionable world is called "beggar's
pride," is often the noblest and   most honorable
pride that a mortal can foster.   It is the just appreciation of true and false worth, of inherent or acci-
dental wealth — contempt of empty titles,   of the
fringed and bordered garments of vain coxcombs, of
filled chests, of well-fed blockheads, and a high value
for unobtrusive virtue without glitter — for merit
without boast — for wisdom without charlatanery.

You ask what I intend to do.   I am going in a
few weeks to Paris.   I shall show myself to my rela-

tions, to the ministers. I possess some knowledge, am experienced, may be made of use — I shall sue for some appointment, civil or military, be the emolument ever so small. I will make myself happy on bread and water, but must be active and of use.

And if sometimes a sorrowful day comes — then, Bellisle, I think of the idol of my dreams — and am again happy. The world in which such an angelic being dwells must be of all worlds the best.

THE COUNTESS KÖNIGSMARK TO COUNTESS JULIA B.

Petersburg, 2d September 1715.

HOWEVER melancholy the cause may be, I congratulate myself on being able to weave a thread of acquaintance with your ladyship; with a lady whose mind, whose kindness of heart must be almost unequalled; for our beloved Grand Duchess Christina herself never speaks of you without admiration; and at the mention of your name her eyes beam with the sweet enthusiasm of friendship, even from her bed of sickness.

Yes, our adored princess is ill. By her order I take up the pen to tell you this, and also the reason why our gracious princess has never replied for some months to your various letters so full of friendship.

You had the happiness of being the playfellow of her youth: you are now her only and best-loved confidante. I have only been raised by the most terrible misfortunes to the rank of your rival, and thus to the opportunity of continuing the confidential intercourse between our gifted friend and yourself.

Her unhappy relations with her husband, the Grand-duke Alexis, are no longer unknown to you. But you can scarcely know what unceasing sacrifices the Grand-duchess has made in order to win the favour of her husband; with what angelic meekness she has borne his undeserved harshness; with what indescribable patience she has met his implacable cruelty; how, without intermission, she has ever been his first mediator with his Majesty the Emperor, when the latter has threatened his son in an outbreak of his terrific anger; how, filled with touching devotion, she loads her husband with kindness whilst she bears the most shameful ill-treatment from him. She is indeed like the balsam-tree, which sheds its delicious fragrance over the murderous hand by which it is broken.

But all caresses, all tears, all kindnesses, are fruitless in touching the heart of the Czarovitch. Presents that he has received from the hands of his lovely wife, work that she has herself done for him during her hours of solitude, he has given within the hour to his Finn mistress, who did not blush to appear publicly adorned with the beautiful work of the Grand Duchess. Parties that she arranged in honor of her husband, were either never attended by him at all, or were turned into occasions for heaping bitter mortification upon her who lived, and did, all for him, and for him only.

Whoever knows the stubborn, wild disposition of the Czarovitch; whoever knows the hatred which, partly owing to the shutting of his mother in a cloister by the Emperor, partly owing to those who surrounded him during the frequent absences of the Emperor, he has conceived for all the undertakings of his father; whoever knows also that he hated the beautiful and talented Princess von Wolfenbüttel for the same reason, because she was presented to him by the hand of his father — whoever knows all this can never hope for a reconciliation between this unfortunate and illustrious couple.   The Czarovitch, daily in the company of low people, without education, without principle, without perception, daily ruining his energies by uncontrolled indulgence in brandy, becomes daily more unrestrained, rougher, more tyrannical. Nothing but his only too just dread of the Emperor, his father, keeps him from even greater excesses.

Under such circumstances, the afflicted Grand-duchess is without any hope but that of being formally separated from her persecutor, or of bearing with fortitude this life of sorrow even to her grave. The Czarovitch himself confessed to her with terrible candour that he would detest her so long as she was his wife. He intimated himself to her that, from his heart, he wished for a dissolution of this marriage; but, owing to the inflexibility of the Emperor, he could never hope to obtain his consent to it.

The Grand-duchess condescended to bestow her confidence on me. A quiet attempt was to be made to learn the sentiments of the Emperor with regard to the separation. I addressed myself to Prince Menzikoff to elicit them from this favourite of the sovereign. The opportunity offered. Menzikoff with his characteristic dexterity, let fall a few casual words. But these aroused the fury of the Emperor to so fearful a degree, that Menzikoff never again had courage to make a similar trial.

"Woe betide Alexis!" cried the Czar. "If until now I have spared this ill-advised, obstinate, unworthy

son, who breaks his father's heart a thousand times a
day, the punishment he so fully deserves, it is from
affection and esteem for his wife. Woe to him if ever
this angelic being fails him!"

Although Menzikoff swore solemnly to the Emperor
that the thought of a separation had never entered the
mind of the Grand-duke, that it was only his own
idea, yet he appeared to retain his displeasure against
his son. At least thus his harsh dealings with his son
from that day would imply; and these have embittered
the Grand-duke to madness against his wife.

Be prepared then now, dearest Countess, to hear
what is most dreadful. An attempt has been made to
put the Grand Duchess out of the world by poison.
Happily this wicked act has not altogether been successful. The Grand-duchess partook of but very little
of the poisoned soup: the fortunate arrival of the imperial physician-in-ordinary at the very moment in which
the princess perceived the effect of the poison; the
promptitude with which he discovered the mischief,
and the potency of his remedies, averted the great
misfortune.

All was effected with the greatest secresy, and
must remain secret. The health of the suffering Grand-
duchess is returning. Perhaps even in a few weeks
she may again enjoy the gratification of being able to
write to you herself.

Never in any court of Europe has there been a
more amiable and a more unhappy princess; never a
woman who by her beauty, her virtues, and her
talents was more deserving, or has received less than
she. I assure you I am in despair, and bewildered.
The Emperor will not allow himself to be persuaded,

the Grand-duke will not change, and the most innocent, the noblest, of our sex is the victim of these circumstances.

Not on one single occasion has the Czarovitch
honored his wife with a visit during her illness; not
once paid so much attention to appearances as to have
sent inquiries for her health. And only remember, in
addition, that in a few months the Grand-duchess expects her accouchment again.

I conjure you, if perchance by some bright thought
you can advise us in this painful position, do not
delay. I can see no help — this saintly being will
sooner or later be destroyed by nameless barbarities.
Therefore prepare yourself always to hear the most
fearful tidings.

CHEVALIER D'AUBANT TO LAURENCE BELLISLE.

Paris, 2d October 1715.

For eight long weeks, my dear Bellisle, I have
already been walking the pavements of Paris: am on
the run from early morning till midnight; yawn half
the day in the antechambers of the great; write humble
remonstrances and petitions; feed myself with hopes
and possibilities, with shrugs and sympathizing expressions, and remain and am as before, the poor, unem-
ployed Chevalier d'Aubant, and do not advance a
step.

People praise my work, discover talent in me
— and that is all. If an empty office falls for elec-
tion, behold some other fellow springs stoutly forward,
and plants himself just where I would like to seat myself — and always one to whom I probably am fully

equal in knowledge, in activity, in goodness of disposition, or indeed ten times superior.

Ah! I know very well what is wanting in me. Adorn yourself with the wisdom of Solomon, with the virtues of a seraph, and unite in yourself the learning of all the academies, you will be nothing, and be esteemed as nothing more than a costly medal, which for the trade and exchange of life is neither current nor useful. Gold is the gloss which gives its glitter to virtue, its merit to wisdom. Gold is the moral alembic in which mud is transformed into pearls, folly into grace, weakness into heroism, frivolity into greatness of mind.

Well then, this universal tincture is wanting — then I must resign myself.

"But your relations, your friends in Paris," you will say. Ah, dear Bellisle, these good people are endlessly kind. They invite me to their parties, where they can sparkle in their superfluities; they will squander a couple of thousand thalers on a single meal, without feeling any remorse; but to render a true service when it consists only of a plain, simple, kindly action — no one thinks of this.

Such is the world; who can change it?

And now what further to begin upon? I do not know. I am so desolate that I lack even a counsellor; and yet good advice is the cheapest thing in the world, and one of which even the miser can be profuse.

But no, I will not be unjust. My old, faithful servant, Claude, who has never forsaken me, and whom I will never forsake, gives me fresh advice every day, and is never weary of it. He sometimes suggests that I shall be appointed colonel somewhere, or at the least captain: sometimes, that I shall stake in the lottery; sometimes, that I shall become a member of the imperial council; sometimes, that I shall marry a widow with ten manors.

To-day — I had scarcely finished my frugal meal — he came running in at full speed, and cried: "Captain! good news! now we will snap our fingers at the world!"

"The world will not care for that," replied I.

"Will you have a marquisate, or a barony, a large or a small principality?",

"A large one, at the least."

"Now thank Heaven, captain, that you *will* have it; it is help for us all. Make me then your minister, or what you will, for I have always been nearest to you; and you will not find a truer man under sun, moon, and stars, than your old Claude. Your horses shall be the handsomest a thousand miles round. Leave me to take care of that."

"But where is my principality, Claude?"

"In the new world, captain: there — wait — yes — on the Mississippi, in the large kingdom of Louisiana, not far from America. Every one is rushing there now. I have spoken with sixteen families to-day at the ordinary; they have come from a distance; there are Germans and Swiss among them. All are going to Louisiana. You can obtain as much land as you like there without paying a sou for it; can take as many slaves as there are Americans, and can live like a king."

"You are a fool, Claude."

"But truly a fool who is not to be outweighed with

gold.   The ship's captain, de Blaizot,   lives in the
Rue Richelieu, number 595, on the second floor.   He
is raising levies for Louisiana. You must apply to him.
He has a map of the district on his table, and appor-
tions to every one who comes to him, a holding on it.
If you will allow me, I will go to him without delay,
and will take possession of a whole province for us,
such as shall form a principality.   I beg you; water,
wine, forests for nothing; nothing is wanting to build
quickly as many towns as the whole of France contains — nothing but the will."

"The will, I have in good truth."

"Now, Captain, the game is won.   Reflect, Captain,
what this means, a completely new world! still quite
new, and not one hundredth part so consumed and used
up as our world in this country.   Doubtless pure gold
lies there beneath the earth in masses; the trees there
are so large that our largest oaks would appear but as
branches beside them.   The people themselves told me
this.   Here, for ready money one can hardly get enough
to eat; the throng of men is so great.   There, there
are really very few people: everything therefore must
be dog-cheap.   With one livre there, I shall prepare a
feast; with two livres, I shall build a palace which will
go near to compare with the Tuileries.   For an old
iron nail, the stupid savages will give me a pot full of
unstamped ducats: for a pipe of tobacco, for a little
bit of glass, I can obtain more slaves than I want.
You must know, Captain, the savages do not understand all these things yet; an old, dirty pane of glass
is to them as valuable as a jewel.   But, as I said, we
must make haste before other people come to teach
them better.   In my life, no one shall enlighten the

people and make them wise, if honest folk are thereby to run a noose for themselves!"

Claude ran on thus for a whole hour on the delights of Louisiana, and I almost laughed myself into a headache. It is certain that Captain Blaizot is beating up colonists for Louisiana, and that the recruiting gentlemen are not deficient in their puffs for decoying people to their solitary Canaan.

For to-day I calmed my happiness-intoxicated minister of state, Claude, by the promise of visiting the captain to-morrow myself, and of selecting my principality with my own eyes. But by to-morrow Claude will assuredly have some other plan.

And I, like him! Man is not made happy so much by what he possesses, as by what he hopes. And I am happy, as a demigod!

Do not distress yourself, dear Bellisle, on account of my fate. A sound heart in a sound body, a free spirit in a free breast, — the world listens to these.

Long since, all accounts from Petersburg have been wanting to me. In vain do I turn over the pages of all the newspapers, and seek for "Russia" among the articles. None name the name best worth notice in the North: my dreams alone speak to me. My horizon must soon clear. Winter approaches: I must make my choice.

THE GRAND-DUCHESS TO THE COUNTESS JULIA.

Petersburg, 5th October 1715.

THE first offering of my renewed strength shall be made to you, beloved Julia; perhaps it also may be the last: and should it be so, do not mourn, but congratulate your friend that she has reached the goal.

The kind Königsmark has told you of my illness, and of its cause. You know that my life will again be attempted — but I know that it will eventually be impossible for me to escape the snares of my assassins. And who can assure me that even already a secret, slow, poison is not creeping through my veins?

No one but Königsmark, yourself, and my acknowledged murderer, know of this frightful event. One of my cooks has become invisible since. I shall not have him pursued: the remembrance of his deed will pursue the wretch.

I feel the near approach of the end of my course. I long for it. To lose such a life is gain.

Oh, Julia, how all has changed since we parted from each other! Ah! could I then have foreseen all, I should have died in the bosom of my lovely home.

Endowed with a taste for every beauty of nature, charmed at the return of every coming spring, inspired by the stirring descriptions which travellers gave us of the majesty of the Alps, of the magic land of Italy, I longed with indescribable yearning to be able once to see this wondrous garden of the earth: my wish remained unfulfilled.

The reluctant daughter of a prince was banished for ever into the cold, sad, deserts of the most remote districts of our quarter of the globe, as out of Paradise into a country over which the anger of the Creator was brooding. Possessing a heart whose ardent sisterly affection poured itself forth to every one, and ever asked for affection in return, Fate exiled me among semi-barbarians who know only their own rude instincts, and do not comprehend me. I see them eager for quarrels and murders; and only contented when their understandings are clouded by intoxicating liquors. They do but differ from the surrounding Tartars in that they have obtained a knowledge of some small portion of the luxury of civilized Europe. Could I reign supreme over these forests, I would still prefer the condition of the poorest subject in kindly Germany.

I must break off. My strength fails me. But I take up my pen again, dearest Julia, to bid you fare-well. This sheet shall be to you the mute witness of the constancy which binds my heart to you, till death shall sever the bond. Truly it is the token — a last, unintelligible, faltering — the token of my death, at which I might well myself be alarmed. For a thousand emotions still glow within me; I would gladly tell them to you, but I am paralysed. I can only strew cold, dead, words over this sacred page. It is my winter now. Thus the eternal sun continues to glow within itself while glimmering dimly behind the pale December clouds; but, instead of the warming rays of heaven, snow-flakes are scattered over the chilled world.

Believe me, Julia, notwithstanding my youth I part without grief from a life in which I have every-where found thorns, have everywhere heard discords. In these words I do not complain of the great Creator, but of the folly of man who confuses the order of the Creator. But this folly, is not it also a melancholy necessity of nature? Does not the path of truth also lead first through the labyrinth of error? Was it not the arrangement and will of nature that man should be unwearied in seeking to extend his happiness? and was it not his own fault if from want of knowledge he chose the wrong means?

Man, in his natural condition, without development of his dormant powers, desires, and passions, still only an animal with few memories and few hopes — and man in his highest state of perfection, in which with cultivated mind and refined feelings he again conceives an affection for the laws of nature, and destroys despotism — these alone are happy. All who wander between these two conditions, the immense mass of the semi-savage — and from the banks of the Tagus to those of the Ladoga I see only these semi-savages — are miserable through perplexities, things contrary to nature, and contradiction in their desires and arrangements of the unbending ordinances of nature.

Ah! Julia, perhaps you scarcely understand me. From this distance I can only point at my death wound.

Soar with me above the busy throng of poor mortals, and observe their ways and deeds! What do you see? Behold everywhere sighs, everywhere tears, everywhere cares and sorrow! Why are the happy so few? They live isolated and alone, and are on their guard against having too many points of contact with the world.

All are unanimous that the happy are few in number; yes, the sufferers even know the cause of their misery. But who ventures on the great moral mutiny which would free the world from its woe? Who has courage enough to throw off the fetters which prevent him from entering into his Paradise? Who proclaims war against venerable, all-powerful prejudices, and

brings about a reconciliation between degenerate mankind and nature?

Consider the self-formed plans and arrangements
of mortals — are not they the work of desires which
are contrary to reason? Consider their sacred things
before which they kneel in worship — are they not
insane prejudices?

In order to please their deities they separate husbands and wives, renounce the holiest and noblest
feelings with bleeding hearts; condemn themselves in
cloisters to perpetual imprisonment, to labours which
are of use to neither heaven nor earth; and the powerful ones of the earth defend barbarities at which the
rude child of nature, equally with the perfectly wise
man, would shudder — and call theirs a holy life,
pleasing to God!

Others, in order to prepare for themselves dwellings
in the regions of a better world, mark their road towards eternal life with streams of the blood of their
brethren. With their dagger in their hand, and the
name of God on their lips, they persecute their fellow-
citizens who will not join in their belief or their fancies.
Even when nations have adopted milder customs, and
repudiate religious wars, they do not blush to hate
those of another faith with a sort of christian compassion, and to exclude them at arm's length from the
rights of community of citizenship.

Insatiable ambition devised the worldly privileges
and disadvantages of birth. Men, formed of the same
dust, placed in the same country, subject to equal weal
and woe, separate themselves in their madness as though
they were beings of different kinds, and honor and
despise each other, as though it could not but be so.

The nobleman looks down with pity on the citizen, the count on the nobleman, the petty prince on the count, the king on the prince; and each calls it profanation to enter into relationship with those over whose cradle a lower title hung.

And yet the queen and the peasant, the day-labourer and the emperor, call themselves all children of God, and equal in His sight, and moulder in the grave in the same manner, and all leave their titles behind on a heap of ashes.

Thus by countless barriers, sometimes from public opinion, sometimes from wealth or poverty, sometimes from self-prescribed laws of honor and disgrace, sometimes from the dark or fair color of the skin, the human race are separated from each other, dismembered, loveless, joyless, continually opposed, ever degenerating more entirely.

Oh, my Julia, you do not understand why I say this to you! — But read it, and re-read it, and perhaps from the fragments of these thoughts a bright anticipation may arise before you, like a spirit from the grave, which may one day comfort you and dry the tears from your eyes when I can no longer dry them for you.

If I could see you; ah, Julia, if I could but see you once more! It is my last wish, which no hope will crown. I would lay my pale cheek on your heart, and die amid thoughts of the bright days of my childhood, and pass away to the new childhood of second life.

Do not weep, my darling! Sooner or later, if the

power of Heaven should not thwart my wish, I will appear before you again — not I myself, but my spirit! It shall speak to you; and ah! perhaps it may understand your replies. Doubt this spiritual appearance: yet one day I will remind you of my words.

Farewell! — do not forget your friend. The thought of your love will lighten my last, heavy struggle, and in a happier life it will be the first of my joys.

Farewell! I ever throw the sheet down, ever to take it up again, and the intensity of my pain prevents. me from telling you what I suffer. Love me for ever. Spirits cannot be parted.

Yet one thing more, beloved Julia, I must say to you. Look upon what I have confided to you as a sacred legacy from your friend.

It is now . . . .

THE COUNTESS KÖNIGSMARK TO THE COUNTESS JULIA.

Petersburg, 9th November 1715.

THAT I only now inform you, my dearest Countess, of what the whole of Europe has already learned from newspapers and messengers of mourning, forgive on account of my inexpressible grief. I will not try either to depict it to you or to console you. The angelic Princess, who lived like a saint, and died like a saint, and already long ago was filled with presentiments of her death — she is truly deserving of the offering of our tears. But I ought not to be silent to you respecting some of the immediate circumstances of her death of which indeed I was a witness.

On the 22d of October I was summoned to the

5*

late Grand-duchess. Her long-expected accouchement
had already taken place. She had given birth to a
prince, who received at his baptism the name of Peter,
and the title of Grand-duke. The news of this birth
filled all Petersburg with joy. Never had his Majesty
the Emperor appeared so delighted. Only one solitary
man failed to join in the universal rejoicing, and this
single unfeeling being was — Oh! you can guess who.

But the public joy was speedily clouded by the
intelligence of the indisposition of the Grand-duchess.
She fell a victim to her long-continued sufferings.
When she felt the approach of death she only requested to see the Czar. She thanked him for his
fatherly kindness, and took an eternal farewell of him
and of her children. She commended them both to the
Emperor, and then gave them over to the Czarovitch,
her husband. He took the children· with him to his
apartment, and returned no more to his dying wife,
did not even make any inquiries after her health, but
repaired to one of his country houses.

The physicians still wished to persuade the Princess
to take some medicines; but she exclaimed with deep
emotion; "Do not trouble me any longer! Let me die
in peace. I have no longer any reason to wish to
live!"

She yielded up her spirit on the first of November.
By her express request her body was not opened and
embalmed, but was laid silently in the grave.* This
was also ordered by her husband, the Grand-duke, to
whom her death was announced by special messengers.

---

* Note. — This account of the death of the Princess von Wolfenbüttel,
wife of the Czarovitch, agrees in all respects, word for word, with that
which Peter Henry Bruce has narrated.

On the 7th November the funeral ceremony took place in the Cathedral with all the pomp and tokens of respect which were due to her exalted rank.

The fearful day on which her husband had ill-used her so frightfully with blows and kicks, and had left her fainting and bathed in blood — I do not know whether the sainted one has ever written to you of similar events which alas! occurred too often — and the attempt to poison her which was only frustrated by her youthful vigour and the prompt aid of the physician, these without doubt were the chief causes of her early death. She was scarcely twenty-one years old!

I refrain from all observations on the occurrences, by which the daughter of one of the noblest of the princely houses of Germany was abandoned to the brutality of a monster, and by which a Princess possessed of the rarest advantages of heart and intellect, with whose beauty and virtues no one in all the courts of Europe could vie, was unpardonably and cruelly killed.

Oh, how wretched is the domestic life of the great, even whilst, dazzled by external glitter, the ignorant mob stare at them as enviable demi-gods. What crimes does not the purple often cover, for what atrocities does not the princely crown often serve as a shield against the indignant verdict of the world! Could the eye of a pious pauper pierce into the dark secrets of many a wealthy house, shuddering he would turn back to his dry crust, and with a grateful look bless his beggar's staff.

Among the papers which the sainted Grand-duchess left behind her, I have found a long, unfinished letter which she had destined for you in her lifetime, my dearest Countess. I inclose it in this letter, as a precious remembrance of faithful love.

Let us sorrowfully revere the memory of the exalted sufferer, and cement the bond of friendship over her grave.

CHEVALIER D'AUBANT TO LAURENCE BELLISLE.

Paris, 7th November 1715.

How deeply, beloved Bellisle, your unexampled friendship affects me! An act like yours belongs only in these days to fairy fables. You give up to me and to my possible descendants the half of your large fortune; present me with the beautiful estate at Bordeaux which fell to you with your last inheritance, and for all this ask nothing but my consent. I could not, for I was too much overcome, I could not refrain from reading to some of my relatives your letter, priceless record of the goodness of man's heart. All were — not touched — but astonished. They congratulated me. "Has this man any children?" others inquired. "Certainly; indeed both a son and a daughter!" I replied. The amazement became still greater. An old, very wealthy, childless cousin shook his head at them all, as though he could not believe the story. He asked a hundred questions about you; and all the hundred questions, as I at last perceived, had only this for their end and object, to ascertain whether you did not now and then suffer from weakness of mind, and cloudiness of understanding.

You see, my Bellisle, how incredible your act is to common minds. All these people also imagine that they know what friendship is. There are among them several gentlemen who have taken pleasure in reading poetic effusions, and who even bemoan themselves over the lack of true friends, and the absence of the tenderer and nobler sentiments among men. But that they should ever watch any one who is dear to them to see whether, and how, he suffers; that they should devote any, even a small, portion of their fortune to place him whom they love in more prosperous circumstances, this never occurs to these gentle, sublime spirits either waking or sleeping. They write you the most feeling epistles; they swear fidelity to you in time of need and of death; they call every one their own enemy who dares to annoy you; they profess themselves in the most solemn terms ready to shed their blood for you, if occasion require; they would esteem their own lives as nothing, if thereby they could promote your happiness. — But, my dear friend, you must not expect one farthing of money: and if a couple of hundred louisd'or could release you from purgatory and death! —

Yet all fancy themselves sufficiently good-hearted to be true friends, and to have true friends; but assuredly not one among them remembers ever to have either performed or received any great proof of friendship.

But no more about these poor sinners who, if they read in a book stories of highminded friends, or see them represented on the stage, clap their hands in ecstasy; or, touched with sorrow, weep their eyes red; yet in reality would not like to apply the hundredth part of their possessions to the maintenance of a true-hearted man.

Yes, my beloved Bellisle, I do thank you. Your gift is worth more, at least I esteem it more highly than if you had sacrificed your life for me. Do not misunderstand my words. One can much more easily find people who, transported by the attractive enthusiasm of mutual affection, will sacrifice their lives for each other, than any who would give to a friend their goods and possessions, or even a very nominal portion of them. All enthusiasm, even if its secret spring has been only self-love, soon forgets its obscure origin, and annihilates mean and greedy selfishness. The payment of money on the contrary requires cold blood: there egotism again has its say, and talks and calculates so long that the bags of gold almost consecrated to a friend find their way back to the secret coffers. Then this tender-hearted friend bethinks him of some poetical tirade; weeps also, if it is not to be avoided, some bitter tears of melancholy on your heart, and bemoans the cruelty of remorseless fate.

And now, beloved Bellisle, one more request at the end of my incessant chattering. Your kindness would raise me above all cares as to my means of life; and would place me in a position to be able to live according to my rank and my birth, and even in considerable style. But in the possession of this gift I should be less happy than I now am — permit me then to give it back to you without using any ceremony about it. I will retain nothing but the ceaseless obligation of gratitude to you — ah, that I could show it!

Do not be angry with me, that I return your present. If poverty should press me, I would without hesitation turn to you and ask your aid; I would look upon your possessions as part of my own, just as I possess nothing which does not also belong to you.

But I am still in the spring-time of my life; I feel my own powers, and I am not yet robbed of the means of earning for myself what I shall need for freeing my later life from care. And a little tree planted by our own hand affords us higher pleasure than a whole forest given to us by chance.

And — why should I conceal it from you? — I love you too much to be able to endure to be vanquished by you in the grandest proof of friendship. I should fear to love you less if I were obliged to revere you as my benefactor. Nothing must destroy our equal terms, neither be exalted above the other, if we would retain unaltered the affectionate feelings which hitherto have warmed our hearts.

And now for a strange adventure!

The day before yesterday as I was passing through the court of the Louvre — it was late and twilight — an acquaintance made me go with him to a neighbouring billiard-table.

I found a great crowd there. In every room gaming-tables were set out. I went from one to another.

"Do you know red-coat yonder?" asked my acquaintance, and pointed stealthily on one side. Not far from me stood a small, broad-shouldered, man in a scarlet frock-coat whose colour contrasted strangely with the coal-black, unpowdered hair, and the pale, bony face. He was watching the card-players.

"I do not know him," was my answer.

"He never takes his eyes off you," said my acquaintance.

I paid no further attention to him, took some punch, and went into the next room. There I found the red-coat again, and certainly remarked that, from time to time, he looked keenly at me with his large, prominent eyes. Neither the man, nor his looks, pleased me. I hastened into the billiard-saloon; the red-coat was there also. I stood in front of the chimney-piece. My offensive spy planted himself by me. I began to converse with him: his speech betrayed him a foreigner. By his pronunciation I should have taken him for an Englishman, if he had not had such a repulsive, gipsy-like face. He replied to me for the most part very laconically. After a while he suddenly pulled out his watch, turned towards me, and said: "The wife of the Czarovitch, the Princess von Wolfenbüttel, is dead!" I was struck with a chill as he uttered the words. He turned away from me. I sought for him in the crowd. He had fled. None knew him of all those who were present: every one said he had been seen there for the first time on that evening.

I hastened immediately to the secretary of the Russian embassy, whom I knew very well. Still trembling with horror, I imparted the frightful news to him; I asked him for confirmation or contradiction. He laughed and said: "The last couriers announced the good health of the Princess von Wolfenbüttel, and that her accouchement was daily expected."

Oh! I was happy as a god at these words. What object could the red-coat have had in imposing on me with this horrible story? And even if he knew me, as he must have done, how could he know the secret of my heart, and what I feel towards the angelic Christina?

But the stupid jest is already forgotten. I wish you may never see such a gipsy fellow even in dreams.

CHEVALIER D'AUBANT TO LAURENCE BELLISLE.

Paris, 18th December 1715.

IF none of your prized letters have been answered by me for six weeks, oh! forgive me, — I have not been myself — I have been the prey of a boundless sorrow which, at last, with kindly force robbed me of consciousness. I have struggled with a terrible fever. To-day is only the third day on which I have ventured to leave my bed for a few hours. With a weary, trembling hand I can tell you of my convalescence. Thanks for it to the good doctor who lives in the same house with me, and to the attendance of my faithful Claude.

She lives no longer! Oh, Bellisle! the only one, the most heavenly of women — she lives no longer!

Do not blame my immoderate grief; only when I give myself up to it does it become more endurable.

I may not, I cannot, tell you what I have suffered since I took the ill-fated newspaper into my hands, and read the detailed account of the death of the Grand Duchess; how, stunned, I staggered back leaning on Claude's arm through the streets to my house, how there I sank down powerless, and soon lost all consciousness.

Ever since I had seen Christina for the first time in her paternal woods, I had lived, breathed, for her alone. A wonderful change had passed over my being; the whole world had become full of charms for me for the sake of this its brightest ornament, and every phenomenon of nature more full of meaning.

To picture her to myself in the glory of her ineffable attractions, to imagine her present with me in the important moments of my life, to see her radiant in the background of all my dreams as their most blessed object, once more again to be able to attend her court either in Germany or in Russia, to be able to live in her service — all this had become a necessity to me, the end of all my thoughts and acts, my existence itself.

Love — what in intercourse with women we call love — was not my feeling. It was a continual rapture in remembering the most perfect and most lovely being that ever trod the wondrous circle of creation.

And now must I thus suddenly extinguish all my hopes, and twine the image of my sacred one with thoughts of the past alone, of death, of decay . . .

Ah, Bellisle! the great change has fallen upon me. Behind me, lies the springtime of my existence in the far distance; before me, perpetual winter. Brightness and beauty have vanished from nature. I live for nothing but for lagging death.

Alas! that I must needs experience this hour, this position! That all my illusions are torn from me, which, like a veil, had hitherto so beneficently concealed from me my own misery and the misery of life. Creation with all its splendours is a gigantic fermentation, throwing up being after being, like a transient froth which sinks down again into the leaven.

Where hast thou, oh, Nature! in the whole realm of thy mysteries one single balsam for the never-healing wounds of the heart which thou hast created so sensitive a thing? Wherefore didst thou call my name in the obscure world of sleeping germs and substances, and summon me forth from the still unconsciousness of nonentity? Canst thou repay us with thy thousand joys for one single pang that we must endure? Fearful iron despotism of nature, who, because she wills it, commands us to live instead of not to live; throws mingled roses and thorns in our path; and kills us when she chooses.

Paris, 3d January 1716.

It may be as you say, dear Bellisle, that my last letter betokened still a very feverish pulse. Your kindness is inexhaustible. Your ideas reanimate mine. I will try all I can to bring myself back to my former cheerfulness: I will forcibly throw myself into illusions, and pass the rest of my life, as if in a state of intoxication; for indeed this poor existence is not worth enjoying when insipid. All men feel this as soon as they have outgrown the cloudy, confused, age of childhood, and begin to see and to think more clearly. Indeed why do the proclivities of nations also correspond with this, confusing their intellects for a longer or a shorter time with wine, and the juice of the grape and of the palm-tree—with beer, strong waters, opiates, and tobacco plants? It must then be a very generally felt pleasure that we should not enjoy the world, this weary, prosaic, world, as it is placed before us.

Europe pleases me not; I shall seek a home in some new part of the world; it would be quite indifferent to me if I were to become a new Robinson in an uninhabited island. What does it signify after all where my dust lies? I am alive, and a time will come when I shall be no more.

You will say, "Change yourself, but not your hemisphere." The old common-place has lost its force with me. I am free; why should I live amongst sleeping men if I would be awake — among triflers if I would be in earnest? Europe disgusts me with her semi-culture. I would live amongst wise men, or among the simple children of nature: both are equally worthy of love because they walk in simplicity, integrity; and are natural. The nations of our quarter of the globe are still in their boys' clothes; and are, like boys, awkward, full of contradictions, and rich in undigested school-wisdom. Every one *seems*, no one *is*.

My bargain with the ship-captain de Blaizot is concluded. I am quitting Europe, and going to Louisiana. I shall build my house on the beautiful banks of the Mississippi, and be the chief of a little colony who have elected me as their leader. There are six mechanics who are willing to go to North America at their own cost: they are entering my service. I have already given considerable commissions in Bordeaux for the purchase of seed, cattle, agricultural and domestic utensils. Next month I shall take my departure from Paris, and in March we are to embark.

Do not suppose that I am hastening thither, like many others, to collect stores of precious metals such as Ponce de Leon must have found there. They may rest in peace thousands of years yet, for me; I will not destroy the repose of one Indian for their sake. No passion, except those which religious zeal engenders, is so frightful, so destructive of everything, is more cruel in its working, more worthless in its object, than the thirst for gold.

Millions of men fall victims to it; millions traverse distant seas, and perish miserably amidst their hopes in the wastes of a foreign land. Unfortunates! And if they had scraped together heaps of gold, and had dragged it back to Europe, would they have been more light-hearted, happier, richer? Could they have done more than satisfy their hunger, defend themselves against frost and heat with clothes, sleep peacefully? What is a ton of gold with an ailing body? What is a whole Potosi with a sick heart?

No, I do not leave my native shores for this. I yearn for a happier life. I would be the founder of a happy society which, flourishing through industry, wise through instruction, shall, by civil and religious freedom become powerful and enviable. I will go far into the interior of the country, at a distance from the colonies of covetous Europeans, and from the troubled sea-coasts. I will enter into a treaty with my Indian neighbours, and our simple bond shall be more sacred than the repeated treaties of the cunning politicians of Europe.

Sivray, 20th February 1716.

From the ravishing banks of the Charente, already ninety miles distant from Paris, I write to you. The first flowers of the young spring must smile at me from the banks of a foreign isle; nothing will detain me, were it even the whole of France replete with charms, as a fairy land.

Perhaps you are astonished, my dear friend, to see me, distant from the accustomed streets, reposing in a poor, inconsiderable little town. You are right. You will be still more surprised when I tell you that already for nine complete days I have been scouring this country in all directions like a hunter following on the track of much-coveted game. But — you laugh more and more — witchcraft surrounds me everywhere. I no longer know whether I am dreaming, whether I am awake, whether I am raving. Things supernatural become realities; my dreams embody themselves, and angels, whom I have beheld in the raptures of imagination, move around me here as human beings on earth.

Attended by Claude, I quitted the capital. My mind was already wandering amid those plains of the Mississippi which lie in the same latitude with Egypt, the blessed Yemen, Hindostan and China. I already saw myself there in my philosophical solitude, surrounded by my huts, my plantations, and my flocks; saw my garden adorned with all the flowers with which eternal spring strews the earth within the tropics; and beheld, amid the sacred gloom of a grove planted by myself, the monument I shall erect to the memory of my adored princess. She is no more, but I still live, and live and breathe for her alone. I shall weep for her so long as my eyes have tears; I cannot forget the never-to-be-forgotten one; and no joy is so dear to my heart as the silent, hopeless, ever restless yearning for her.

We then arrived at Poitiers. Here I took a day's rest in order to visit in passing an old companion in arms, Colonel Brouin. It was in the morning. I did not find him at home. A guide conducted me round the city to show me its curiosities and antiquities.

The finest part of Poitiers is by the gate St. Lazare. Here ruins of the sunken Roman works raise themselves up on different sides; there is also an old ruined castle not far from which a stream runs into the river Clain.

The landscape all around possesses much beauty and a romantic appearance. Tired, I seated myself, not far from the castle, on a broken piece of wall; and, whilst my well-informed Cicerone related to me the ancient glories of Poitiers, how the Emperor Augustus himself built it, how in former days famous councils of the Church had been held here, and how even in the time of Charles VII. the parliament of Paris had fled hither, I meditated upon the transitoriness and perishableness of all earthly things. The fortunate Augustus and the unfortunate Charles, the pious men of the councils, and the Demosthenes of the Parliament are no more, and their works have passed away also. All had cares, possessions, and sufferings, like ourselves; and died after a life poor in joys and full of anxieties. And I reflected on the teaching of the Church concerning the resurrection and restoration of all things. Then my soul trembled with joy. Amid the millions there, would *the one* of all others stand glorified, and amid millions I should see her.

And whilst I was thus thinking, — oh, Bellisle! — she stepped out from behind the half-buried walls round the castle, in the midst of some ladies and gentlemen, went down the path towards the stream where a little boat awaited her, rowed with her companions down the stream, where amid bushes, and the windings of the river she vanished before I could recover from my amazement, my unspeakable perplexity. "Was it she herself? Was it her spirit? Was it hallucination? Was it a wondrous fancy of nature who had created her most lovely work a second time in order that the most precious link in the chain of her creations should not be wanting by the death of the Grand Duchess?

Christina is no more, and yet I saw her; for she it was. Her figure, her grace, her countenance, her luxuriant light-brown hair, her movements — all was herself!

I sprang up and hastened to the river-bank, but it was already too late. I asked the guide the names of the party. The stupid fellow did not know what to answer. Instead of telling me these, he chattered through several stories about a large stone which was lying in Poitiers on four other stones, and wished to conduct me thither. I ran along the bank to try and discover the boat in the distance, but the brushwood prevented me from advancing.

I returned to the city like a madman. Colonel Brouin received me affectionately; but vainly did I inquire the names of the persons who had excited in me so lively an interest.

Do not pronounce sentence on me too hastily, Bellisle. Read this letter to the end. What I believe to have seen is more than a mere illusion!

On the evening of the same day — I do not know what festival the people of Poitiers were celebrating — I went to mass with Brouin and his family. We entered the interior of a handsome, old, gothic church whose large bold proportions, whose pillars, vaulted roofs, and hundred altars, were lighted up by the brilliance of countless lamps and torches. We could scarcely find room for our party, so great was the crowd. Whether from the solemnity of the place, or the splendour of the lights, or the effect of the music, and of the voices of the choir sometimes broken in upon by the majestic tones of the organ, suffice it to say that I was soon filled with sensations of the deepest melancholy. The image of Christina hovered around me; my yearnings became more intense, and I again experienced all the nameless pangs which had almost destroyed me when I had heard the account of her death and interment. My eyes swam with tears; and, with a trembling voice, I sighed to Heaven: "Oh! wherefore hast Thou given me such a heart, and such a burden of grief?"

When I again cast down my eyes they wandered sideways to the seats of the ladies; and, Bellisle, there I again beheld the same form which had appeared to me this morning at the old castle. Her feeling eye rested on me! Bellisle, on me! She it was again, the Grand-duchess herself in every feature, every movement, only I might say more blooming, brighter, more lovely, than when I last saw her in Petersburg, when grief was already leading her slowly to the grave. As in the morning so now, she was dressed in deep black, and wore a few flowers at her breast.

My stedfast gaze was rivetted on the wondrous form. She perceived it, appeared to be moved, and hastily dropped her black veil over her heavenly countenance. And yet it seemed to me that, from behind the darkness of her veil, her eyes were still watching me.

But I almost lost my consciousness at this poetic moment of my existence, at this point of light and radiance in the gloomy picture of my life. How shall

6*

I describe my condition to you? I did not remember the enormous inconsistency of the Russian Grand-duchess sleeping the deep sleep of death in the imperial grave at Petersburg, whilst at the same time hearing mass in a church in Poitiers. I no longer saw the church with its brilliant altars, its arches and niches veiled in gloom; but it was to me as though I were breathing the air of the outer precincts of Heaven, where blessed spirits, all clad in their earthly forms, had assembled, in sweet anticipation, ere receiving their summons to the most holy place. And the effulgence of the rays that fell around me in the shadowy gloom, and on the worshippers all, and the chorus of sacred harmonies above, were blended in my dream, my celestial vision. I found nothing unintelligible in it; and if a deity had ordained this to be my eternal state, I should have been the happiest of all created beings.

The time flew past. Every one left the church. Even the wondrous image resembling Christina seemed to be preparing for departure. "Who is the lady yonder in black?" I anxiously inquired of Colonel Brouin who was next me.

"I do not know her."

"A stranger, then?"

"Very probably; for I have never before seen her in Poitiers. The young lady next her, with whom she is in conversation, is a daughter from the hotel of the Golden Star."

"Are you well acquainted with her?"

"I have met her several times at balls. She dances splendidly."

"Dear Colonel, I entreat you, ask your acquaintance the name and native country of the black lady."

"With pleasure."

During our talk the ladies had already become lost in the crowd. How gladly would I have hastened after her! but I was obliged to make some sacrifice to decorum.

I gave the Colonel no rest on the following morning until we started together for the Golden Star Hotel. The Colonel inquired of the pretty daughter of the landlord about the strange lady.

"She comes from Lyons," was the reply; "Her father's name is de l'Ecluse; he appears to be a merchant. He ordered horses to be put to early this morning, and went away with his amiable daughter."

"Whither?" cried I.

"We do not know. He was inquiring yesterday about the road to Sivray," answered the young lady. "It would seem," she added as she glanced archly at me, "that you knew each other in Lyons, and have met here in our city unexpectedly. Were not you yesterday evening with the Colonel at the church of St. Eustatius?"

I replied in the affirmative.

"Well then, Mademoiselle de l'Ecluse was questioning me about you. I could only tell her that you were a stranger."

This was all that we could learn respecting the unknown, who with her father had scarcely remained two days in Poitiers.

Brouin's entreaties were all in vain. I took my departure on the same morning for Sivray. Wherever I arrived, I inquired for the merchant of Lyons and his travelling companion. Sometimes I was directed to the right, sometimes to the left. Continually I fancied I had discovered the track; continually I found myself again mistaken, until I gave up all hope of ever being able to clear up the perplexing adventure.

To-morrow I shall go from here. Say if you will, my Bellisle, that the force of a vivid imagination has played me a trick; that, on account of some resemblance, I have mistaken a pretty girl of Lyons for a spiritual apparition; that there is nothing less astonishing than that a lady, unceasingly followed by the eyes of a man, should at last become curious enough to ask the name of this man — still I never shall forget the day at Poitiers. To it also will I erect a monument in my hermitage by the Mississippi.

Bordeaux, 13th March 1716.

WHEN I had only just returned from paying my first visits in this prosperous trading-town, the banker M. Duchat appeared at the door and asked whether I wished to receive the sums of money lying for me at his office in bills of exchange or in coin?

"What sums of money?" Before I came to Bordeaux M. Duchat had had no correspondence either with myself, or with any of my intimate friends. I had not even received a card from him through you, dear Bellisle. I expressed to him my astonishment: I maintained that he was completely mistaken in the person. He showed me a letter without address or signature, and asked me whether I was the Chevalier d'Aubant described in it? Whether I had been in the Russian service? Whether I had determined upon going to Louisiana with Captain de Blaizot? I did not deny it; and he then pointed out to me that I had a capital of 150,000 livres to receive from him. Further information he would not give me. But that the order for it came, as he asserted, from London, where not a soul knew that the Chevalier d'Aubant would arrive at Bordeaux in March in order to take ship for America — that is certainly an invention.

Who is my unknown benefactor? Oh, Bellisle, can I guess any one but you? A friend, like you alone, is capable of giving to his friend so regal a present, as his farewell. Yes, I accept the sum of money; but, I pray, increase its value by owning that you are the giver.

Santa Cruz, 8th July 1716.

OH, Bellisle! the strangest fatality that ever provoked a mortal, persecutes me. The boundless ocean divides me from the shores of Europe; yet what I saw there, I see again here: and what enchanted me there exercises its powerful witchery over me here. The course of my life resembles a beautiful ghost-story; the same wondrous form that ravished me in the plains of Germany, that I beheld radiant at the Court of the Russian Emperor as Grand-duchess, that startled me on the banks of the Clain, that inspired me in the Temple at Poitiers, — utters my name amid the palms of Teneriffe.

But I will narrate all in quiet order, so that you may not again chide me for the confusion in my letters. You will already have received my last letter which I wrote to you from Funchal in Madeira: we were obliged to remain there for several days on account of contrary winds. Captain de Blaizot at last, early on the morning of the third of July, ordered the

anchor to be weighed: towards evening on the fourth
we could already, in the dim distance on the horizon,
see the island of Teneriffe which however we did not
reach till the following day.

The captain wished to lay in supplies of wine at
this island. Therefore we were obliged to wait there
for a few days. I went on shore with de Blaizot;
and, on beholding the majestic peak which rears its
conical form into the very clouds, had nothing less in
view than to visit this far-famed mountain. But the
Captain deterred me from doing so. Yet I lost nothing;
for thereby I beheld the unearthly beloved one.

Yesterday was a glorious day. In the evening I
betook myself to the shore called "The Almeida,"
where, beneath the shade of lofty palm and chestnut-
trees, I enjoyed a delicious hour of dreamings over
my future. The contemplation of the ever restless,
boundless ocean; and then again, on the other side of
the town, of the gently swelling mountain whose
highest summit was encircled by a coronet of floating
silvery clouds; the light, pure air in which I imagined
I breathed more freely and healthfully, the aromatic
perfume which surrounded me from innumerable shrubs,
plants, and bushes of novel forms, the busy hum of
workpeople, porters, and sailors on the beach, all
formed a new and beautiful picture to me, such as
I had never before seen, and as made my heart swell
with tender emotions.

When behold! — I had arrived at the end of the
Almeida, near the quay, which is built far out into the
sea — the same man, whom in my letters from Paris,
I called "redcoat," came striding breathlessly along with
a parcel under his arm. It was the same gipsy face,

only instead of the scarlet coat he wore a light-green travelling dress. He ran past me, looked at me, stood in astonishment, and cried, "Chevalier, you here! Welcome to Teneriffe! Whither lies your route?"

I answered as hurriedly as he asked, "To Louisiana, to New Orleans."

"Good luck!" cried he, and ran off, along the quay. The haste of this strange person vexed me. I called after him. He did not hear me. I would gladly have spoken with him. I followed him slowly. The sides of the wharf were crowded with boats which were landing, and pushing off. I saw my greencoat spring into one of these boats; in it there were two ladies and an old gentleman. I stepped nearer. The boat was already loosed from the ring, and rowing seawards. I heard a female voice call "D'Aubant!" from the vessel. Oh, my friend, all grew misty before my eyes; it was the Lyonnese divinity, the Grand Duchess, the maiden of the German forest, call her what you will.

With the speed of a bird the boat flew forwards, and was lost among the ships which lay at anchor in the roadstead. Unhappy me! all presence of mind and all self-possession had left me. Too late I determined to hasten after the strange man, and at last to unravel the incomprehensible enigma. I ran up and down the quay, and sought to hire a boat at any price. I found nearly all engaged; the captains wanted others; whilst again with others I had some trouble in making myself understood by the sailors, who only spoke Spanish.

When at last I had obtained a boat, I saw three large vessels with spread sails putting out to sea. A land-wind, which at Teneriffe is a rarity for voyagers, favoured them. I trembled at the thought that one of these might be bearing away the mysterious Unknown. I came to the anchorage, and inquired from ship to ship, and my fears found confirmation.

The ladies had gone on board the French ship, called the Dolphin, which was among those that had sailed. All that they could tell me was, that the commander of the Dolphin had only delayed his departure on account of these ladies, and had his anchor already weighed on their arrival.

It was dark when I once more stepped on shore — I ran back to the Almeida like a desperate man, and (I do not blush to acknowledge it) gave vent to my grief in a thousand tears. My eyes found no sleep that night.

As soon as morning dawned I went out to make inquiry where the ladies might have been found during their stay in the island. It was in Santa Cruz itself that they had lived, in a private house. The owner of the house, a wine-merchant, knew nothing more to tell me than that the lady who interested me so much was the daughter of a German who was on the voyage to his relations in the West Indies. The second lady he had engaged as attendant to his daughter; and another person, a man, who by the description given of him can be none other than my redcoat of Paris, or Greencoat of Teneriffe, appeared to be the servant of Herr Walter, who called him simply Paul.

So far went my enlightening, if that can be called enlightening which only increased my perplexity. I obtained without difficulty that the room should be shown to me which the lovely Miss Walter had

occupied. I entered it with quiet awe, as the holiest
of temples. Her spirit seemed to me yet to speak
from the simple furniture and ornaments, and each
appeared to be beautified, and to be rendered of importance, because it had been consecrated by her use.
This floor had supported her, this arm-chair received
her, this mirror reflected her heavenly form. I searched
all with looks of inquiry and sacred awe, and sought
for traces and reliques like a pilgrim who treads the
holy ground of Jerusalem, and beholds the sepulchre
in which his Redeemer lay.

On a side-table lay some torn-up papers, one of
which contained these broken German words: —

"Oblivion from dark Lethe's kindly flood.

Hope, the green coronal of fays . . ."

One could see by the character of the manuscript
that a female hand had traced them. The wine-
merchant also affirmed that he had once found the
lovely stranger writing in this room. This was enough
for me. The little sheet, with its touching lines, became
my treasure.

Bellisle, Bellisle, who is this wonderful being who
crosses my path under ever-changing forms and names
in the most different countries of the world. It is not
only *one* — are they more? I no longer think the
latter, since on the quay I heard my name spoken by
her. The daughter of Walter, and the Lyonnese de
l'Ecluse, are the same. The daughter of Walter, and
the wife of the Grand-duke Alexis, are marvellously
connected in my ideas through the so-called Paul, who
is her servant, and who in Paris announced to me —
why specially to me? — the death of the Princess
von Wolfenbüttel before the embassy was informed of

it.   Bellisle, do not strange secrets exist here?   Who
knows the history, veiled from the world, of many a
princely house?   The wife of the Czarovitch is dead;
her body has been laid in the Imperial burying-place
— but yet this princess is still living, and wandering
about under this sky! The Princess von Wolfenbüttel
at this moment is sailing over the waves of ocean between the tropics, whilst Europe is mourning her.

I cannot now rest on earth until I shall have un-
ravelled the mystery.

As the rocking boat bore her away across the
water, she uttered my name in sweet tones — and
this call summons me to follow her — through deserts,
through paradises, — it is ever resounding in my ears,
and the quenched flame of my life bursts forth again
with renewed force.

The Dolphin bore her to the shores of America.
She can then be traced. I will ceaselessly and restlessly
journey from port to port, from country to country,
until I discover her track; and then, an Arcadia will
bloom for me, and that world will not deceive me!

Perhaps you may not receive any letters from me
for a long time, send yours for me always to Bilaxi;
or, if you prefer it, to the new colony on the Mississippi, New Orleans. Some day, tired with my adventures, I shall certainly return thither.

BOOK THE SECOND.

FROM THE DIARIES OF AUGUSTINE HOLDEN.

1.

THE palms cast their soft shade over the window of my hut; an unknown mountain with its snowy summit glitters in the distant horizon; a nameless stream roars in the ravine amid rocks and uprooted trunks of trees; Nature, in a strange garb, surrounds me with an enchanting mixture of colour; I do not even know yonder trees that wave their dark enormous branches in the breeze; nor that copse at the foot of the hill; and the flowers that spring up in the meadow are all unfamiliar.

All is well with me here; here a new life is beginning, here is my rest, my security.

Receive a greeting from me, thou wondrous, thou friendly solitude, I will be thine inhabitant. I will call you sisters, ye kindly savages; for ye cradle your children and your dead amid the branches of the trees. Thus one day your hands shall rock me in eternal sleep amid the cool boughs. Fear not the frail woman of Europe. Extend your hands to me, ye children of nature, let me come into your huts, thus simply twined with poles, and branches, and roofed with leaves; I will learn the songs of your women, and teach you the skilled works of my fatherland. I will be the witness of your feasts, your dances, and will adorn your victor with loveliest pearls of crystal, and enrich your peaceful dwellings with all useful furniture.

2.

Julia! oh, my Julia! for you it is to whom I talk in thought: to you I dedicate these pages of my diary, this fruit of loneliness and sadness. Julia, though you are living at an immeasurable distance from me, and weep for me as one weeps for the dead, your friend is wandering beneath a foreign sky, and still loves you; and, with feelings of tenderness, engraves your name on the cedars of a strange hemisphere.

I see you turn pale, and with trembling hands lock up the papers which one day — when both our lives shall be hastening to a close, and Europe shall long have forgotten me, and the remembrance of me shall only be preserved by your true love — in that day, will perhaps become your property.

Why do you faint and tremble? Have you forgotten the promise that, after a long time, my spirit should appear to you? You shrink back and doubt? Oh, my Julia! do you no longer recognize the trace of my hand? It is the same hand which twined so many posies for you in the garden of our childhood; the same that, with its soft pressure, swore everlasting friendship for you; it is the same that once enclosed yours convulsively, and would not let you go until we were made to part.

Yes, Julia, I am alive. My exalted kindred, my prospects, remain behind. I resigned my name itself to the dust of the grave: Augustine Holden is a new-born being.

In front of my door, where once chamberlains and countesses awaited my orders, Indian women are now sitting, who are nursing their children. In place of concerts and masquerades, I listen to the song of a savage who is wandering alone in the forest, or to the warbling of an unknown bird; or watch the dance of the natives in the moonlight. A mossy couch is spread instead of my velvet cushions; and my table is covered with maize, vegetables, and the cooling fruits of the torrid zone. And yet, Julia, do not pity me; for I am happy! No tear of home-sickness for Europe has yet fallen from my eyes since I have trodden the soil of America.

There is heaven in my heart, oh Julia! and a new feeling has been disclosed to me of the value of life. I move with rapture through the green twilight of these enormous forests; sit with thrilling joy on the declivities by these lonely waterfalls; breathe more freely in this mild air amid balmy shrubs, and weep tears of pleasing melancholy only when in the evening old Herbert's flute sounds through the listening solitude, and revives in my imagination the loved forms of my deserted children, their smiles, their sweet caresses, their innocent wiles. Ah, Julia — to be able only to look at those fair little beings once more — only to be able to stand unrecognized among a crowd of other spectators and watch their games from a distance — this is my last burning wish. But they scarcely knew their mother; they will never mourn her loss. Only I bewail your lot, oh my Natalie! my Peter!

3.

Only to you, beloved one, will I reveal the secret of my life. But I conjure you throw these sheets into the flames, that no profane eyes may wander over them, and that the treachery may never renew the grief of my parents. Ah! what would console them if they knew that their loved child was living among savages in the interior of America? Who would rescue the few who, filled with compassion, managed my flight? Would they not, if it were not too late, claim me again in my home? Would they not cause the whole of this solitude to be searched in order to find me? I tremble at the awful possibility — I should resolve rather to die than to behold the shores of Europe again.

Believe it, Julia, only the most frightful events could have induced me to choose such an extraordinary line of conduct. I had fought a great fight, and had wept tears of blood over the cradle of my forsaken children. May God forgive my husband!

Every evening I fell asleep with tears, every morning I awoke with feelings of dread from my restless, uneasy slumber. Scarcely a day passed in which I did not endure outrages, and the most torturing threats, from my husband. It was a blessing to me when he avoided me. And when he came my grief began anew. For the most part he only showed himself when, overcome with brandy, without sense or feeling, he wished to give vent upon me to the wrath which the exasperated Boyards, lifeguards, and priests, had excited in him towards his father: or when he returned from the convent where his mother with her detestable lover Glebof had been devising plots and intrigues against the Emperor; or from his aunt, the Princess Mary, who shared in the hatred against her Imperial brother felt by the deposed Czarina.

"Patience! patience!" he often cried, "the Czar is not made of iron. When once I ascend the throne, madam, our marriage will be at an end; and I will send you into the same convent in which my innocent mother is now pining. I will have the Lord High Chancellor, Count Goloskin, impaled alive as a reward for his meddling; for it is entirely his fault that I was obliged to marry a Wolfenbüttel. And I will also have Prince Menzikoff and his brother-in-law impaled alive for company for Goloskin. The favourites of the Czar shall learn to catch sables in Siberia, and all the accursed foreigners with their new customs and refinements, these fortune-hunters, idlers, and adventurers — I will drive them out of Russia with a rod of iron as troublesome vermin, and they shall be presented with charity in knouts on their way home."

He often repeated this to me — swore it to me with the most frightful imprecations. Once I clung caressingly and weeping to his neck to soothe his displeasure: he threw me off as though I were an insolent beggar, and gave me a blow on the face that stunned me. Ah, Julia! this is not the first ill-usage that I have been obliged to bear during my life; I, who from my childish years, had always been petted by thousands; I, the darling of my parents; I, the Princess! — No; and if I could I would not depict to you the feelings under which at that time I was pining away.

To no soul did I disclose my mortification, which was afterwards repeated all too often. Perhaps I might have been able to sweeten my bitter lot if I had joined in the railings of my husband against his father's favourites, against the wisest and most virtuous people in the land; if I had begun to lead a dissipated life amid all the monks and dissolute voluptuaries who surrounded my husband; and had entered into sisterhood with the infamous woman who had enchained him. But I could not.

No being is more deserving of pity than the defenceless woman who trembles unceasingly before the man from whom she ought to receive protection. No more pitiable condition can be endured. The unfortunate creature stands alone in the world by the side of her murderer; his name is hers, his honor is hers. She must conceal the cruelties of her tormentor that she may not tarnish her own fame with the world. She must praise the lips that abuse her; she must caress the hand that strikes her. United with him in the thousand little domestic relations of life, each becomes for her a fresh thorn in the martyr's crown.

For a long time, long, I was able to bear all my misery. For years I sought every means of touching the unfeeling heart. I opposed my love to his hatred; my tears to his curses; my caresses to his brutality; my calmness to his excitement; to his meannesses the honest pride with which innocence, and consciousness of right, arm us; — I did not conquer.

My gentleness only increased the roughness of his mood; my earnestness drove him to frenzy.

Once, you know it, the Countess von Königsmark found me when thus ill-treated. Her compassion

restored my powers. He had often offered me a separation; but, afraid of the Emperor's anger, had never
ventured to speak a word of it openly. I ventured to
have the proposal for a separation made known to the
monarch. Prince Menzikoff was discreetly to suggest
the idea to him. Menzikoff's art was lost upon the
Emperor's immoveable temperament.

The Czar, who sees no enemy more to be dreaded
than an undutiful son who, ever to be found in the
midst of the malcontents, the darling of the foolish
people and of the affronted priests, threatens to bring
to nothing the great work of his father, the Czar would
sooner lay down his arms before Charles XII. than
indulge a wish and inclination of this son.

In letters written by my own hand I imploringly
entreated my dear father in Germany to give his consent, and his noble, princely word for my deliverance.
With paternal sternness he refused his unhappy daughter.
Thus was I sacrificed to the honor of my house; not
even once was the favor accorded me of returning
sometimes to Wolfenbüttel.

Left thus to myself and my despair, I gave up all
hopes of a happy life. My husband redoubled his
barbarities. My youthful strength baffled the pains
he took to ripen me for death by grief and sorrow.

Then I was poisoned, and — saved.

4.

Filled with deeper gloom than ever — it was a
melancholy evening, wind and rain were beating against
the window of my lonely apartment — I pondered
one day upon my fate, contemplated the joyless present

and the fearful possibilities of the future. I bewildered myself with plans suggested by despair; and lamented that the skill of the physician had rescued my wretched life from the perils of poison.

"What have I?" thus I said to myself, "What have I to hope? Is there peace for me anywhere except in the grave? Will not the cruel Czarovitch, whom I am forced to call husband, will not he take some other means of ridding himself of me? Sooner or later, I must fall by his means. To one who has once learned the horrors of his cruel deeds, no further crime can appear impossible. He may present death to me in my favourite dish; pour it into my wine; strangle me at his side in my sleep.

What should I have to expect if such a savage were once to ascend the throne of his father? Death, or perpetual imprisonment. Who is my protector? I am forsaken by every one.

The sleep of death is sweet. God have mercy upon my little child — my life is useless to her. My death will perhaps stagger the cruel man, and make him a tender father who was no tender husband."

Quickly the resolve to suicide was ripened. I went to my medicine press, and took out the bottle labelled Opium. I filled a glass. I ordered my daughter Natalie to be brought to me that I might bless her once again. I took the lovely being to my heart; I wept bitterly; she fell asleep amid my tears.

When I had given back the child, I ordered the ladies in waiting to leave me alone, and not to return until the following morning, as I wished to go to sleep. They obeyed. I locked the door. I sank on my knees to pray. But I could not raise my hands in prayer; my soul seemed numbed.

"Murderess of yourself and of the child within your breast, can you address your Creator whilst you meditate a crime?" Thus spoke a voice within me. I could not pray. I sank down weeping, my forehead touching the ground.

"Nay, oh my God! my Creator!" I stammered, "I will remain faithful to Thee, I will bear my sufferings, and drain the bitter cup -- forgive a weak, despairing woman!"

Thus I lay. All was still and dark around. I was wearied and faint. Strength failed me to raise myself; between sleep and fainting, in a beneficent trance, I gradually lost all consciousness.

Green, bright islands floated before me as in a morning-dream. They bore me up: I wandered through unknown meadows, and over pathless and flowery pastures, and from every branch of the trees the songs of birds resounded, whilst right and left the drooping blossoms danced in purple and silver colours in the breeze around my head. Ah! it seemed to me as though I were again living and moving in the exquisite spring-time of fair Germany; and my breast expanded with long drawn respiration, as though I would drink in the whole heaven at one draught.

"But where am I then?" I inquired of an old man who, venerable for his snow-white locks and beard, dressed in white clothes like a Brahmin from the Ganges, was wandering near me.

"This is America!" said he, "and here you shall live like one of the blessed."

Hot tears of joy rushed to my eyes. "Escaped then from the vast, wintry prison of Russia? I am free — there is no longer any Russia, any Czarovitch for me! — And here I shall henceforth live like one of the blessed." Thus thought I; and I bent down and kissed the flowery soil of America.

My dream vanished, and sleep fled away. I arose from the carpet. It was already about midnight. I threw myself on the bed in my clothes, to renew the sweet dream.

Julia, if inspirations are given to us from Heaven — and why should I doubt it? why should not the Father of the universe speak to His suffering children as of old; He, who now, as then, directs their thoughts? — then that was a heavenly voice which said; "This is America; and you shall live like one of the blessed." I awoke late in the morning more cheerful; but my heart was full of deep, painful, indescribable yearnings for the glowing land of the distant hemisphere.

The Countess von Königsmark visited me. She was alarmed at the pallor of my countenance. Her eyes grew dim. She kissed my hand with the fervour of lively sympathy, and I felt her warm tears fall on it.

"No," cried she, "my Princess, I cannot bear it. I cannot see you dying away under the barbarities of your husband. Tell me what to do, and though it cost me my life, I will rescue you. Fly to Wolfen-büttel, to the protection of your noble parents: I will take upon myself to contrive your escape. Not a soul shall be aware of it until you shall have reached German soil."

I embraced the kind-hearted woman in silence, and

gave her the harsh letter from my father in which he had prohibited my return home.

"He may do so!" cried she. "But if once you are in Wolfenbüttel he will not thrust you out."

"But he will deliver me back again at Petersburg, and my whole life will be marked with the stain of disgrace. How could he withstand the imperious demand of the Emperor? Yes, dear Königsmark. You deserve my confidence. I feel that I can no longer drag on this miserable existence. If I were but at rest about the fate of my child, and of this other that lives within my breast — my resolve would be taken at once."

"What can you fear for your children? The Czar will not desert them. The whole affection of the sovereign, now devoted to you, will extend itself to his grandchildren. He will know how to secure their destiny, even if the Grand-duke should be as unnatural a father as he is unnatural a son. And suppose, dear Princess, that you remain in Petersburg, are your children therefore the better protected? Or if you fall a prey to your grief, and leave this life young — will your children be aided by that? I conjure you, save yourself! In Petersburg your life is daily in danger."

"I know it, Countess. I will save myself."

"And how?"

"By a novel, voluntary death. Do not be alarmed. I will venture on no self-murder. But I will die, to Petersburg, to Europe — I will fly across the sea, and conceal myself beneath a strange name in the interior of a distant quarter of the globe, in unknown districts, where the foot of a European has never trod.

"'There I shall almost enter on a new life; begin as a child to lisp a new language, to form new ties, to learn new things. I shall walk in a new world as in a new planet; and, like one dead, only remember the past dimly, as a former state of existence on the planet earth.

"I shall hear nothing more of my friends, of my children, my parents, of anything that happens in the known world. Nothing more will be seen of me; I shall be mourned and forgotten, as one buried. I shall be as one of the happy departed spirits, without having experienced death. You shudder at this thought, dear Königsmark! It affords me unspeakable pleasure. It is self-murder without sin. I shall fulfil a sacred duty, and save my life without wounding the prejudices of the world, or the ideas of princely honor of my relations. All depends only on the concealment of my flight. Should the secret ever be betrayed, my relations would truly be inconsolable, less perhaps on the score of my fate than of the fancied disgrace I should cast upon our house. Men, unaware of my wretchedness and of all the thousand causes of my desperate resolution, would place me in the rank of adventurers; and, instead of respecting the courage with which I broke through this prejudice in order to recover my lost peace and freedom, would condemn me in their hardness of heart."

In this way I spoke to the Countess. There was little trouble in persuading her to assist, or in dispelling her many fears about the bold plan. She swore perfect silence; and arranged all that was necessary for my flight which was to take place after my accouchement, and immediately that I should have gained the strength needful for so long a journey.

5.

My old, faithful servant, Herbert, a man of probity and great courage, was the first whom I admitted into our secret. His help was indispensable: I could not throw myself upon the wide world without an attendant. From my childish years he had been my friend, my confidant: I had to thank him for much of my most valuable knowledge. I honored him too much as a tender father to have been able to treat him as a servant of the court. In former times he had been the witness of my joyousness; since the day of my betrothal, the witness of my grief. Often he would stand at a distance and watch me, his countenance marked with pain: often when I complained to him, he knew how to inspire me with renewed courage; often when I would despair, he knew how to rekindle my hopes by his representations. It seemed to me as though his were the noble form of my heavenly dream through whom my guardian angel had spoken to me.

Herbert, when I had disclosed the great undertaking to him, stood perplexed and speechless before me.

"Why are you silent, dear Herbert?" I inquired of him.

"Gracious Princess, the thought is terrible. You, accustomed to the glitter of a court, to a thousand little indispensable comforts, to the enjoyments which art and science afford in the refined world, you would choose your dwelling-place among hordes of wild Indians, in the unknown deserts of a strange quarter of the globe?"

"Life, freedom, repose, and poverty are sweeter than sorrow amid gold and silks. Herbert, I will, I must save my life. I ask you, would you rather follow your Princess to the grave, or to another part of the world? We will fly, Herbert. I will cease to be a Princess. I will call you father; I will be your daughter. There will be some fair corner of the earth where we may dwell in seclusion and untroubled ease, concealed from man. I lose my children; you, nothing. What rivets you to the Russian desert that you do not wish to exchange it for the blooming solitude of a milder clime?"

"Nothing!" cried Herbert, and he fell on his knees before me, pressed my hand to his lips, and swore fidelity to me till death. As soon as the following day he must, so we had agreed, ask openly for his discharge, in order that, removed from Petersburg, he might be able to accelerate the arrangements for my flight, without exciting suspicion by his disappearance, later on, at the time of my pretended death.

Oh! how endless after these days was every hour to me! And yet it was not without fear and pain that I beheld the weeks pass by, as though they flew too quickly. I, at the same time, wished for and dreaded the great *dénouement;* the hour of my deliverance was to bring the eternal loss of my little Natalie.

Fair, gentle angel, I still see thee dancing on my knee, in my arms — alas! thy mother answers thy shouts of childish glee with deep sighs; thy mother meets thy sweet laughter, thy loving glances, with a tear-stained countenance. Happy innocent! thou dost not yet comprehend the language of grief — soon thou wilt no longer remember thy desolate mother — but I, often shall I wander on the shores of ocean, and extend my maternal arms towards the east, and in tender, sorrow-stricken tones utter a thousand times, thy name — Natalie!

6.

The nearer the time of my accouchement approached, the more rare became the visits of my husband. This was satisfactory to me. I dreamed of the happiness of freedom — I prepared busily for the great journey. The Countess Königsmárk provided me with new clothes, with letters of exchange, and addresses: I furnished myself with gold and with jewels: my faithful Herbert also had already placed some capital in safety.

On the 22d October I gave birth to a young prince who received at baptism the name of his illustrious grandfather. How undisguised, how touching, was the joy of the noble emperor! Alexis alone, my husband, remained unmoved, without feeling, cold.

I felt myself wonderfully strong and well. I should have been able to leave my bed within a few days if the good Königsmark had not set limits to my impatience. Thus now, in order to keep every one in the dark as to my intentions, I played the part of one dangerously ill; and, inexperienced in the art of deceit, my anxiety to become free assisted my unskilfulness.

Among all those who surrounded my sick bed, the grief of no single person was so great, so inconsolable, as that of one of my maids in waiting; by name,

Agatha von Dienholm. She was an amiable girl of my own age, of an impoverished but noble family, without parents, without near relations. At the re-commendation of Königsmark I had taken this good girl. She repaid my friendship with boundless grati-tude, with an attachment which is seldom equalled. It was not unknown to me that she had inexorably banished from her a young and distinguished officer of one of the best houses in Petersburg who had soli-cited her hand, and to whom she was at least not indifferent, because in a company of other officers he had spoken against me to the advantage of the Czar-ovitch.

When they began to be doubtful about my life, she was overpowered with the greatest distress. She appeared no more at my bedside. I inquired for her, and learned that she herself was ill from grief about me.

How could I leave such great love unrequited? I resolved to make her the confidante of my secret, and the companion of my pilgrimage. The Countess von Königsmark hastened to her, prepared her for the great disclosure, and acquainted her with my inten-tions.

Agatha, leaning on the arm of the Countess, en-tered my apartment. She was pale and looked ill: but love and delight beamed on me from her lovely, expressive eyes. She fell on her knees by my bed — without a word, without tears; but her bosom heaved quickly, and bore witness to what a storm was stirring her heart. She pressed her burning lips on my hand: I was myself uneasy about the good girl, and also about the concealment of my plan.

"Will you, dear Agatha, be my sister for the future?" I said softly to her.

She sighed aloud and deeply; looked towards heaven, and then with tenderness at me; and faltered half breathlessly, "Faithful —— for ever! for ever!" Then she took a knife from the table, and cried: "I will pierce myself to the heart if I ever forsake you; my Princess, I swear it!"

I dismissed her; and on the same day she went about amongst the others, already recovered. She appeared elevated, happier: she bore heaven within her heart, on her countenance a feigned anxiety.

Wherefore did I enjoy the love of so many strangers; wherefore did that single being hate me to whom my fate had bound me?

7.

The day for my flight was already fixed. The Countess von Königsmark, truest of friends, was security for my successful escape, and for the carrying out of the general delusion. Herbert had provided sledges everywhere, and delayed mine in a forest near the capital; whilst couriers remained in readiness to announce my death throughout Europe.

As a dying person, I said farewell to all my court. I refused to receive fresh aid from the hands of the despairing physicians, and only with anxious longings requested to see the Emperor once more.

He came, and with him my husband. My children rested in my arms for the last time. Oh, what a bitter leave-taking! The Emperor yielded to his feelings of grief; he would not hear one word of thanks from my lips for his affection; he blessed me and my children, and swore to me henceforth to be their all.

My heart was breaking: I sobbed aloud, "Oh, my children! my children!" — I embraced them alternately a hundred times, and bathed them with my tears, and a hundred times I took them again. At this fearful moment I almost lost recollection and resolution. I thought the most miserable life more endurable than eternal separation from these cherubs. The Emperor perceived my deep emotion: he was fearful that my death would be hastened by it. He bade the Countess Königsmark to carry the lovely beings away. My husband accompanied them. But once before he left, he silently and sullenly extended his hand to me. Ah! if I had seen in his face one tender sign of one single feeling of pain, one soft emotion, I should have thrown up my part, and have renewed my old life in Russia. But his expression was dark. To be witness of my death was rather painful and uncomfortable than a cause for grief.

The pressure of his hand was faint, and as if compelled by decorum. He appeared to be angry with himself that no tears would come to his eyes to display to his father, the afflicted Emperor.

He went away, and was forgotten by me, as soon as his back was turned: Ah, my heart only called for my children.

I sank back exhausted. I was left alone: the Countess Königsmark, only, staid to watch me. Her words restored my lost courage. I slept for a short time, and felt myself strengthened. After midnight the tidings of my death were spread. My husband had already quitted Petersburg, and betaken himself with his companions to a country-seat. He received the intelligence of my release, and gave orders, as I had myself desired, that my body should be buried privately. The coffin came. Agatha and Königsmark laid me in it, and concealed my face. Many of my court requested to look at me once more. Weeping, they surrounded the bier. From time to time Königsmark raised the veil from my face, whilst the grief of the spectators became ever increased, and my death undoubted in case of any future suspicions.

I was dressed at night, when my closed coffin was borne to its resting-place, conducted from my house by Königsmark. I remained concealed in her palace. On the third night, faithful father Herbert appeared at the gate of the city. Agatha von Dienholm and I left Petersburg in man's clothes, of the old costume. A deep snow had fallen: but the storm had ceased. The stars twinkled brightly.

Herbert himself drove the sledge: he flew over the snow with the speed of a bird, noiselessly as if among clouds. No one spoke. I trembled continually lest I should be betrayed and overtaken. Often I secretly wished it, that I might again be near my children, if even in a dungeon. Unspeakable anguish, and the deeply gnawing agony of a mother's love, distracted my heart. Agatha, loving girl, clung timidly to me; the happiness of being necessary to her Princess seemed to her immeasurable. I pressed her hand in mine. "Oh my Princess! my Princess!" she whispered: "how much I love you! how willingly would I die for you! how gladly!"

"I am no longer your Princess! Do not forget

your part. Call me your friend, your sister; for now I am so, and your equal!"

I put my arm round her: only at my repeated requests would the timid girl do the same. I felt her blushes, and the excitement of her honest heart, in which the tenderest love was still struggling with her habitual respect.

Morning dawned, after a long, terrible night. We found ourselves in the wilds of a forest. The tired horses trotted along more slowly. At last we reached a mean, lonely house in the woods, at which Herbert made a halt. He conducted us within. A pair of old people received us hospitably. Herbert named Agatha and me his sons.

8.

OH happiness of an unobserved life of seclusion, of being unknown except by the few kind hearts that love us, what happiness on earth can compare with thine! The old Russian, with his wife, and a sturdy young fellow their son, had lived in this hut already many years without having left it, except on a high feast-day when they visited the church of a village seven wersts distant from here. The old man and his son made all kinds of wooden utensils which the latter then carried away for sale, and exchanged for the means of life, for clothes, and for a little money. How the quiet contentment and frugality of these poor people charmed me! All that their heart could desire lay within the inclosure of their hut. They knew nothing of the splendour or the misery of the great, they knew nothing of the events which convulse the world, or of the terrible fermentings which, cast into the hearts of men, desolate happy families and bathe the throne in a sea of blood.

Whilst Herbert was taking care of our horses, the amiable Agatha became my head cook. She prepared a clean and simple meal for us. I admired her skill, her industry. When we were left alone in the little room I approached her, clasped her in my arms, and imprinted a kiss on her lips. An enchanting blush suffused her face: glowing, and with timidity, she returned the sisterly kiss, looked at me with swimming eyes, and faltered gently, "Oh, my God!"

"Like these old people," said I, "we shall find a solitude, prettier than this; we shall be happy. Mere peaceful existence in the world will be an enjoyment to us; in the affection of isolated and kind neighbours we shall forget the flattering of faded courtiers, the servile adoration of a mob of subjects: we shall hear no more of wars, of treacheries, of cabals, and of all that vexes poor humanity, in which men behave with childish greediness, with which they poison their wretched lives; nothing more of the vanity of coxcombs, of the strife of ambition, of the privileged sins and follies of the great, of the blindness of the rude mob, and all beside that fills the papers. The morning and evening glow will be our newspapers, for they will announce to us a bright or a gloomy day: the forest our opera-house; mountains and seas our theatres; health our cook; the boundless heaven, the vaulted roof of our church. Ah, dear friend, can you also rejoice heartily with me in this calm happiness?"

She smiled at me, kissed me blushing, and said: "I no longer rejoice in hope, for that which I never dared to hope has already come to me.   Oh, how gladly shall I avoid the world, that great hospital, wherein almost all, small and great, are fevered with some anxiety; for gold, for admiration, for revenge, for immortality, for high places, for dainties, for fine clothes and tormenting frivolities.   Whoever is able to renounce all the vanities which are unnecessary for life, he has what he needs — peace in his heart.   And this has come to me."

We remained nearly the whole day in the hut in perfect security.   We slept there as peacefully, as soundly, as though Russia no longer had danger for us.   In the evening we quitted our old hosts, and continued our journey over the snow.

Herbert knew the way perfectly: everywhere he avoided the large roads: we travelled for the most part at night; rested generally in lonely huts or poor villages; saw but few people; and changed, sometimes our dress, sometimes our names, in order to remain undiscovered. But all this made our flight very tedious: the nights soon became too dark, the days too stormy, and the roads were too much snowed up to be recognized.   We had already been fourteen long days in these eternal wilds, wandering through unfrequented steppes and dark forests through whose labyrinths we should never have found our way without a guide taken from one village to another, and yet we had not reached the boundary of the Russian empire.   Herbert comforted us day after day; but day after day our hopes were deceived.

At last one evening Herbert said: "Be at rest; we shall to-night sleep in the last Russian village.   It is called Kwadoszlaw, and cannot be more than ten wersts from us. To-morrow we shall travel on Polish ground." I danced for joy. "Nay," cried I, "this very night we must be in Poland. Till then I cannot breathe freely."

We arrived at Kwadoszlaw late. It was dark, and snowing hard. Herbert wished to stop; but I gave him no rest till he continued the journey towards the next village. He inquired its name. It was called Nieszospesda.

We sought for a guide; but the people there were so unaccommodating that not one would offer himself, and we, let us promise what remuneration we would, could not obtain one.

I urged the continuance of our journey, notwith-standing; for we had not come far that day. We soon found ourselves in an extensive forest. Till now, we had followed the scarcely perceptible track of a sledge that had preceded us; but it became more and more faint; the wind blew the snow in our faces, so that at last it became impossible to find a trace of the vehicle. We had already wandered too far out of the way to venture to hope that we could return to the place we had left. Wind and snow had obliterated our tracks. We were half stiffened with the frost, and were obliged to warm ourselves by trotting every now and then by the side of the sledge. I suffered much, still more suffered the good Agatha who had not, like me, through mingled hope, anguish and fear, obtained the strength of desperation: and who had besides, on this day, adopted the clumsy dress of a Russian peasant.

We had driven about in the forest for some hours without coming to the end of it. Herbert, as he could nowhere see any outlet in front of him, had got down to investigate the country in advance. Agatha and I awaited his return in the sledge.

To our no small horror a strange man on foot unexpectedly appeared close to us. I spoke to him: he made no answer but went towards the horses, swung himself up, and gallopped off with us, sideways into the wood.

Surprise and terror almost deprived us of our senses. We shouted Herbert's name; we heard his answering shout in the distance; but soon we could no longer distinguish even this. I sank back powerless in Agatha's arms, and did not come to myself until the moment at which the sledge stopped.

I opened my eyes. We were in a wide plain outside the forest; the wind and snow continued. The churl who had carried us off, had sprung down off the horse, and disappeared. Probably he had only wished to make use of our horses that he might shorten his journey on foot, and get more quickly out of the wood.

Nothing remained but to return to the forest to seek our lost friend. The deep tracks in the snow marked the long road by which we had come. In half an hour we reached the wood. We called Herbert's name countless times; but our cries of distress were only answered by the roaring of the wind amid the black firs. We drove deeper into the forest for another half hour: not a trace, not a sign of the unfortunate Herbert. Where should we seek him? We had to fear for ourselves lest we might get into a false track. Perhaps the unhappy man was already numbed with cold, and frozen to death in the snow; perhaps he had been attacked, and torn in pieces,

by wolves; and we, without a counsellor, without assistance, were alone in this wilderness, our strength and
courage exhausted!

Never before had I found myself in so fearful a
situation. Our numbed hands had scarcely strength
enough to guide the reins of our wearied horses.
Agatha advised that we should return into the open
country, in the hope of discovering some human habit-
ation, if we were to follow the foot-tracks of the man
who had carried us off. From thence we might, with
the return of day, send out some people acquainted
with the country in search of Herbert. I took her
advice: and indeed, by following the track of the run-
away, we reached at daybreak a small, poor village
half buried in snow.

9.

We stopped at an old house built of brick, which
was the best in the whole village. A pack of dogs
surrounded our carriage barking until a dirty, ragged
boy who came out of the house reduced them to
silence, and listened to our pitiful story which I related to him as well as I could in the Russian language. He left us without making any answer,
re-appeared in a few minutes, and conducted us into
a hot room which resembled a stall, where several
men-servants and maids were lying about on soft
straw.

For an hour we were here obliged to wait our fate
with patience. The sleepers awoke themselves; our
horses were led into shelter, and ourselves at last into
a large room where a stout, broad-shouldered man,

who wore an immense moustache, announced himself as the stern Lord of Horodok.

He spoke to Agatha first in Russian, then in Polish. The good girl, knowing neither of these languages, answered in French, then in German, and was not understood. I would have replied for her, but he ordered me to be silent. "You are no Russian, in spite of your dress!" said he; then whispered a few words in the ear of his servant, and desired Agatha to be taken out of the apartment. In vain I opposed this strange proceeding.

"I know you well!" the dreadful man said to me. "You have escaped from Petersburg. I suspected you from the beginning."

This speech completed my distress. I already saw myself discovered, betrayed, sought for, and delivered up in Petersburg. I spoke of Agatha as my sister; related our nocturnal adventure, and how we had lost our father in the forest. I only entreated to be allowed to go in search of him. The nobleman shook his head; he ordered me to be conducted into the adjoining room, whither after some little time Agatha also was brought; she sobbed bitterly. With the help of a servant who spoke broken German, the Lord of Horodok had also examined her; and as she gave herself out to be a maiden in the service of my father, the suspicion of the old village tyrant was increased by the contradiction in our stories.

We were treated as prisoners, our little possessions were brought from the sledge into the room; we were provided with food and something to drink, and were left alone till towards evening. We only learned that the stern lord, to whom they gave the title of Starost, had gone out hunting with some strangers.

Sometimes we determined to escape at nightfall; sometimes, to await the course of things with heroic composure. One plan succeeded another; but most of all were we concerned about our good Herbert.

When it became dusk we heard the hunters returning. Wild noises soon sounded from the room next to ours. We heard the clatter of winecups, and peals of rough laughter. The Starost, whose voice we could distinguish above all the others, was talking of us. What made me most uneasy was his supposition that we were Swedish spies, or vagabonds who had been carrying on our business as pickpockets in Petersburg. He would, he said, send us and the old man whom we called our father to the authorities of the nearest Russian town on the following day. They seemed to have found Herbert also.

Whilst I was explaining the speech of the Starost to poor trembling Agatha, the door was opened. The company, excited by wine and brandy, pressed in upon us, and began to examine us. Agatha wept; but I loaded the Starost with reproaches for his rude treatment of unoffending travellers, and demanded to be taken to my father.

A well-grown young man approached Agatha, and, as he put his hand under her chin and turned her face upwards, said to her in French: "You are indeed neither a peasant nor a criminal, fair girl!"

"And you, Sir," I answered, "appear to be neither a robber, nor capable of deeming those barbarities lawful which are practised upon travellers in the dominions of the king of Poland. We came to claim the hospitality and the famed generosity of the Poles; but instead, we have been subjected to all kinds of ill-usage."

The young man looked sideways at me with a smile; then again at Agatha, who, abashed, cast her eyes on the ground.

"Follow me. I will set you free, if you wish!" he said at last; and as he laid his hand on Agatha's shoulder, he added: "Do not weep, fair maid!"

He then turned with a laugh to the Starost, and cried: "Wladislaw, you have played a pretty joke on me!"

"What do you mean, Janinsky?" exclaimed the Starost.

"You have imprisoned the painter about whom Captain Osterow wrote to me, and whom I have been so anxiously expecting. These two young people belong to him. Where is he? I must speak to him."

With this he left us. The whole company followed him. Half an hour had scarcely passed when Janinsky returned, laughing slily, and leading our Herbert.

"The horses," said Janinsky, "are harnessed. You can follow me to my castle, and enjoy there every comfort so long as you like to remain with me and rest yourselves."

Now that I saw Herbert once more, I believed myself to have escaped for ever from danger. As soon as we were alone, we told him of our adventure, our distress, our anxieties about him. He related his story which was very similar to ours; as soon as he found the tracks of our sledge in the snow, guided by them, he had come to Horodok.

Tired as we all then were, we did not hesitate a moment in quitting this hateful place, and travelling with the unknown Janinsky whose friendly exterior promised us at least a better fate.

10.

We started on our way amid chilling flakes of snow. Janinsky's sledge went in front. At last, a little before midnight we reached a large village called Sloboda, on one side of which rose an extensive and ancient building, adorned with several small towers. The moon shone feebly through the grey clouds of snow, and cast a melancholy light on the castle, which, with its buttresses, little towers, and narrow windows, resembled a large prison. All around it ran a moat over which was a bridge.

"Ah!" whispered Agatha to me, "I do not hope much good from this flight."

Our host was very attentive in helping us out of the vehicle: he then took Agatha with him, and conducted her into the castle. Herbert and I followed.

Supper was laid in a large room decked with old tapestry. There reigned everywhere an order and cleanliness that infused new confidence into our minds.

"How rejoiced I am," said Janinsky, "to have rescued you from your strange imprisonment by the Starost. He is really a good fellow, but somewhat rough; and besides a mortal enemy to the king of Sweden. He is rich in lands and dependents; but since he has lost his wife, his house has become like a beggar's inn, and he rolls and revels in mire and dirt to his heart's content. One must humour his strange fancies; and, since he is a man of importance, take care to keep on neighbourly terms with him. Forget the fright which this strange fellow has occasioned you; nothing shall be wanting on my part to render your stay with me more agreeable to you. I have also taken journeys in Europe, and know how pleasant it is to find hospitable shelter, especially in wild, inhospitable countries like ours."

We thanked him for his great politeness, and Herbert took out his pocket-book. "Here," said he, showing him a Russian passport, "You will learn from this who we are. You will see from it that I am a French nobleman called Laborde, and that these two are my daughters. The dressing of one in man's clothes, and of the other in the costume of a Russian peasant, was a whim of these merry maidens which I willingly indulged. I am convinced of your generosity, Sir; and we esteem ourselves happy to have unexpectedly made so agreeable an acquaintance by means of this rough 'mischance.'"

Janinsky glanced through the passport; and apologized to me and to Agatha because, misled by our disguises, he had perhaps not behaved to us with becoming respect. There was a cover also laid at the table for Agatha. Meantime I remarked that Janinsky appeared to have grown much more grave since Herbert had made this disclosure. On this day we needed repose more than food. A maid conducted Agatha and me to a small room in an upper story of the house, where we fell into a peaceful slumber under the protection of our noble host's ancestors, whose half-faded portraits hung all round the walls.

The next morning Herbert brought us an invitation from our kind entertainer to stay a few days with him until our horses, exhausted with their great exertions, should have recovered. Besides the weather was even more stormy than before: we ourselves needed rest to recruit our strength. No one would know us in this country which was very seldom visited by travellers; and this gave the addition of a delightful feeling of security to the pleasures of repose.

We agreed. Janinsky appeared charmed, as though he were our debtor, not we his. "Ah!" said he, "how seldom does it fall to my lot to see people from the civilized world! If I had never become acquainted with other countries, and other wants, I should have been satisfied to be like my neighbours, whose highest good lies in hunting, in gaming, and in carousing. But now I am no longer at home in my own home. The death of my father made me the inheritor of his property: but sooner or later I must move from it, and go back again to Warsaw or Dresden, unless in some happy hour Heaven will conduct an amiable companion to me, who will enliven my solitude."

Janinsky was a handsome man; the national features of Poland were unusually advantageous to his figure. He spoke Polish, French, and Russian; and possessed a select little library of Latin and French authors. He was fond of music; and played the flute and harpsichord with ease. Thus ennui could never overtake us in Janinsky's castle. I read: Agatha sat at the harpsichord: Janinsky accompanied her expressive strains with the flute: Herbert wrote, and turned over the leaves of the maps.

Our host occupied himself with Agatha more than with any of us. His eyes were fixed unchangingly upon her: to her he knew how to say a thousand things that betrayed deep feeling; he loved best to listen to her words; and her wishes always came to him with the greatest force.

Agatha received these attentions as habitual politeness; but they were the traitor tokens of a soulfelt passion which Janinsky made most evident when he wished most carefully to conceal it.

When on the evening of the second day he was standing beside Agatha at the harpsichord — they were alone together in the room — he suddenly stopped his accompaniment. She looked up at him. His eyes were filled with tears. He turned away, and moved towards the window.

"Are you not well?" asked Agatha, rising.

"How can I be well?" he cried with emotion. "You will go away to-morrow, and leave me alone again? Why did you appear in my hermitage, like a being from a better world, to give me for a moment a glimpse of Heaven that ever after I might feel more keenly the misery of this life? Oh lady, lady, I am very unhappy!"

Agatha, surprised and confused, did not know how to reply. He took her hand, pressed it to his lips, and raised his tear-dimmed eyes towards Heaven.

"Do not be angry with me, nor with my sorrow, lady!" he continued. "Had I seen you in a large town, in the brilliant circle of a court, my heart would still have singled you from amid the thousands of your sex, and would still have spoken; you only could be dear to me amid all. And now I dwell in this desert, far removed from all congenial, all kindly, society. In vain I long for something better. My days flow on in wearying monotony. I was beginning to become a commonplace man; and to drill my warm, only too-tenderly-feeling, heart in the paths of dull every-day custom. Ah! what I had dreamed of only as impossible, became suddenly a wonderful reality. I saw you: a heavenly apparition could not have sent a deeper thrill through my heart. I have become transformed. I see *you* alone; I recognize *you* alone; and all around me has become as strange as though I now beheld all for the first time. Do not be angry with me, lady; that I am not worthy of you — that, indeed, I feel; I am too undistinguished for you. Among the millions whom you have seen, you have seen millions like me."

With these words he led her back to the harpsichord, and took up his flute. Agatha, trembling, struck but single notes. She was not angry with him; but did not know whether he had given her pleasure.

Meanwhile father Herbert came into the room. Janinsky went towards him.

"You will leave me again to-morrow?" he said. "But remember that you are my debtor. I count upon your acknowledgment: I shall consider the little service which I have rendered to you as repaid, if you will grant my request to you to remain two days longer in Sloboda. I cannot possibly reconcile myself to the thought of losing you so soon."

Herbert smiled. "How gladly," said he, "would we increase our debt to you, if pressing family affairs did not make it a duty to hasten on our journey."

But the ardent Janinsky would not allow himself to be repulsed: he urged our delay with friendly vehemence; he knew so well how to depict the perils

of a journey during the present cold weather, the in-
security of the roads from the wolves that the frost
was driving out of the forests to seek for food in the
inhabited districts, that at last Herbert hesitated, and
asked at least for time to think about it.

When Herbert, as soon as we were alone, made
the proposal to Agatha and me, I perceived that during
the present rough winter weather he would be better
pleased to remain a couple of days longer at Sloboda
than to leave.

Agatha, instead of expressing any opinion in answer
to my questions, replied by silent blushes.

Thus we staid on in Sloboda.

11.

The promised two days gradually lengthened into
six.   Janinsky was the happiest of men, and kindness
itself.   Agatha took pleasure in conversing with him,
when he kept silence on the subject of his love: I observed that she sang better and with more expression
to his harpsichord than formerly to mine: that her
whole being seemed to be inspired with a higher tone.
To me, she became more loveable than ever: her voice
had in it something indescribably tender and touching;
her glances lingered longer and dreamily on objects
around her; had she possessed a deadly enemy, he must
have sunk on her heart melted to love.

I only was the ever restless one, and moved about
in unceasing fear.   Every strange figure, every traveller who wandered over the waste of snow, filled me
with mortal anxiety. — Ah! and my forsaken children,
the princely deserted ones!   I was ever with them in

spirit; I dreamed of their lovely forms alone — how gladly would I have paid the forfeit of my joyless life for one single kiss from their lips.

On the evening of the sixth day, kind Agatha came into the room to me. Her eyes were full of tears, yet she was smiling. "I have been talking to Father Herbert," said she; "he will decide upon leaving early to-morrow, if you agree to our departure."

"At any moment — now — I am ready!"

"But Janinsky must not know it — not until in the morning we suddenly say our farewell. He would throw a thousand obstacles in the way, to prevent our leaving," said she, and she turned from me, blushing.

Her behaviour struck me. I clasped her in my arms; I inquired the cause of her embarrassment, and the secret of her tears. I half guessed it. "You have committed a robbery in the desert!" I said, laughing.

"He has asked Herbert for my hand," replied Agatha, "in the belief that Herbert is really my father. Herbert in vain represented to him that he could not separate himself from his daughter; that I could not live in these wastes. He will convert his property and possessions into money, will leave Poland, will follow us, and settle himself with us in France."

"And you, Agatha?"

"I am sorry for it. He is such a good man; but full of wild enthusiasm. Therefore we must make haste and leave Sloboda."

Herbert confirmed what Agatha said. In order to put Janinsky off entirely, he had told him that he would decide Agatha's fate nowhere but on French ground. On the following morning, as soon as Herbert had quietly prepared every thing for our departure,

and the horses were put to, we disclosed to the unfortunate lover our intention of leaving him. The
sledge had already been brought round.

Janinsky stood pale and speechless before us. His
eyes wandered alternately from one of us to another,
and seemed to ask; "Part? Can you mean this? Do
you desire Janinsky's death?" We all said what our
gratitude dictated. Herbert drew a costly ring from
his finger, and intreated him to accept it as a remembrance. He pushed away Herbert's hand. He went
to the window, saw our sledge standing ready; came
back to us; pressed Herbert's hand, then mine; then
fell on his knees before Agatha, and clasped her hand
to his heart with fervour. We did not see poor, kind
Janinsky again.

We were all deeply moved. We all hoped he
would return. But we soon heard from one of his
servants that he had flung himself on a horse, and had
quitted Sloboda.

Herbert and I stood beside the sledge. Agatha
still remained in the house. I went back to seek her.
When I entered the room in which Janinsky had left
us, I found her sitting in an arm-chair, sobbing, her
face buried. On a little table near her she had written
with a piece of chalk, "For ever, Janinsky."

I drew near, and took her hand. She was startled
and sought to hide her grief from me. But I had read
those words in which she had written the history of
her heart.

"Do you wish to remain here?" I asked.

She sprang up, and led me to the sledge, without
speaking a word.

We seated ourselves in it and departed.

12.

IT was a gloomy winter's day: the sky, one un-broken grey cloud from which snow and rain poured down upon us. Dusky woods rose up from the snow-covered plain like black islands. Every now and then the melancholy clang of a village bell sounded in the distance. And woods, and clouds, and huts, seemed to fly past us like the figures of a monotonous dream.

Agatha lay almost clinging to me. I did not venture to disturb her thoughts and reveries. The poor child had come from this strange adventure with a wounded heart. Out of love for me she had given up him whom she loved.

Oh, Julia, how completely is our whole life a mingled dream; more of shadow than of substance; more of anticipation than of enjoyment. We appear without knowing from whence: and wander for a long time among thorns and roses, and meet and exchange greetings with many strange beings; we would gladly form ties of the heart with many, but we see them vanish never to return again; and the tide of time, and mysterious Fate, bear us on further and further until we sink down tired and exhausted, and give back to earth our borrowed dust.

People take pleasure in laughing at the eternal love, the unchangeable friendship in which youth delights: they call them the enthusiasms of romance, excitability, over-refinement, sentimentality. But I will not be displeased with Agatha's tears.

Youth is more noble, both in its arts and senti-ments, than later age. It is still wandering in the paths of uprightness pure as it rose from the hands of nature and the pious teachings of the nursery, unacquainted with the crimes and depravities of man; it desires what is great, what is good; its enthusiasm is the noblest. Blackened by the smoke of the passions, later age pursues its way; is no longer holy itself, and sees no holiness around it; revels in the pleasures of sense or with eager mind rushes after a phantom; or else barters its best feelings for gold, and stigmatizes all that no longer appears attractive, as folly and childish trifles. Virtue, sacred to a child, and even to young boys and girls, is to age only worldly prudence. Later age no longer values the beautiful, but only the useful.

Oh! tell me then as we are grown-up people, and must think and feel as such, which enthusiasm is the nobler? Is it the ungoverned striving for the gratification of the senses? Is it the strife for self-abnegation, magnanimity, friendship, truth, and the virtues of the soul?

Let us leave exalted thoughts in our children; let us not voluntarily destroy them sooner than sad destiny would perhaps have done.

Now I will, be my destiny on earth and beyond the grave what it may, I will always disagree with the idle talk of degenerate man; I will not covet riches, if I can but preserve myself from a life of poverty; will not struggle for worldly honor, if one heart will but truly love me; will not draw distinctions between the royal purple and the beggar's smock, but between hearts alone, and will make my world below what it should be; not what it became in Europe, owing to uncontrolled passions.

We live once more; oh, Julia, why should I

sacrifice this life to the caprices and opinions of men, and not devote it to myself? Why should I be the slave of their passions and of their prejudices, when the mightiest among them is unable to compensate me for one pang, or to grant me one hour of renewed life when my appointed time shall have run its course.

13.

WHEN after two days we reached the first little town, — its name has escaped me — we found in it a travelling carriage with every possible convenience, which the Posting-master said had already been waiting some time for us.

This, too, was an arrangement made by the foresight of Herbert, so that we should not be delayed too long anywhere. He had, unknown to me, sent on a man called Paulovitch to make preparations for us; a man whose fidelity and prudence had been proved; who had already made several journeys; who, impoverished by misfortunes of all kinds, had been left without employment, and now desired to link his fate indissolubly with that of Herbert. Herbert told me that Paulovitch was waiting for us in Paris, and was making preparations there for our voyage to America.

So we hastened without delays through Poland, and travelled through Germany without staying longer in any one place than was necessary for recruiting our wearied powers by a night's rest.

I read in the papers the account of my death and burial. My flight from Petersburg had remained a secret. — Oh, my tenderly-loved parents! — My darling Julia! — At the moment at which you were weeping

9*

over my death, how near I was to you! Sobbing, I stretched forth my arms towards every district that belonged to you; and amid a thousand tears, gently faltered the farewell to you, and the blessing, that you could not hear. Whilst you were clothing yourselves in mourning your unhappy friend and daughter was praying for you, and for peace and consolation for you to Him who can alone bestow peace and consolation. But to you I am dead, and thus shall remain — my destiny wills it so.

At last, after an unspeakably long journey we reached the capital of France. Here the good Paulovitch had engaged a pleasant dwelling for us: and told us that he had agreed with the sea-captain de la Bretonne, who was at the port of l'Orient, for the sum for which he would take us, among some hundred other Germans, to America. These Germans were, for the most part, people in poor circumstances who had resolved to quit their country in order to seek their fortunes in a foreign climate on the founding of a new colony in Louisiana.

But our departure could not take place until the month of May. I was afraid lest during this time I might be discovered in Paris. Even the enormous crowd of this little world in which I at first thought I might lead an unobserved life, was all the more dangerous because travellers from among all nations of Europe streamed hither.

How easily in the neighbourhood of the court might I be recognized and betrayed by some inquisitive person who might have seen me in Petersburg or Wolfenbüttel.

Father Herbert, who had now adopted the name of de l'Ecluse, thought my fears well-founded. We

quitted Paris in order, according to our restless, uncertain habits, to visit some other parts of the kingdom
before our voyage.

But even in these wanderings I was not secure
from betrayal; where I believed myself the most secure
of concealment my danger was the greatest. ˎ

For instance, whilst we were in Poitiers, it occurred
to me to attend an evening-mass in the church there,
in company with the amiable daughter of our landlord.

I was praying with fervour, oh my Julia! for you,
and for my children, and for my princely parents. —
An unexpected sight recalled me from the abstraction
of devotion, and riveted my attention irresistibly.

Not far from me, in the circle of the men, stood —
oh! with what pleasure I write his name who reminds
me again of the happy hours of my childhood — the
Chevalier d'Aubant. I was frightened, and yet I
could scarcely withdraw my eyes from him.

It was D'Aubant who long ago — ah, Julia! I
recall the day with sadness — I was celebrating your
birthday, and we heedless girls, with childish glee, had
been scouring the green forest wilderness — appeared
like a guardian ˏ angel in our perplexity; d'Aubant,
who afterwards in dismal Petersburg thought so nobly
as to hazard his life for the honor of a Princess degraded by the jests of the mob — whose image I can
never recal without beholding it radiant with the
heavenly rosy tints of my childhood — whose name I
never utter without gratitude, for that he shed his own
blood for me without one hope of reward.

He it was! Julia, I trembled. My half-extinguished
life glowed again with wondrous and delicious warmth.

D'Aubant seemed at this moment a good genius who wished to appear to me once more on the very borders of my native quarter of the world, as an adieu before Fate should bear me away for ever.

At the sight of him I forgot myself and my danger. He did not observe me. His countenance expressed manly melancholy. You remember his tall figure, and the gentle, intellectual expression of his face! How often did the apparition of the "handsome forest-god," as you were pleased to call him, give occasion to merry banterings among us!

Oh! what did I not feel! Ten years seemed to have vanished out of my life. I was again wandering in the meadow with you, and you were again crowning me with wild flowers for our evening dance at our country-house.

Suddenly he turned round. He perceived me, and I thought I read in his eyes the greatest astonishment, such as would be excited in his mind by the sight of one supposed to be dead. I was aroused from my reverie, and concealed my face in the folds of my veil. I was almost fainting. Like a detected criminal I longed for flight and freedom. The ground seemed to burn beneath my feet, and the thousands assembled in the church seemed to fix their eyes on me only, and to whisper to each other; "See! there is the Princess that ran away!"

It was impossible to leave the church immediately, on account of the crowd, much as I begged my companion to do so. And d'Aubant's gaze remained perpetually fixed on me; my eyes were continually meeting his; and feelings of mingled fear and pleasure pervaded my heart, as heat and cold to one ill with fever. As soon as I again reached home I sent for Herbert. Agatha observed my embarrassment, my anxiety. Herbert, the same. I concealed nothing from them. I told them about d'Aubant. His name had not been unknown to them since the time of his flight from Petersburg. We resolved unanimously to quit Poitiers at once. I had no sleep that night. I continually pictured myself betrayed, the house surrounded, and myself taken back to the prison at Petersburg, — and in the midst of my death agony the form of d'Aubant stood again before me, and with him the Elysium of my former life again bloomed forth, and I could not then hate the man who might wish to betray me and carry me away.

This single night in Poitiers appeared to me to be longer and more eventful than my whole life before.

We had already left Poitiers when morning dawned on the following day.

14.

As soon as the month of May set in, we embarked under the name of a German family travelling to their relations in the West Indies. Paulovitch was now called Paul; Herbert, our careful father, bore the name of Walter. The former, whilst we others had been moving about in different provinces of France, had, with admirable diligence, purchased in l'Orient everything that could serve to render a long sea-voyage more pleasant, and everything that could be useful to us in a distant part of the world.

The guns thundered their farewell in the harbour. The wind filled our sails. The sailors shouted. The batteries of Port Louis thundered back their adieux. The ship sped, as if flying, over the dusky, dancing waves of ocean. The shores of Europe disappeared.

Agatha stood on the deck in deep melancholy. Her lips trembled as though she were speaking to the vanishing continent; tears filled her eyes. Poor Agatha! Her heart was wandering amid the wastes of Poland, and hovering over the sorrowing Janinsky in wintry Sloboda.

Herbert leaned against a mast with folded arms and drooping head, in an attitude of dejection. For my sake, he had separated himself from his native country, and was now to pass the close of his virtuous life in a distant wilderness. He heard neither the roars of the guns, nor the hurrahs of the sailors. But now and then his breast seemed to heave with a sigh.

And amid the din and the noise of the sailors arose all at once an anthem from men, women, and children. They were Germans and Swiss who had embarked in order to seek in Louisiana that good fortune which would not smile upon them in the old world. They sat crowded together; and with a loud voice sang a psalm to God their Father, and commended to Him the dear Fatherland that was unable to provide for them. And all eyes gazed at the shore; and, looking on it, wept tears of farewell.

Melancholy overcame me also. My silent, earnest prayer arose to Heaven for my children amid the hymns of these unfortunate people; and my tears were united with theirs.

Natalie, oh Natalie, beloved daughter, and thou too, my unhappy babe, whose tears a mother's love may never dry; yet once more, fare ye well! Thus I ejaculated; and I saw the shores of Europe grow fainter and more dim on the horizon. Like an enormous coffin, our native continent sank beneath the waves with all its treasures, and all its pangs; with all its tearful, and all its joyful, hours. At this solemn moment my heart yearned only for my children — they also were going from me for ever. I moved, a solitary, over the ocean; like a departed spirit which, transported to a distant place, sees with a shudder the world vanishing before it like a vapour — that world, which indeed has had many sorrows, but also many treasures.

I sat on the deck, lost in my reflections. The moon had risen, for our departure took place late in the day; a death-like stillness reigned all around; on all sides only sea and sky, darkness and moonlight. This solemnly attractive scene riveted me by its novelty, and diverted my grief.

Agatha came up to me, and asked, timidly, "My Augustine, do I disturb you? You are sad. Has repentance overtaken you so soon? Are you leaving Europe unwillingly?"

I drew the kind girl to me, and answered: "No, willingly. For no one loves me there, and no one protected me there. And those who do love and protect me, are accompanying me to the new world. I only mourn for my children, and for my Julia. They are lost to me. And yet if I had not left them, they would still have been lost to me. Then now, good-night, thou past! Welcome to me, thou Stranger Future! I come to meet thee with a clear heart. Whoever has nothing to fear, has only to hope."

Agatha pressed her face to my heart, and sobbed

deeply. "You are weeping?" I asked her. "Do you yearn for home?"

After a long silence she murmured the name Janinsky.

My eyes became dimmed with tears. I kissed the young girl's hot brow, but answered nothing. What could I have replied to a word that told so much? Agatha loved. Janinsky was the idol of her first passion. True and devoted, she had sacrificed to me her tenderest feelings, and now this was confessed when she was sunk in hopeless despair at the possibility of happiness.

Yes, it is indeed the greatest sacrifice cheerfully to allow one's heart to break whilst killing one's love. Under heaven nothing makes us so happy as this passion, which is indeed one with the feeling of immortality. He who sacrifices his love, makes also a sacrifice of immortality. Without love, Eternity becomes empty and worthless.

15.

AND now we sped on over the clear, ever-moving ocean, from island to island. We became accustomed to the incommodious life of voyagers; to the confusing rocking to and fro of the ship; to the strange, restless monotony of the sea. No landscape with its flower-sprinkled meadows, no mountain with its vast proportions, gives us so perfect an emblem of isolated and restless life, of eternity, as the sea. Here all is motion, and unwearied. The waves dance beneath us; around us flutter the ship's gay pennons; above us float the clouds. Almighty nature is in a state of half-pleasing, half-terrifying excitement; and man, who controls the unruly elements, appears nowhere in more potent grandeur than here.

We saw the Canary Isles — we remained for some days at Teneriffe, at the foot of the Peak. A new world presented itself to us even here, a new vegetable kingdom, and men of a different colour. We deemed ourselves already widely separated from Europe. Agatha lamented more quietly for Janinsky, and began to smile again as formerly. I had almost forgotten Russia and Germany, the remembrance of all that had once given me joy and sorrow became fainter — I looked back on the past as on a long, sad dream, or as the spirit of one dead might look back on its earthly career.

I could not have believed that I should again here, a third time, have been reminded so unexpectedly, in so astonishing a manner, of the happiest hours of my life, of you, oh my Julia! and of my far-distant, lovely home.

The ship's captain suddenly decided upon quitting Teneriffe again with the fair wind. We left the shore hastily. We had got into the boat and were waiting for the return of our brave Paul. He arrived breathless, embarked in the boat with us, and the sailors pushed off.

Julia! at this very moment — I was sitting with my face turned towards the shore — a young man appeared on the quay, exactly like d'Aubant. I was frightened — no, I cannot call it fright — it was an indescribable mixture of amazement, pleasure, and sadness, that overpowered me. I seized Agatha's hand. "It is d'Aubant! surely d'Aubant!" I cried.

He appeared as though he had seen me, had recognized me; but his behaviour was quite inexplicable. He ran about the quay in distress; he extended his arms towards the sea, and towards us: I could have wished that some accident should befal our boat, and compel it to return. We reached the ship. The anchor was weighed on our arrival. Swiftly we dashed into the wide waste of waters; I stood on the deck; I gazed back at the flowery shores of Teneriffe. And when they grew dim in the blue distance, I gazed on; and it seemed to me as though I could still distinguish d'Aubant's form, as he extended his arms, and, as a voice said to me, ever towards *me*. When at evening nothing more could be seen than the lofty, solitary Peak, rising like a pyramid from the depths of the waters, methought this mountain statue only appeared above the horizon to mark the spot where d'Aubant was sorrowing.

Paul knew d'Aubant in Petersburg. Paul told me that it really was d'Aubant who had appeared on the shore, that he had exchanged a few words with him; that d'Aubant was travelling to America in order to settle in Louisiana.

In Louisiana! Then is he also an unfortunate?

I could almost blush for the interest which this man excites in my heart. For each of the moments in which I have seen him possesses considerable importance in memory. But it is not him of whom I so delight to dream with the repose of melancholy, with a feeling of longing; it is at the recollection of my happy days, during which he appeared for the first time, that I lament. Now, cut off from my former world, every trifle from it is so new, so important to me! Thus on a raw winter's day in the North, one plant blossoming in the window affords us more pleasure than a bed filled with flowers in the summer. Ah, Julia, I like to think of d'Aubant. When my heart is filled with gratitude, this is the least it owes to the noble-minded man who shed his blood for my honor. To remember him is to remember you and my lost paradise.

16.

Written at Port-au-Prince.

THE sea-air did not agree with our good Herbert. He was taken ill. We mourned over him as over a father. I thanked God with tears of joy when, after a long, tedious voyage, we at last saw dry land again. It was St. Domingo, the richest of all the West Indian islands, but girt round with crags and dangerous rocks. Our vessel came to land. I left the ship with the few who had followed me to this foreign land, and we did not return to it again. For Father Herbert has lain sick here for twelve weeks. Woe betide me, if I should lose him! He is my second father, my teacher, my guardian angel, my guide. I should stand alone in the wilderness of the wide world. Agatha is a sweet child; but, herself, needs counsel and protection.

Oh, Alexis, Alexis! thou hast driven me here, my husband! Far from my children, far from my home, I, the daughter of Wolfenbüttel, wander in distant climes. You could weep no tears at my death; how would you feel if you could see the forsaken one here?

We live in a pretty country-house near the sea, not far from the town; it belongs to a colonist of property. He is a good old man, always ready with cheerful suggestions. His daughter, who is married to a young planter, manages the household affairs. She is the mother of two charming boys, who are the great delight of their old grandfather. We soon became quite domesticated in this family. We are as fond of each other as if we had been acquainted for many years. The two lovely boys especially cling to me. I also am a mother; and alas! the kisses which I lavish on them belong to the loved and distant cherubs from whom I may never hear the sweet name of mother. Oh, Julia! what can be more bitter than the woe of an unfortunate mother!

They use every device to detain us wanderers in St. Domingo. Every day they urge upon us to settle here. The old Deroy, for this is the name of our kind host, wishes to sell to us a pretty plantation in his own neighbourhood.

No, we are still too near Europe; every week, ships arrive from that continent now become so terrible to me. The curiosity of travellers makes them traverse the whole island. How easily I might be discovered and betrayed!

I will go to Louisiana. Thither my yearnings draw me. There, under the shade of groves centuries and centuries old, I shall live concealed and forgotten; there I shall belong to myself only. And perhaps — oh, Julia! — sweet is the illusion! — it comes to me as a prophecy that I shall not be lonely in these solitudes.

What have I, poor wretch, with which to give any charm to my impoverished life, but dreams! I will cling to their bright hopes with childlike ardour, even though they may never be fulfilled.

As soon as Father Herbert shall have recovered, we will seek the plains of Louisiana.

17.

Oh, wondrous power of love! What no one could have believed, or could have dreamed, has come to pass! Julia! I am giddy with joy. Agatha's lover, the hospitable Pole, Janinsky, is in St. Domingo. With incomprehensible success he followed on our track through the whole of Europe and across the ocean, as soon as he had converted his lands and possessions into money. It is not a little romantic. But be it so, if the good man feels happy in his enthusiasm. I almost suspect that Agatha had entered into a fuller understanding with him than she allowed me to know; and that perhaps she herself, like another Ariadne, gave to him, her Theseus, the gossamer clue through the labyrinth.

Suffice it, he is here. A messager came from the town to Herr Walter. Herbert bears this name in St. Domingo. The man brought him a letter. Herbert was still too weak to read it himself. Agatha and I were standing by his bed. I opened the letter and read it to him. Before I had finished, Agatha sank down almost insensible. Janinsky announced himself by this letter.

As soon as the amiable girl had revived, we held counsel together. But Agatha said nothing. She seated herself at the window, with the letter in her hand: there she remained silent, and in deep emotion. She only gazed at the letter, and did not read it. I had fears for her health. I tried to calm her, but she did not hear me, she only stared at the mute sheet of paper, and heaved a sigh from time to time.

I wrote an answer to this bold adventurer in Herbert's name, and requested him to postpone his visit for a few days because Agatha was over-agitated. I had scarcely ended my note when the door opened. Janinsky himself entered. I was startled. Agatha, with a cry, sprang from her chair, became as pale as death, staggered towards him with half-closed eyes like a dying person seeking the last long rest, and fell, unconscious, into his arms.

We restored her to life with difficulty. It was not until the following day that she could see and speak to her friend with composure.

The invalid Herbert would have reproached Janinsky. "No," cried Janinsky, "it is for me to reproach you. Why did you make your appearance in my hermitage with your amiable daughter, and rob me of my peace and happiness for ever? I saw her, I loved her; and the conviction that I did not love Agatha without return, only made me more miserable. I have succeeded in finding you out in spite of all your representations and concealments. I am now here. Will you be hardhearted any longer? If you will not be my father, well then reject me. But I will follow you to all parts of the world like your shadow until my devotion, my constancy, touch your heart. Do you disdain me as your son, then I will be your slave. You will not again get rid of me."

In this manner the man spoke, and *how* he spoke! His whole form was full of inspiration. Triumph, rapture, melancholy, and anxiety spoke at the same moment in his voice, in his smile, and in the tear which fell from his flashing eyes like a ray of light.

Herbert looked at me with an inquiring glance, and then extended his hand in a friendly manner to Janinsky. "Such constancy is deserving of the highest reward!" said I. — Janinsky threw himself at my feet, covered my hand with ardent kisses, and cried; "Do not forsake me; do not spurn the unhappy Janinsky!"

And when Herbert said; "Well then, Janinsky, I will give my daughter to you, if she can give you her love," Janinsky sprang up, and talked like an enthusiast, or like one whose senses have left him. He wept, he laughed, he related the perils of his journey, he pronounced Agatha's name, he entreated her love, although Agatha was no longer present; he loaded Herbert and me with thanks and blessings, described a storm which he had encountered at sea, and then again folded his hands towards heaven as though he would repeat his thanks to God that he had attained his goal.

It was not to be thought of to send the ecstatic enthusiast back to the town. We received him into the house.

On the following day Agatha gave him her promise of unchanging love, and also, with glowing cheeks, the kiss that was due reward of such incredible constancy. How intensely happy they both are! In the happiness of these lovers I find my own budding again. Janinsky will settle with us in fair Louisiana.

We unceasingly dream of the Elysium that awaits us there.

18.

FATHER HERBERT's health returned at last, by degrees. After seven months of pain he was but just able to leave his sick bed; — we resolved so soon as he should be perfectly restored to celebrate the marriage of the lovers.

Oh, my Julia! I now take up my pen to describe to you one of the most fearful hours of my life.

On earth no joy may ripen; our hearts may cling to no happiness. Hope, which rests, like a new born babe, smiling on our breast, is in the next hour killed by some treacherous dagger. We do not belong to this world. She herself repulses us with cruel severity when we would love her best. "Our home is beyond the stars, not beneath them," says the good Herbert when he would comfort me. Alas! and what can we do with our infirmities? Why do we bear about such hearts in our breasts?

Janinsky, Agatha, Madame Almas, the daughter of the old Deroy, with her two fine boys, Augustus and Charles, and I, were going one afternoon through the fertile plains. Rain during the night had freshened the air, and a cool east-wind blew from the sea. We wandered through the sugar and indigo plantations, looked at the work of the slaves, and visited several huts in a kindly manner.

Tired with our long wanderings we rested on some soft greensward beneath cocoa-nut-trees and the elm-leaved guava. The sun had already sunk behind the hill, its last rays were resting with a ruddy glow on the bushes and rocks. An aromatic odour from a thousand unknown shrubs was borne around us by the breath of the east-wind.

Janinsky said, "Why is this splendour so transitory? Why does not Heaven grant us endless life? We are called on to behold scenes full of wonders; and ere we have fully enjoyed them, the curtain has already fallen."

"Life here below is only the prologue to the eternal scene," I replied; "It only foreshadows and arouses our expectation for what is to follow. If the prologue be so full of pleasure, how earnestly should we not wish that the curtain would fall, so that the real drama may begin?"

Janinsky pressed Agatha's hand to his throbbing heart: and she smiled tenderly on her much-loved adorer. "Should we wish that the curtain would fall?" she asked him.

"I have attained sufficient, Agatha!" he exclaimed. "For Agatha loves me. And my highest aim is won: the world can never make me happier. Sooner or later, one day or other, we must have done with all below; blessed the man who falls asleep in the midst of joys! And if this life be only the prologue, oh, my Agatha! what shall we be in eternity?"

In such conversation minutes and hours flew by. The risen moon and the growing darkness warned us to return home.

We chose the shortest path which lay by the sea-beach; the boys ran on merrily along it.

A sudden storm of wind arose before we could reach home. Trees and bushes cracked wildly: the dust was blown up in great clouds from the ground, the waves beat with sullen roar against the rocks.

The convulsion of nature became every second more and more fearful. We redoubled our speed; but we were still a long way from home.

"My children! my children!" sighed Madame Almas in alarm.

"They are certainly at home now!" said Janinsky. "For they have left us a long time."

"And they know the road!" added the young mother, trying to calm herself.

The force of the storm almost threw us down. Moonlight, darkness, and clouds of dust, confused us so that we could hardly see where we walked. The sea roared furiously, and broken branches were blown down from the tottering trees.

It seemed to me as though the whole earth trembled, as though the furious hurricane would loosen the rock-rooted St. Domingo from the depths of ocean, and crush the island to powder.

"Only one quarter of a mile!" said young Madame Almas, who showed us our road. Motherly tenderness made her active and bold. She flew on always far in advance of us through darkness and storm; we could scarcely keep near her. When we did come up with her we only heard her murmur the words, "My children! my children!"

Suddenly she stood still, wrung her hands, and cried; "Oh my God! we may not venture on this road so close to the sea. In floods, and in storms like this, large waves often sweep over the narrow footpath. Go back!" But before we could resolve what to do, she cried, "But first I will go to the dangerous part, to see whether my children have past it."

She went: we followed her. When we came out

from between the rocks whose walls had protected us
for a short distance from the gusts of wind, the boiling
sea which was foaming high, opened to our view; and
every now and then a gigantic wave dashed against
the wall of rock on which the footpath was made.

The waves were breaking in frightful fury from
the ocean to the shore, hundreds upon hundreds, like
eager warriors who storm a strong fortress and rush on
furiously over the corpses of their fallen front ranks.
The pale moon glimmered through the scudding clouds,
and cast a dismal light over the strife of the enraged
elements.

I was trembling on Janinsky's arm; Agatha was
also trembling, overpowered by fear. But Janinsky
tenderly comforted us.

When we came near the place he desired us to
stand quiet. Amid the confusing noise of the waves
we could scarcely hear our own voices.

"Be still!" exclaimed the trembling Almas; "is
not that the cry of a child?"

A cold shudder ran over all of us. We listened;
we distinguished clearly a piteous moan; but we said
to the anxious mother; "No, we cannot hear it. The
wind is whistling in the clefts and bushes."

"But I must go across!" cried the despairing
mother. Janinsky seized hold of her, and as this last
wave receded, he carried her quickly across the path in
safety. Then he came back, watched for the favorable
moment, and carried his Agatha across. He came
again, and took me also.

On that side little Charles was already sitting in
the house, at the window, and crying; his mother
threw herself on her knees before him in mortal agony

and cried, "Where is your brother Augustus?" The boy sobbed and pointed with his hand to the foaming flood.

."Almighty God!" cried she, and she sprang up, and stretched out her arms towards the sea, as though imploring the pitiless ocean to yield up its precious booty. Meantime the moon emerged again from the clouds. We now plainly saw poor Augustus in the water, not far from the shore. He was holding on to the broken branch of a tree which hung into the waves, his little arms firmly clasped round it. Every now and then a wave swept over him.

When his mother perceived him, she flew with out-stretched arms towards the foaming sea, and threw herself into the water to save the lovely darling of her heart, unmindful of her own weakness. The waves broke with a roar over them both. We all stood aghast. I staggered fainting against the rock.

The noble-minded Janinsky alone preserved his presence of mind. He watched the tide, entreated us to remain quiet, and when he saw the dress of the poor Almas above the waves, he sprang quickly into the water.

Agatha, shuddering, threw her arms round my neck. All strength forsook her. She sank on the damp ground at my side like one lifeless. I cried out some-times the name of Almas; sometimes that of Janinsky. And when I saw how Janinsky, battling with the waves, conquering their force, seized the dress of Almas, and brought his prize to shore, my heart once more beat high and joyfully.

Just as the trembling Almas was brought to land and laid down at my feet by Janinsky, her husband

and her father, who had come to meet us full of anxiety, appeared on the scene. They had heard my cries, quickened their steps, and now hastened to restore the half-dead lady and Agatha to life.

But Janinsky did not loiter in his noble and fearful task. For the second time he flung himself into the sea. The boy, with his dying strength, was still moaning and hanging on to the drooping branch. Each wave that rolled over him threatened to wash him away. His deliverer appeared, dragged him from the tree, fought his way back with him towards the shore; and as soon as he was near enough slung him with incredible strength on to dry land, where his father received him.

But the waves carried Janinsky back from the shore: only once did he stretch his arms over the flood — and we saw him no more.

Oh, Julia! we never saw him again. We raised a fearful cry. Storm and sea howled in concert with us. But the noble-hearted man remained invisible — our cry, our search, was in vain.

Slaves were sent for, and torches, ropes, and ladders. Several negroes ventured their own lives in the water, to seek the lost one. The hoary-headed Deroy promised his freedom as a reward to any slave who should recover Janinsky for us. He offered the reward in vain.

We women were taken into the house, together with the children. The men continued their search. Alas! it was not until the fifth day after that Janinsky's body was found on a rock far distant from this spot where we had last seen him.

Thus death amid the waves was the reward of his

heroic virtue. Thus this high-minded man had left his home and all he possessed, inspired by true love, had wandered over land and sea, had found his beloved one again, being guided by a propitious star, that he might close his life before her eyes.

19.

FIVE sad months have passed since Janinsky's death. In a few days we shall embark for New Orleans. Herbert, although not completely restored, is yet strong enough to venture on the fatigues of a fresh voyage. The unhealthy climate of St. Domingo would kill him, if we were to remain longer.

And my Agatha, the ill-fated bride, has fought her fight, and conquered. She, even more than I, longs for the solitudes of Louisiana, there to mourn for her Janinsky with the same imperishable love with which he once loved her. She is a sweet picture of melancholy, and dearer to me than ever.

Good-night then, thou noisy world! from whom we all part with wounded hearts! — Receive me, ye peaceful wilds of the stranger, and give me the long-wished-for repose. There, the terrible vicissitudes of fate cease to exist. There our days will flow on in calm monotony, like a tranquil dream, in conventual stillness, until they restore our dust into the peaceful bosom of Earth.

When the rosy tints of morning beam through the forest, and the birds awake to song, I will devote my earliest hours in prayer to the Father of the universe: then by household duties, I will seek to add beauty to the life of those who with self-sacrifice have followed me into this solitude. I shall see them happy, and when they smile, what can be wanting to my peace? I will study the wonders of Nature: examine the formation, the peculiarities, and the virtues of the beautiful vegetable world, from the tall cedar down to the moss, from the palm to the blades of grass. Then shall I behold God, then shall become more full of trust in Him. Soon shall I make the barren field fruitful; soon arrange secluded walks that I may surprise my loved ones; soon watch the labours and daily work of the insects; soon delight myself with the sublime melody of the roaring waterfall.

And when night with her spiritual beauty steals over the plains of Louisiana, when the firmament reveals its thousand suns, and sheds a grave influence over the silent world; then will I devote my meditations, my hopes, to eternity. It shall no longer be to me a stranger. My eyes shall grow dim in death amid tears of joy.

Permit me to greet you, ye sacred solitudes, un-desecrated yet by ambition, by the dissipations, the thirst for gold, of Europeans!

Receive me into your cool shades; I no more belong to the tumults and to the passions of the world: henceforth I will live in my own innocent heart.

BOOK THE THIRD.

1.

THE CHEVALIER D'AUBANT TO HIS FRIEND BELLISLE.

Christinenthal, 24th April 1718.

You will think, dear Bellisle, that I have long since been swallowed up by the Ocean, or killed and eaten by Indians, that I have not written to you for so long. For I see by my diary that fifteen full months have passed since I sent my last letter to you from Bilaxi. But when one is taking possession of a new world, and is founding new states — and when in these new states all diligences, posts, and couriers are still wanting, you may well forgive me. Take also into account the little vanity that I would not write to you until I could do so from my own estate. Yet why do I say *mine?* No; all generously as you conceal and disguise yourself, to you alone am I indebted for all; you, by your loan, have made me the happiest man in the world; and so I write to you not from *my* but from *your* property. When I die, all will fall in to you: and, if you so will it, not before. Notwithstanding that I am sole ruler and king of Christinenthal, a settlement of a clan of powerful nomads allied with native Indians, I have also the honor to be the protector of a European, and the protector of an Indian, colony in my neighbourhood, whose head is called king. Thus I might indeed with full justice assume the imperial title, if in this country one were not far behind the follies of European citizens.

I have much to tell you; amongst other things exactly where beneath our moon my, or rather your, renowned empire is situated. For alas! you will not yet find it on the maps, although what concerns the great, can never be kept in silence; but first I must relate to you my whole Robinsonade.

When we sailed from Pensacola, along the coasts of West Florida, all we emigrants looked with vehement longing for the enchanting appearance of the much-lauded Louisiana. We dreamed of the shores already painted to us in all their beauty, with their green hills, rich plains, and enormous forests; and resolved carefully to observe, as we passed by, which were the most convenient landing-places, and what part was best adapted for the establishment of a colony. But alas! we found ourselves atrociously deceived. A long, low, barren coast extends for fifty or sixty miles from Pensacola; nothing but bare sand everywhere, on which here and there a stunted pine or meagre bush showed some little green.

At last the captain landed in the most dismal and barren district of the coast. A few miserable huts lay around, in which some half-naked, half-starved people lived — remnant of a former colony founded here! At this sight the courage of all of us fell: we looked for a melancholy future; our proud expectations melted into nothing before the reality. Many of the emigrants were very near returning to Europe in the ship which was to sail direct from Bilaxi to our native quarter of the world.

Meanwhile the captain of our ship consoled us all:

"Wait," said he, "till you have seen New Orleans! Our settlement is not to be in this frightful Bilaxi." What was to be done? We attended to him. I gave my last letter to you to go to Europe by the returning ship.

At length we reached the mouth of the gigantic river Mississippi, of which every tongue in Europe is now talking. It has many mouths; but most of them have but little water; in some, it fails completely at certain seasons of the year. The banks are everywhere flat and low; and appear for some distance, as along the greater part of the coast, to be formed by the sea and river. There is scarcely any stone found there; all is mud, sand, sedge, and decayed wood, such as the Mississippi from its distant, and not yet discovered source, has collected on its vast course hither, and washes down towards the ocean. This marshy ground leaves nothing on all sides but an inordinate quantity of reeds, which seem to multiply year by year and are impassable. Here the trees uprooted by the floods of the Mississippi, or broken by the force of storms in unknown regions, lie in a confused mass: mud and sand fill up the spaces between them, and thus widen the low banks considerably; or form large islands full of sedge and rushes in the mouth of the Mississippi, which are the abodes of all kinds of vermin; and during the hot seasons of the year, the air far around is poisoned with their horrible exhalations.

This gave us no very charming ideas of the Paradise called New Orleans. But we were not yet there! We sailed up the Mississippi. For ten or twelve miles we still saw nothing but the flat, inhospitable, sedgy banks, bordered with reeds, drift, and a few plants.

Often we had a difficulty in forcing our way through the immense mass of roots of trees entwined with each other which extended quite across the passage. And in order to get on more quickly, the boats were lowered.

But even with the boats, which were fitted up with sails and rudder, we went on intolerably slowly. We had continually to struggle with the drift and floating timber: and the recurring calms in this hot temperature did us at the same time a very ill turn. However the shore improved on both sides, otherwise I should have supposed the whole of Louisiana to be a lake of mud and rushes. Right and left rose thick, dark forests which filled us with solemn awe. Not a ray of sun penetrated them. I have never in my life seen such tall and ponderous trees collected in such enormous masses. There were not wanting everywhere wild fruits, a multitude of unfamiliar birds, and many red deer which every now and then we saw straying from the thickets of the surrounding plains.

At last after two days — for our voyage was always made zig-zag — we arrived, by a narrow passage which they call the English, at New Orleans.

When we were told we were now at our resting-place and destination, we rubbed our eyes in astonishment: for in spite of all our efforts, not one of us could discover New Orleans, nor anything that at all resembled so famed a place. On the eastern bank of the river where it described a large curve, in which all the ships landed passengers, ruined huts made of wood and reeds stood all around. Here and again indeed a building might be seen, built of wood and baked clay, which had something of an European aspect. The want of all large and solid houses was explained to me thus, that the ground was not firm enough to bear massive buildings. And this was the capital of Louisiana!

My faithful Claude would not yet credit this. In a capital, he expected at least to be able to discover some two dozen church-towers in the distance, ancient gates, market-places, and palaces; and bustle and stir in the principal streets. He shook his head, and said: "I would not give a sou for this capital, Sir. The village in which I had the honor to be born, if it were placed here, would be a real Paris."

I thought so also; but what was to be done? — we were all presented to the governor. I handed my letters of introduction to him. He was very courteous; and urged that I should temporarily lodge myself in his house until I should have found a situation to please me for my settlement. This was indeed not to be refused; for inns there were none anywhere in New Orleans. The other emigrants were obliged to build huts in order to get shelter. The poor people made wry faces. Things appeared to them to be as little prosperous as they did to my prime minister, Claude.

The governor was very kind to me. He is one of a distinguished French family who are reduced in circumstances. He looks upon his residence here as an exile. Probably he also had formed large expectations, and had proposed to bring back considerable treasure from the enormous gold-mines of St. Barbara which are so celebrated in Europe, but which no one is acquainted with in this country. His wife talks unceasingly of Paris with rapture and with tears; she finds life here among the wild inhabitants of the country, and the

fortune-seeking emigrants from all nations, very tedious
Her daughter Adelaide, a young merry beauty of sixteen summers, seems to content herself the best in this
foreign-land.   She cultivates her garden, dances by
herself when no one will dance with her, teaches an
old negro to sing French opera airs, and plays the
guitar charmingly. But I have not seen the fair girl
of whom I am writing this to you, for a year past;
however she writes me a pretty letter now and then;
quarrels with me and makes it up again; and plays
all her little freaks of good temper and ill temper
upon me, as if I were her doll. And I do not misunderstand the dear little girl, nor leave her without
an answer.

On the very first day after my arrival, I applied
myself to searching the district in order to build a
house for myself somewhere. My travelling-com-
panions, who wished to make me their chief, tormented
me from morning till night to provide for them. They
had all lost courage, and stood about in great trouble,
picking their teeth.

Nothing around pleased me; nor can I now understand how it could have occurred to any one to found
the principal town of Louisiana — this central point
of communication between France and her colonies in
this country — in such a district, and at thirty miles
distant from the sea.

New Orleans is situated on a large island which
may be some fifty or sixty miles in length. It is
formed by the Mississippi, a branch of the sea, the
lake Pont Chartrain, and by the Manchal. But the
greater part of this island is quite incapable of cultivation, lies within the inundations of the Mississippi,

and has a wet, swampy soil. They had tried the cultivation of the sugar-cane; but the occasional appearance of frost during the rainy season, even though slight, destroyed the crops. Tolerably successful attempts were made with the cotton-plant; but the indigo plantations succeeded the best, and this is certain at some time to become as important an export as tobacco. The land is very productive of anything that requires a damp soil. Grain does well; fruit-trees thrive better; in this climate they blossom twice in the year: but only the smaller portion of the fruit comes to maturity, because most of it falls before its time, being eaten by insects. Pomegranates, figs, and peaches grow everywhere in wonderful profusion; and are generally separated by marshes, standing water, or ditches.

Without any difficulty I obtained permission from the governor to set off on new discoveries, and to establish a new colony wherever I might please, for myself and all those who had come out with me.

At the head of twenty-five armed men who were all provided with the necessaries of life for several days, I crossed over to the right bank of the Mississippi, and advanced up the great river. The further we went, the prettier and the drier became the country; the banks ceased to be so low, and consisted chiefly of limestone rock. Every now and then impenetrable bush compelled us to go a long way round: sometimes we halted in extensive forests where enormous cedars, interspersed with fruit-trees, grew in wild beauty; sometimes we wandered over exquisitely luxuriant meadows and plains formed by the hand of nature. Whilst industrious, over-peopled Europe is offering unfruitful tracts of land for sale at high prices, the most enchanting and fertile plains are lying here unused; beautiful kingdoms without owners or inhabitants, with only some wandering hordes of wild Indians to traverse them, who live by hunting and fishing. It would be inexplicable to me why there has been no movement of people in the interior of America from the North to the magnificent South, if I were not acquainted with the roughness and stupidity of those who inhabit the northerly portion of this vast hemisphere. We met here and there a solitary Indian. They had retained their natural kindness of heart. We presented them with numerous trifles, and they hunted venison and wild fowl for us. The guide whom I had brought with us from New Orleans, was able to make himself tolerably well understood in their language, which has but few words. They belonged to the large tribe of Natchitoches.

We had left the Mississippi, and had taken a north-east direction that we might seek the banks of the Red River, which rises in the mountains of New America, and empties its waters into the Mississippi. We reached our destination without difficulty, and our trouble was agreeably rewarded by the discovery of one of the most attractive of landscapes. In the midst of an amphitheatre of hills, which were adorned with large woods, a wonderfully beautiful and fruitful plain opened on our view, large enough to contain and provide food for ten villages. It was divided into two nearly equal portions by the Red River. The monotony of the level ground was broken by several copses which were scattered in different parts, and which tended to increase the fertility of the meadows; whilst in the centre of the landscape rose a precipitous rock, which, lying between the Red River and two of its tributaries that flowed into it at this point, had the appearance of an island.

When we had forced our way through the brush-wood to the summit of the hill, and were looking down over the beautiful country with rapture, I exclaimed; "Here let us build our huts! This lovely country will one day receive my dust; I give it the name of Christinenthal. These surrounding forests will preserve us hidden from the world; these fruitful fields will gratefully reward our industry; the hill, fortified scientifically, will protect our colony against plundering incursions of the savages; and the Red River affords us excellent communication with New Orleans, whither we will send the superfluities of our labour.

All shouted approbation. We struck straight through the forest, the shortest road back to the capital, in order to make the necessary preparations for the new settlement. But, as we were obliged sometimes to throw bridges over streams and woodland torrents, sometimes to hew our way through woods amid which no mortal foot had wandered since the days of the creation, more than ten days elapsed ere we saw New Orleans again. When we arrived, the news of our discoveries and intentions soon spread. Within five days ninety-seven men had applied to me, of whom thirty-four were married, and of them eighteen had children.

The governor, although he would gladly have had us nearer, had nothing to object to our project. I learned that another colony was also in its infancy not far from our Christinenthal, and also on the bank of the Red River, about thirty miles from its mouth, and ten miles from the Spanish frontier-fort Adayes. We had then European neighbours: and the hope of being able to reciprocate assistance in case of need.

It is true that we had already whilst in Europe provided ourselves abundantly with such necessaries as are requisite for founding a colony in these un-inhabited regions; and yet we were in want of a thousand things, especially horses, sheep, and cattle. It was only by the outlay of a large sum of money that I succeeded in collecting a tolerable number of them. Others of my more wealthy colonists journeyed to Adayes in order to obtain cattle at a moderate price. All this delayed us a long time, eager as was our desire to establish our new home.

At last we all quitted New Orleans. I made the journey again by land, at the head of my colony; twenty men of the others came by water up the Mississippi and the Red River in three newly built boats, provided with sails, that they might explore the rivers and the navigation.

They arrived at Christinenthal four days later than we did, because they had several times been obliged to draw their boats, which were besides of heavy build, up the river.

Our occupations were shared. The new comers had to a man elected me as their chief; the governor had confirmed this, had conferred on me magisterial powers, and had bound me by oath and allegiance in the name of our sovereign the king of France, who was living some thousands of miles from us. First of all we provided for our security. The hill was our fortress; we surrounded the little level places on it with mounds and palisades; and levelled a road up it for horse and

11*

man. There I took up my abode, which at first was a mere hut. There was no want of wood, lime, or sand. Whilst the materials for building were being procured, I traced out the plan for the establishment of the whole colony, measured the land, apportioned the fields, which at first were of necessity sown with grain, rice, and maize for our most pressing needs; in the meantime others went out hunting and fishing; the women attended to the cooking.

All our works went on as well as we could wish; contentment and harmony reigned in our little state. At the end of a year of industry we had not only built our houses, stables, and store-houses; but had also profitable crops on our fields. Certainly we were obliged to be very frugal during the time of our heaviest labour; but the pleasure that we received on the perfecting of our realm, sweetened every hardship.

We entered into an alliance with the Spaniards in Adayes, and with the colony Roland on the Red River. The natives of the country also visited us from time to time, and stared with astonishment at what we were carrying on in their country. A chief of the Natchitoches from the so-called Black River came himself to visit me, accompanied by some hundred of his warlike subjects. I made them all presents and concluded a friendly treaty with them.

But before three months had passed this treaty involved us in a fourteen days' quarrel which cost our colony two brave men who lost their lives, besides that several were wounded.

A wild tribe of the nation of Arkansas took arms against the Natchitoches on the Black River. These latter defended themselves, but were defeated, and desired succour. Willingly or unwillingly, we were compelled to come to their aid; partly in order to obtain rest for ourselves from future attacks from the victors, partly in order to gain respect and esteem from the natives.

The colony, whom I ordered to assemble, were unanimous with me in deciding that we must help the Natchitoches. We crossed, a party of eighty men strong, into their territory over the Red River which itself served as a guide to us, and provided us with the necessaries of life. We found their army on an eminence. Their king appeared very wanting in courage. The Akansas had crossed the Black River, and had burned all the dwellings of our allies; they were also, as we had been told, much stronger in forces than these latter. A death-blow which had been dealt by one of the Natchitoches to a man of importance among the Akansas had given rise to the dispute.

I wished to act as mediator and peacemaker between the two nations. I sent one of our colonists, accompanied by two principal Natchitoches, to the King of Akansas with an invitation to return across the Black River, and to acknowledge me umpire of the quarrel. I promised to judge with fairness. But our messengers of peace returned from the camp of the Akansas insulted and wounded. It was necessary that a victory should establish my position with these children of the desert. I divided our colonists into four bands, appealed to their courage, and urged on them the necessity of making ourselves respected among these nations for the sake of our own safety in time to come.

The Akansas were already storming the hill before I had completed all my arrangements for attack or defence. The Natchitoches fought like desperate men; and rushed upon their enemies with terrific cries. We followed them slowly in different directions. Suddenly our muskets rattled shots among the Akansas from behind every bush. The savages of both nations ceased their strife in terror: the king of the Natchitoches pointed out to me the king of the Akansas, adorned with a high feather, and surrounded by his bravest warriors. I gave orders to the guard who were with me to advance, and to shoot the King in the midst of his attendants. It was done. A fearful horror took possession of the astounded Akansas. They fled with howls. Nothing now remained but for the Natchitoches to pursue them, and to kill and make prisoners. Pursuers and pursued swam through the floods of the Black River in deadly confusion. We Europeans, less nimble and less expert than these children of nature, occupied a whole day in constructing a bridge of rafts across the river.

In company with the Natchitoches, who were intoxicated with victory, we reached the huts of the Akansas after three long days' journey. They had prepared these for a last stand in defence of their possessions. They fought with fury; but the fire of our muskets was too terrible for them. The Natchitoches gained the victory, burned the huts of their enemies, and massacred women, children, and prisoners with inhuman cruelty. The Akansas sued for peace. I willingly granted it. The people of the Natchitoches did homage to me as their protector and supreme lord. They entered into a formal agreement with the colony; that, for the protection extended to them, they should yearly bring us a considerable number of hides.

We returned home to our people in smiling Chris-tinenthal. Besides this treaty, we had the advantage of having received from the Natchitoches over two hundred slaves who could render substantial service in the plantations.

Since that time the repose of peace has returned to the forests of Louisiana. The humbled tribe of the Akansas has migrated about three hundred miles further into the wilds towards the source of the Akansa river. Our possessions are bounded by friendly colonies, and peaceable tribes. I never lived so free from care, so pleasantly, as in this solitude, where my work is for all, where every one honors and loves me.

My house is built on the hill, and supplied with every convenience from New Orleans. Five majestic cypresses overshadow my dwelling, which is surrounded by a flower garden, in which the entire flora of the district blooms, and exhales a balsamic perfume around my windows. Sometimes I visit the forests to hunt in them; sometimes I visit my plantations on the Red River, where I have a pretty house in the centre of my property, in which my tenant lives with his family and some slaves who love me as a father. My good Claude, who has married the daughter of a poor colonist, manages my little housekeeping with the aid of his young wife.

I do not long to be at home in your world: I have prepared happiness for myself by my own skill. The calm joys of life dwell beneath my roof; but per-secuting anxieties, the lean ghost of the passions, I have left on the other side of the ocean. The most precious of all the possessions that I brought with me from Europe is my little library. It consists of a collection of the classical writings of the Greeks, Romans, Italians, English, and French; and the principal works on all the sciences.

The governor with his wife and daughter promised long ago to pay me a visit. This little change will be a pleasure to me. I shall then learn much news from Europe.

2.

D'AUBANT TO BELLISLE.

Christinenthal, in July 1718.

Oh Bellisle! Bellisle! lament or praise my fate. I am the happiest and the most miserable of all mortals. Yes, Bellisle, my peace is destroyed; I have lost my philosophical composure for ever. I love a female form before whom every quarter of the globe bows the knee, who is Queen of all wherever she appears, and by whose presence this romantic solitude is changed into a land of enchantments.

My neighbours, when in the evening they assembled on my ground, had often rallied me with good tempered jokes on my bachelor life; Claude had already often after his fashion described to me the happiness which he experienced as a married man, and had always specially talked to me of the governor's pretty daughter, my little friend Adelaide. I had indeed myself thought now and then of Adelaide. But alas! I could not love her, so faithfully did my constant memory still preserve the image of that Unknown one whose form had appeared to me again so fabulously, whose name adorned my colony.

The colony Roland is two days' journey from here.

I had long determined to visit it, and to knit the bond of friendship more closely with my neighbours.

About five weeks ago I started on my way thither, attended by my faithful Claude, two colonists and some natives. We chose the shorter of the roads; and, for the sake of convenience, the journey by water.

Only on the morning of the third day did we reach the colony, which is incomparably larger, richer, and older than ours, although the soil, and the situation of the properties are not to be compared in excellence with ours.

When we had made our boat safe and had landed, men, women, and children poured down from the fields and houses, to stare at us. We soon made ourselves familiar with all; said who we were, and from whence, and wherefore we had come. With kind-hearted rejoicings the householders pressed around us; each would lodge us hospitably in his hut. We were the not unmoved witnesses of the most pleasing, friendly dispute among these kind people; who at last, after much to say both for and against, agreed to divide the strangers among them. Wherever we passed, all stretched out a hand to us, and cried: "Welcome here! Come, we entreat you, into our house, and let us show you hospitality." And the women hastened in-doors, and brought us refreshments of all kinds.

We were all separated. A venerable grey-headed man, accompanied by his children and grandchildren, took possession of me. His house stood under the shade of lofty palm-trees. Here seats were arranged, and wine and fruits were brought. The whole family reclined around me. It seemed to me as if I were living in the days of innocence of the primeval world in the East.

We talked of our settlements, of our flocks. Even the civilized peopling of this district had raised the price of slaves and of plots of ground considerably. Certainly there were not wanting unfruitful plains, and tracts of forest; but partly their situation, and partly the enormous expense of bringing them under cultivation, prevented the attempt to do this.

"Then I shall not be able to buy land and settle amongst you!" said I.

A granddaughter of the old man, called Lucia, came up to me, laughing, and replied, "For you, kind stranger, our country will always have space sufficient. I pray you, stay with us!" And the glance which her beautiful, bright eyes cast upon me, entreated me more irresistibly than her sweet voice. Her figure so slender and graceful, the native, artless beauty of her movements, the softness and loveliness of her features enchanted me completely.

"You could chain me to this spot, fair maiden," said I, "if my home had not been already chosen." And I told them of the arrangements of the colony Christinenthal, and of its fertility, and of the reasonable price of property there.

"Then you might take the German stranger with his daughters to your home," answered Lucia. "For I am sorry for them, because they cannot find a property here to their mind."

"Yours is a happy thought, Lucia!" said the old man. "We will send to invite the German stranger, or seek him ourselves. It would be a help to him, and the news will gladden him. For it is hard that the old man should have taken such a long journey to us, with his children, in vain."

We wandered till midday through the plantations of Lucia's grandfather; truly I learned a great deal from the conversation of this old man whose experiences became the rule of my agricultural undertakings: but the lovely, merry Lucia distracted my attention all too much. My eyes and my heart were ever with her, and I felt that if I ever should choose a wife, she it must be.

On the following morning I went with Lucia's grandfather to find the German stranger. It was agreeable to me to be able to increase our colony. The German lived nearly a mile off, at the opposite end of the settlement, with a planter.

He was absent when we arrived. The planter conducted us into a large, roomy house. We told him the object of our coming. "Well indeed! that will be good news for him!" cried the planter. "Take your dinner with us. He will have returned by then; in the meantime you can talk to his daughters. Herr Holden is a thoroughly good man; and his daughters are most amiable, especially Augustine — she is truly an angel, such as in all my life long I never saw before." He left us; but soon re-appeared, and said; "Follow me, they are outside with my wife under the cocoa-nut-trees."

We went out; our way lay through a little wilderness of flowering shrubs: then across a bridge over a brook to an enclosed garden. When we entered it two young, simply-dressed ladies were standing under the cocoa-nut-trees near a busily occupied matron who was weeding flower-beds. All turned their faces towards us. Suddenly one of the ladies turned away from us as if frightened, seized the arm of the other, and exclaimed "Agatha!"

Both immediately advanced some steps towards us — oh, Bellisle! oh, Bellisle! a delusion played its arts on me — it was the dead Grand-duchess of Russia! It was the same being who had appeared to me in the meadow in Germany — in the church — on the Ocean — oh, Bellisle, it was herself!

I lost presence of mind, and utterance — I bowed in silence — she bowed, and leaned against the stem of the cocoa-nut-tree. Lucia's grandfather opened the conversation. By degrees I regained my senses, and joined in the conversation, though certainly at first very monosyllabically. But she remained silent longer. Her sister Agatha alone uttered a word.

The hours flew like minutes. I trembled — I vowed to myself never again to quit this wonderful being — I was like one in a dream — my mind was filled with rapture and doubt. But I did not venture to tell her how I believed I had already seen her more than once, (like an apparition,) at different times, and in different zones. But every moment I became more convinced that it was she herself again, and none other. And she was affected — I observed her blush, her pallor, her uneasiness, her embarrassment; and how by degrees she grew more self-possessed and cheerful when I became master of myself, and more distant towards her.

Herr Holden, the German refugee, arrived. His daughters flew with eagerness to meet him. They had already long descried him in the distance. They went into the house together. It was not till half an hour afterwards that Herr Holden came out to us.

I found him an intelligent, intellectual man. Our conversation soon turned upon business. I depicted to him the beauties of our colony; I related its history to him; but when I pronounced its name, Christinenthal, his countenance changed. He tried in vain to conceal his consternation from me.

Yes, Bellisle! my Bellisle! it is she, she is alive! The Princess von Wolfenbüttel lives, it is she! The story of her death and burial is to me and to the world an inexplicable mystery. But love and respect alike enjoin me to shut up the secret that she is alive within my own breast. She shall not suspect that I recognize her. I will deny to herself that I have ever seen Petersburg; I will invent a tale, and say it is the history of my life. Thus shall I make her feel more safe; thus she will become reconciled to my presence; thus she will fear no traitor in me, and will make Christinenthal a heaven to me. — I love her, oh Bellisle! — the wife of the inhuman Alexis of Russia — oh! how unfortunate is d'Aubant!

But hear how far my negotiations with Herr Holden, the supposed father of the unfortunate one, prospered.

"To confess honestly to you," he one day said to me, "your description of Christinenthal is charming; but both my daughters have an almost insuperable preference for settling in the colony Roland. But this seems to me to be over-peopled: at least slaves, and desirable properties are all at too high a price for me to be able to maintain my family as I should wish with the capital which is remaining to me after my many misfortunes in Europe. I will only wait for the return of my servant from the Spanish town Adayes. Then I will come with you to Christinenthal, and take the affair into consideration on the spot.

The servant indeed really arrived in a few days from Adayes. And, oh Bellisle! who was it but the gipsy-face again who had at first informed me of the death of the Grand Duchess, and had afterwards made a fool of me at Teneriffe. They call him Paul here. The fellow, when he saw me, did not appear in the least surprised at the sight; called me with perfect indifference by my name, and said he was just as well pleased to be in the enormous English parks of Louisiana, as in the labyrinth of paved streets in Paris.

When we saw each other every day, Augustine and Agatha also became more unconstrained, less anxious, and even friendly. But I — oh I!

On the evening previous to the journey back to the colony Christinenthal — I had gone to take leave of the ladies — we were sitting under the palm-trees by the evening light of the full moon. My gaze rested on the form of the wondrous Augustine, who, beneath the rays of the clear moonlight, resembled a glorified being.

It seemed to me like magic, when I saw her before me who had hovered about me like a guardian angel amid the thunders of battle and in the stormy hours of my destiny; when I saw her, the ideal of my imagination and of my aspirations, embodied in so fair a form; when I saw her, the daughter of a princely German house, nurtured amid the pleasures and luxuries of refinement, seated beneath the palm-trees around the house of an American planter!

I would often have aroused myself from my delirium — I could scarcely believe in the truth of the reality. — When she talked graciously to me, my every nerve throbbed, and my whole being was on fire. But when I would have replied I sank powerless within myself — I only beheld before me the most unfortunate of princesses — my love was turned to reverence and humility.

When we had taken leave, and the daughters were accompanying their father and myself for some part of our way, the princely Augustine leaned on my arm. I suppressed my melancholy.

"Who gave the name Christinenthal to the colony?" she asked softly.

"I gave it," I faltered.

She was silent, and yet it seemed as though she wished to add another question to this.

After a long silence I again turned the conversation to the beauties of my home in Louisiana; I spoke of the happiness which would fulfil my highest desires, if her father could resolve to choose it as his place of settlement. "And indeed," I added with quick emotion, "should his decision go against my wishes, I shall be greatly to be pitied. I should lose my possessions there, and in preference follow you as a beggar into any solitudes."

She smiled at me with indescribable sweetness, pressed her hand lightly on my arm, and lisped, "Let us hope!"

We and Herr Holden, attended by Paul, journeyed on the following morning to Christinenthal by boat. We reached the lovely spot without any adventure. Holden stayed in my house. Hope and love made me eloquent in urging him to purchase. I perceived at last that he had but an imperfect knowledge of agriculture. I offered to join my capital with his, to manage the cultivation of the land for him and myself, to attend to the purchase of properties and slaves, and to make arrangements for him with the governor at New Orleans.

He accepted my proposals. We sketched out together the plan of his house, which was to be near mine on the Red River, on my first estate. He then returned to his family at Colony Roland.

Now I am busy every day with the erection of the building, and in laying out the garden round it. Nature has herself done everything for the adornment of this country. The house will be finished in the spring. But they will not come to Christinenthal before that — an eternity to me! And yet I am so happy, for I work for *the* one who is my all! Her footprints will consecrate the ground which I am ornamenting for her with the loveliest flowers and shrubs of the country: and in these apartments which I am building for her, in these bowers that I twine with flowers, I shall see the Wondrous One!

3.

EXTRACT FROM A LETTER FROM M. BELLISLE TO THE
CHEVALIER D'AUBANT.

Orleans, 5th September 1718.

. . . So much of myself! . . . And now at last for tidings which have made Europe tremble, which are fearful and uncommon in history, and certainly are to you, in your fascinating solitudes, of the highest interest.

The Russian Emperor, Peter the Great, the most superior man of our age, has pronounced sentence of death upon his own son, the Grand-duke Alexis, and has ordered his execution.

The newspapers it is true are all writing of this story, as extraordinary as it is fearful; but I have heard through an officer some more minute particulars which I will not withhold from you. The affair stands thus: —

The estrangement which existed between the Emperor and his son has increased every year. Alexis had, in spite of, or perhaps rather on account of, his rough sullen disposition, numerous followers amongst the people, as well as amongst the higher classes and amongst the discontented spirits. All the enemies of the reforms begun by the Emperor in the establishment and moulding of his vast empire anticipated a universal counter-revolution after his death; the more confidently because the Czarovitch Alexis has concealed neither his hatred against the Emperor, nor his resentment at the Emperor's bold improvements.

At last the Emperor, in order to set his own mind at rest as to the continuance of his changes in the constitution, wrote a very stern letter to the Czarovitch. At the close of many admonitions to reform, he added these significant words: "You have now to choose between the throne and — the cloister."

The Czarovitch, surrounded by his followers, took the resolve of evading the dangerous consequences of a decisive reply. The Emperor was at that time in Copenhagen. Alexis pretended that he was going to join him, and went away with his Finn mistress Euphrosyne; but he took the road to Vienna to put himself under the protection of his brother-in-law, the German Emperor Charles VI. Here he wished to remain until the death of his father. But Alexis soon felt that Vienna would not afford him the needful security if it came to a point. Unhappy wretch! What right had he to consolation and protection at the court of an Empress who heard him condemned by the world as the unfeeling murderer of her sister, the much-to-be-pitied Princess von Wolfenbüttel? He fled to Naples, in order at least to live more within reach of the wastes of a distant part of the world.

No sooner did the Russian monarch hear of the stay of the Prince in Vienna than he sent thither his secret emissary Count Tolstoy, a bold and crafty man, of whom the Emperor always makes use when there is a dangerous affair on hand. Romanzow, the commander of the body-guard, accompanied him. In Vienna they heard that Alexis had already disappeared, and had taken the route to Turin. They pursued him, but discovered no further trace of the Czarovitch. In the hope however of finding him, if he should be living in concealment in Turin, they lingered there for some months. Tolstoy, dressed like a man in private life, led the life of a common citizen, roamed continually through all the inns, churches, taverns, and public places; but always fruitlessly.

One evening he was sitting over his glass of wine in a house of public entertainment in which several friends had assembled, amongst others a Neapolitan. They were drinking freely. Tolstoy pretended to be intoxicated early, threw himself on a sofa which was in the same room, and made as though he were sunk in profound slumber. The others paid no attention to him. The Neapolitan narrated how, some time ago, a young man had arrived in Naples with a lady, how he spoke a language that no one could understand; how he lived so expensively that people surmised he was some northern prince who was travelling privately.

Tolstoy now knew sufficient: he roused himself up again, called for something to drink; showed much good fellowship to all the guests, and attached himself specially to the Neapolitan, whom he invited to his house at noon on the next day. He became more and more intimate with this man; and would not allow him out of his sight until he had been fully informed by him of all that he himself desired to know. He then immediately journeyed with Count Romanzow from Turin to Naples.

The day after their arrival in the capital, their first business was to wait on the governor. After the first courtesies had passed, Tolstoy drew the governor on one side. "His Majesty the Emperor of Russia knows with perfect certainty," he said to him, "that the Czarovitch, his son, is in Naples. The sovereign, as his health is so feeble, is anxious for the speedy return of the Prince, to whom he is much attached, and who is the heir to the throne. He will be particularly indebted to you, Sir, if you will obtain for me a private interview with the young Prince. May I request you to accept my credentials for what I have said." With these words Tolstoy presented to the governor, together with a magnificent diamond, the instructions that he had received from the Emperor.

The governor promised a meeting on the following day, and kept his word. Tolstoy and Romanzow, as they approached the Czarovitch, prostrated themselves

12 *

in the Russian fashion, and kissed his hand respectfully. The Prince expressed himself much concerned
at the occasion of their journey, and inquired how
things had been going on in Russia since he had been
absent. They presented to him a letter from the Emperor. The contents of this letter were, that the
Russian monarch upbraided his son for having violated
his oath and his duty, and for having placed himself
under foreign protection; that he enjoined him to follow
his wishes as they should be made known to him by
Tolstoy and Romanzow, and that he promised him,
"in the name of God and by the day of judgment,"
not to punish him, but to love him more than ever if
he would come back to Russia: but that if this did
not take place, he would proclaim him a traitor and
pronounce his eternal curse on him.

The Prince was very much amazed. But Tolstoy
endeavoured to remove his every fear, and represented
himself as so attached to him, that the Czarovitch and
his companion Euphrosyne gained confidence.

"Indeed!" observed Tolstoy one day to the Prince's
ladylove; "we are in a splendid country here: one
lives here as if one were in heaven. I should like to
remain here always. But it is unfortunate that it is
subject to the Pope, and that our holy religion forbids
us to live among people who belong to the Church of
Rome. Besides, it happens now that the Emperor is
very infirm. If he should die, Alexis will ascend the
throne of Russia; and you, Madam, will then play the
most brilliant part in all Europe. It cannot be otherwise. From affection for you, Madam, and for the
Czarovitch, I must advise that we should quit this
Italian paradise. If it be of importance to you that

his and your reign should be happy and of long dura-
tion, then do not, for the sake of anything in this
world, give the Russians cause to suspect that the
Czarovitch may possibly have wavered for a moment
between the orthodox Greek Church and the Roman
Catholic religion."

Speeches like these did not fail in their aim.   Departure was resolved upon, and on the thirteenth of
February of this year Tolstoy conducted the Prince
within the gates of Moscow.   On the same evening
the repentant Alexis threw himself at his father's feet.
They had a long conversation together.   The joyful
rumour quickly spread through the city that the father
and son were reconciled, and the past forgotten.

But on the next morning but one at daybreak, the
regiment of guards was already under arms; the great
bell of Moscow was heard; the Boyards and privy coun-
cillors were ordered to the palace; the bishops, the
archimandrite, and two priests of the order of St.
Blasius had assembled in the cathedral.   Alexis was
conducted to his father without his sword, like a prisoner.   He prostrated himself humbly before him, and
presented to him a paper in which he declared himself
unworthy of the succession to the throne, and only
entreated his life, as a favour.

A sort of public accusation against the Prince was
then read before the assembled council, in which were
enumerated his intimate relations with the followers of
the old practices and customs, his cruel treatment of
his deceased wife, the unfortunate Princess von Wolfenbüttel, his connexion with Euphrosyne, a person of
low character, his flight to the Roman Emperor
Charles VI., whom he had solicited to protect him by

force of arms, and many other particulars which were termed state crimes. For these the Emperor solemnly disinherited him by a special edict, declared him for ever unworthy of the succession to the throne; and Alexis, shuddering, signed the document with his own hand. Then the procession went to the cathedral. The deed of disinheritance was there read a second time, and the priests signed it also.

But the fate of the Prince was not accomplished. He was imprisoned from this moment, as were all his former followers, fellow-malcontents, and companions in guilt; among them the deposed Czarina herself, his mother; and many others were discovered whose complicity in the oath for the grand Russian counter-revolution was either proved or suspected. They were prosecuted, and sentence pronounced.

This sentence was carried out without mercy. Glebof, the favoured lover of the mother of the Czar-ovitch, was impaled alive: the Boyard Abraham Laper-kin, the uncle of the Czarovitch, brother of the dead Czarina, Alexander Kikin, chief Commissary to the Admiralty, the Bishop of Nostow, and Pustinoi, father confessor to the Czarina, were broken on the wheel, and their heads were publicly exposed; many of the participators in the excesses of the Czarovitch, among whom were found fifty monks and priests, were be-headed.

This fearful slaughter gave rise to the belief that now all was ended. But fresh disclosures proved that the Prince had not yet acknowledged the complete truth. The Emperor assembled a high court of justice formed of the nobility, the clergy, and officers of highest rank both military and naval, governors of provinces, and other persons of station. The prosecution of the Grand-duke Alexis began on the twenty-fifth of June. The Czarovitch was led before his judges, heard his sentence, and was taken back to prison.

On the following day His Majesty the Emperor, attended by all his senators and bishops, together with other persons of eminence, went to the castle, and into the apartment where the Czarovitch was imprisoned. What happened here is a dead secret. But in half an hour the Emperor and his followers quitted the apartments of the Prince again. On every countenance sat gloomy horror. The next news was that the Prince was dangerously ill, that he was seized with convulsion after convulsion. At five o'clock in the afternoon it was said he had died in frightful cramps.

By order of the Emperor the body of his son was embalmed, and placed with all solemnity in the vault by the side of the coffin of the Princess von Wolfenbüttel, his wife.

What do you say, dear Chevalier, to this fearful tale? Peter the Great, in order to preserve his new creations, acted contrary to the feelings of a father's heart; — Alexis, the cruel Alexis, incapable of anything great or good, has reaped already on earth the reward of his manifold crimes and vices, in a way in which the sons of Princes are on this side the grave seldom accustomed to take a part.

Truly, my dear Friend, there is a God! An unseen, almighty arm ordains retribution in the eternal world and judges deeds and thoughts!

As to the sort of death which the Prince was obliged to suffer, I can give you no further nor satisfactory intelligence. It has been set abroad that Alexis was struck down by apoplexy whilst the sentence of death was being announced to him. But other conjectures are mingled with this; many will have it that he was compelled to drink a cup of poison; many again, that he was strangled.

If daylight should suddenly break into the dark secrets of many princely houses; if a spirit of truth were suddenly to sweep away the purple which serves to hide the crimes and the misery of many of the great from the sight of the crowd of their subjects: if we were to see them, the deities of the earth, in their private apartments and sleeping rooms, where, their crowns taken off, they brood over their secret grief; where, abandoned to terrible emotions, they become the prey of these; where they stagger between revenge and repentance, between longings and disgust, between deification and the dagger of the assassin, truly, my d'Aubant, our beggars would not exchange their rags for the grand, princely ermine; but would prefer their crust to the dainty banquet of the palace.

But so it is with men. Fury is their wisdom, passion is their piety. Those on whom birth and fortune have lavished the goods of this world with boundless partiality, possessed of every means of ennobling their existence, and of creating a heaven on earth around them, frequently scarcely comprehend the happiness of a pure heart; deem religion and virtue to be school-room fables, or state engines for securing the obedience of the people; strive against the eternal laws of nature in their foolish pride; and at last fall into despair beneath the unnatural state of things, in which everything appears a contradiction to them, and they to themselves.

For all this, the education of princely children is solely to blame. Even from the cradle they behold the world with dazzled eyes; and, instead of the simple truth — see but the caricatures of art . . . .

4.

D'AUBANT TO BELLISLE.

Christinenthal, 3d April 1719.

NOTHING more, oh my Bellisle, nothing more have I to wish for, nothing more to hope! I stand at the goal, and have won my palms in my earthly career. And were the spirit of eternity to appear to me this day, signing to me to follow him, I should bless this earth and restore my dust to it with smiles, and follow the spirit, calmly and joyfully — perhaps to a still brighter planet.

Yes, Bellisle, the only being who ever enchanted me; the wondrous being who has changed the whole course of my life into an eternal spring; the beauteous sacred one the mere vision of whom leads me nearer to God and to devotional feelings than all the priests with their gifts of eloquence, than all the unravellings and interpretations of philosophers, — yes, Bellisle, she is here. She has already for some weeks hallowed my temple: I am permitted to visit her from time to time.

A few days after her arrival her father, the good Herr Holden, who had long been ill, died. How gladly did I give to the noble-hearted man, on his

dying hand, the oath never to forsake his children, to
be in his stead their friend, their protector, their
counsellor. He was buried beneath the tall cypresses
in their garden. The lovely Augustine and her sister
Agatha were inconsolable. They live in great seclusion. Five young slaves are their companions and
their servants. The mysterious Paul, once so disliked
by me, looks after the affairs of their house and fields.
He visits me daily, and I daily receive intelligence
from him of the welfare of his mistresses.

What is now wanting to render my happiness
complete? Far from the tumult of the world, far from
its follies and its passions, I am living in my self-
created Paradise. Equally removed from the poisonous
effects of luxury, and from the depressing cares of
poverty, I inhabit my own pretty hut covered with
vines, and I overlook my little herds with a contented
mind. The charms of nature which adorn this secluded
Eden with perpetual youth and ever-increasing beauty;
the intercourse with my friendly neighbours who honor
me as their adviser and guide; my library, in which
sages of all nations and of all ages speak to me, and
elevate my mind; these bring pleasures and variety
to my simple life. — And now She has appeared, the
sun of my inner world! My boldest wishes could not
soar higher; I stand on the glittering summit of my
mortal career.

The intelligence which you gave me of the scenes
of bloodshed in Petersburg, and of which I forwarded
an abridgment to Herr Holden at the Colony Roland,
was not new to him. They had received the newspapers from New Orleans sooner than I had.

When the Princess, three weeks after the death of

her supposed father, honored my house for the first time with a visit, accompanied by Agatha and by her slaves, I had prepared for her a little country feast. I had invited several of our planters to the entertainment; and these, in order to make the day more cheerful in their own way, had also brought their daughters and various young men, and music for dancing.

I led Augustine through my house, and showed her my arrangements.

When we entered the room in which my library, my newspapers, and my maps are — Agatha had just left us — she cast a quick glance at all, then turned towards me, and extended her hand to me. I ventured to kiss it with emotion and respect. Augustine was silent; her beautiful eyes swam with tears, and a tender blush overspread her cheeks.

"I am an orphan," she at last said; "the death of my dear father has left me alone and unprotected in a strange part of the globe. But God has not utterly forsaken me. He has guided me to you, dear d'Aubant. You are an honorable man. We can never repay you for what you have already done for us. But, d'Aubant, the Eternal Rewarder lives! Continue to be to us what you have been, our guardian angel, our father!"

I could not answer for some time. I thought of her exalted rank, of her princely birth, and of the brilliance which had once surrounded her — and then of her as the lovely sister of a European Empress, the relative of the most powerful of monarchs; and she, who appeared to have been destined by Heaven from her throne to decide the weal and woe of great nations, she was standing by my side in a hermitage of the new world, full of humility and resignation, and with tears entreating the protection of a man who would once scarcely have ventured to set his foot within the golden halls of her palace.

"Nay," cried I; "I conjure you, speak not thus! You are my mistress. I have no will of my own; I am your subject. This property, these herds, this hut — all that once I called my own, is no longer mine; it belongs to you. My life is only valuable in this that I may employ it in your service."

At this moment she observed a small picture below the mirror. She advanced to look at it. I followed her, and my uneasiness increased when I perceived that she recognized herself in the figure, attired indeed in the very same dress which she had worn in the meadow at Blankenburg, where I had seen her for the first time. She stood for a long while silent and surprised. She dried her eyes, took down the picture with a trembling hand, looked carefully at it again, threw herself into an arm-chair quite overcome, and sobbed aloud.

I was still anxious, in order to spare her, to conceal my secret, and seem as if I did not recognize her. But when she raised her weeping eyes timidly to me, and asked; "D'Aubant, where did you get this? And how long ago?" then I could no longer bear it. I sank down at her feet. "Gracious Princess!" I faltered, "I saw you once in the meadows at Blankenburg; I was the painter of this picture myself. Since those days it has ever been my greatest treasure. I wore it at my heart in many a battle; I brought it hither with me across the ocean. One day it will rest beside me in my shroud."

She returned it to me in silence, hid her face, and

wept bitterly. When she had regained sufficient command over herself, she bade me rise. She silently pressed my hand. "I have long feared it," said she; "D'Aubant, if my approbation be dear to you, forget that you ever saw me under different circumstances. Re-awaken in me none of those unhappy memories. Carry my secret, like your picture, with you to the silent grave. I am no longer a Princess. I have myself chosen this fate, and I elect you to be my confidential friend. D'Aubant, do not forget that you are now the only mortal who can make me repent what I have done."

Thus spoke this noble woman. I willingly took an oath of silence to her: but I did not conceal from her that I had already imparted to you, my Bellisle, many surmises as to the fair Unknown who had appeared to me in such strangely different circumstances in life. I described you and our friendship to her; and the consequences of the disclosure were, that you will only receive this letter and all that I shall in future write to you about this queenly being (for to communicate with you about her in spirit is an inevitable necessity) subject to her permission.

From this day the relations between her and me were determined. None of our thoughts struggled back to the past. I saw her again. I saw her often. Like a rose after a shower of rain at night, her beauty blooms sweetly again from amid the tears of sadness which she sheds to the memory of her faithful, deceased servant, Herbert, whom, under the name of Holden, she revered as a second father.

Oh, Bellisle! if you could see her amid her domestic occupations! A marvellous and exquisite spirit of grace and order pervades all. Whatever she touches, seems to become ennobled under her fingers. All becomes more fascinating and more expressive as it stands in nearer or more distant relation to her; even inanimate objects become eloquent; and the smallest flower in her garden blossoms more brightly as it incloses the wondrous completeness which reigns in the district in which she dwells.

With sublime self-denial she occupies herself busily in this new sphere as though she had been born in it, and had grown up in it from her earliest infancy. Never has the history of the world known a woman who has met the most opposite destinies of life with such heroic courage, such strength of mind as she has done; whose calm fortitude has exchanged a throne and the purple for a hut; and who, with a piety such as saints have not borne within their breasts, wanders here, exalted above her fate, and looks down far below upon the troubled streams of the degeneracy of her age and on confused notions of dignity and of the destiny of man. Never has the world seen a Princess full of such touching humility, nor an inhabitant of a hut radiant with such majesty. The whole colony of Christinenthal look up to her with reverence and affection as to a being who has come from a better world, to bestow happiness on us; her slaves idolize her, — and I, oh Bellisle — do I love her? — love? — No, I may only dare to worship her.

Alas! the painful, — the happy, feelings which often enrapture or annihilate me — she knows them not — she must never suspect them.

One day I shall sink into the grave loving, but unloved! She whom I adore is born a princess. It would need an empire to fill up the chasm which Fate has opened between her and me.

5.

FROM THE DIARY OF AUGUSTINE.

IF, beloved Julia, you could now see my retreat beneath the shade of lofty flower-bearing oaks, and the sublime magnificence of perfected nature which fills me with enthusiasm whenever my eyes stray over its glories; if you could see my daily occupations, nd the peace and joy which reign both around and within me, you would call me the happiest of Earth's daughters.

D'Aubant, generous man, vies with fair, bounteous nature in rendering my home the most beautiful in the world. Where she bestows what is lovely, he adds what is useful; where she provides the useful he adds to it the beauties of art.

My existence flows on in a calm river of holy emotions. The melancholy of memory, the joyful anticipations of the future, and the gentle spells of the present — all blend in sweet concord like the varied tones of an harmonious sound.

I cheer our work-people in the fields; I visit the huts of my colony, am the friend and physician of the sick, the peacemaker among disputants; or I culti- vate our garden, or share with amiable Agatha our little household labours, or we receive visits and enter- tain our welcome guests with the best in our power.

I often go with Agatha and some of our slaves along the brawling river-banks, and explore the plan- tations of this lovely climate; often I wander alone and fearlessly through the dark, solemn forest, and up to the mountain. Nature is the true book of heavenly revelation which the Hand of the Almighty has Itself written; and each line of this unending work contains a fresh wonder.

The part of the globe that I now roam over bears traces everywhere of a later formation and origin. The thousandth part of it has not yet been inhabited or seen by man. Here, as in other parts of the world, the boundless ocean formerly prevailed, as the multitude of petrifactions of ocean products, which in the present day would only be found in the depths of the sea, testify. Only slowly, and in the course of centuries, did the surface of the earth show itself as we now see it. But, what was it before our history? Once, where now the enormous deserts of ice are spread in the neighbourhood of the North Pole, there strayed animals who in these days roar about the torrid zones; and whole races of animals are lost of which we can only discover the monstrous skeletons in secret caverns. Julia, there was a world before this of which our history knows nothing; and we roam over the dust and over the remains of races who saw this earth before the time to which even the account of Moses himself refers. What then was, has perished: the arts of that remote race are annihilated and lost. Perchance they flattered themselves with proud hopes of the immortality of their name! and lo! one alteration of the earth in its course round the sun — and all lay sunk in the ruins of oblivion. For this dry land, which we inhabit, is a new country: and the seas that we sail over are perhaps only the graves of some formerly inhabited quarter of the world.

And thus, like those lost ones of the unknown former world, our nations, our deeds, may one day also vanish by some fearful destruction, even to their faintest traces. Then no Alexander, no Cæsar, no Socrates, no Homer existed. In the lapse of thousands of years perhaps a new race will find our naked bones, and the vestiges of our plantations in newly formed mountains of slate, and say; "This globe once had inhabitants before; they existed before our time!" But the names of Greece and Rome will have perished; they will not know that a Russia, a France, existed; that once a fair empire called Germany flourished, which produced noble princes and philosophers.

Thus, Julia, I sink shuddering beneath the contemplation in thought of eternal nature; the past spreads its dark wings over the whole universe between the constellations; and I fall down, bow my forehead to the dust, and worship God.

And the ways and doings of poor mortals appear to me miserable, and foolish, and unworthy of the human intellect. Their pride rears itself by the side of the withering grass; their effrontery desires that their gigantic buildings shall surpass the web of the spider, and of the wonderful silkworm.

Julia, there is nothing everlasting but God; there is nothing immortal but His works, which we also are; there is nothing beautiful, but nature; there is nothing akin to man, but virtue!

I have torn off the bonds of prejudice; and it seems to me now as though I stood here, like a perfected being, better and nobler, between the world and eternity, between God and man. I acknowledge no splendour in the throne of princes, no disgrace in poverty. Men

are only miserable for this reason that they have not
the courage to be happy!

Oh Julia! would you were with me in the beautiful, secluded world of Louisiana; would that I could
share with you my prospects, my hopes, my happiness!

I do not lament over what is past, nor over what
is lost. That which grieved me is forgotten; those
whom I loved are not lost, but rest in the arms of
God. Over the grave of my faithful Herbert human
eyes weep tears of gratitude; but for his death I do
not mourn.

D'Aubant will be to me what Herbert was — I feel
it; he will be more to me. In him I love the world
of my youth; in him I love you, oh my Julia! He
gives again to all things earthly that surround me,
their value; slighted amid my thousand sufferings.
Yes, it is happiness to be human.

6.

ORAL TRADITIONS.

THE happy colonists lived long in enviable retirement from the rest of the world, and forgotten by
Europe. Their plantations, chiefly of indigo and tobacco, soon attained the most flourishing condition.
Nothing was wanting to make them perfectly contented;
and that which might have appeared to be wanting to
them only increased the value of their position. D'Aubant
saw Augustine daily, and daily learnt to esteem new
virtues in her. Mutual intercourse became a necessity
to them in this solitude. Augustine loved the worthy
man, without knowing it, without acknowledging it to

herself; and d'Aubant's passion for the most amiable of her sex burned unquenchably with a steady flame.

Even the gentle Agatha, who had been near fading away, revived again in youthful bloom, and a French officer who came from New Orleans to inspect the colonies speedily threw her remembrance of the romantic Janinsky into the background.

After half a year's acquaintance Agatha became Madame Desfontaines; and M. Desfontaines, fettered by such fascinating bonds, resigned his appointment, and became a planter in the happy colony.

The governor of New Orleans who had long promised to visit the far-famed Christinenthal, at last kept his word. He came in the middle of the summer, together with his wife, the charming Adelaide his daughter, and a large retinue, to pass at least a month in the new settlement. A number of little festivities were arranged in order to do him honor, and innocent joy appeared to have taken flight from the outer world to this unknown corner of the earth. But this residence of the governor in Christinenthal had an influence over the hitherto unvarying relations between d'Aubant and the planter-princess that they themselves did not expect.

Augustine's cheerfulness faded unperceived. Agatha, as well as d'Aubant, found her leaning on the hillock over Herbert's grave and lost in sorrowful reverie, more often than usual. It was true, she smiled, when a friend appeared before her: true that now, as ever, she enlivened society with her gaiety; but notwithstanding, every one who knew her felt that her smiles and her jokes were forced. No one could penetrate into the secret of her silent grief.

Meanwhile the amusements continued. D'Aubant had less opportunity and less means of watching Augustine. He was occupied with the cares of entertaining his guests. The merry Adelaide danced unceasingly around him, and the governor had a thousand things to arrange with him. The wife of the governor remarked with inward gratification how Adelaide attached herself more and more confidentially to M. d'Aubant. She imparted her little discoveries to the governor; and he, as well as his wife, had great reason to be pleased at them. For the little flirting Adelaide had already wished to give her heart to an engineer, a young, amiable man; this her parents knew, and they did not approve of such a gift. They had sternly prohibited any attachment between Adelaide and the engineer because he was a man of inferior family; this Adelaide knew; and she, on her side, did not approve of the prohibition. Now the dispute appeared likely to be very pleasantly set at rest by an engagement between d'Aubant and Adelaide, and no one in the whole colony had any longer any doubts about it.

D'Aubant certainly denied it boldly whenever the amiable Desfontaines questioned him about it; but notwithstanding he would never betray the truth, nor the secrets of all the little confidences that existed between him and Adelaide.

One fine afternoon the entire party of strangers from New Orleans, and necessarily d'Aubant also, were invited to Augustine's house. Augustine seemed to be more melancholy than usual, despite the pains she took to conceal her depression. The governor and his wife also were graver than common. Even coquettish Adelaide was seen with her eyes red from weeping; d'Aubant was more than usually silent. In a word, the Genius of Mirth had faithlessly fled: every one was living more within himself than among others. Agatha alone tripped innocently from one to another, and could not comprehend the mysterious behaviour of a company among whom fun and merriment used to dwell: and let her question and inquire as much as she would, each one was more reserved than the other.

Augustine regained her composure. She imagined that her depression, over which she had had so little control, had been the cause of the unpleasant feeling among the others. Her guests had dispersed in couples into the garden and into the little parks that led from it. She hastened out to collect the wanderers.

As she was passing a little enclosure, surrounded by shrubs, she saw Adelaide fly with outstretched arms towards d'Aubant, who appeared to be in deep conversation with the engineer: saw how Adelaide embraced him.

Augustine turned quickly away, not to disturb these happy people by her appearance. But d'Aubant had observed the Princess. He left the overjoyed daughter of the governor with her lover, and hastened after his friend.

She was standing leaning against a cypress, and staring gloomily before her. When she heard his steps, and perceived him, she seemed to wish to go to meet him; but strength failed her. She was very pale; she smiled at him, and her eyes became filled with trembling tears.

"Are you not well?" asked d'Aubant anxiously.

"Not quite," she answered; "but it will soon pass off." She pointed to some pieces of moss-covered rock which afforded a resting-place beneath the shade of some overhanging shrubs.

D'Aubant conducted her thither. He seated himself by her side. Both were for a long time silent. Suddenly he seized her hand with an eagerness that startled her, and kissed it with unusual emotion. "Do not make me miserable, Madam," he exclaimed in an agitated voice. "There is some illness, some evil, that is stealing away your life."

She raised her eyes to his face, and noticed tears in his eyes. "Do not be afraid!" she replied: "I am well again now. It was a passing paroxysm — it is quite gone."

A fresh silence followed.

"I have been wishing," he said, after some little time, "to bring you good news. I have succeeded in prevailing on the governor and his wife to give their consent to the engagement between Adelaide and the engineer. It was difficult. But the governor was indeed compelled to give his consent as the two young people had forgotten all appearances in their love and affection, and such open avowals cannot easily be retracted. Come then, take a part in the joy of this happy pair who are now probably reclining at the feet of their parents."

Augustine appeared greatly astonished at this intelligence. She asked many questions; and, leaning on d'Aubant's arm, went to seek the governor. The gloomy silence which had reigned in the circle of friends only an hour ago, had now suddenly vanished: the oppressive secret was removed from every heart.

Congratulations were given and received, and all gave themselves up to joyousness more unreservedly than ever.

Augustine, inspirited by the happiness of her guests, desired to crown the feast. She invited the neighbouring planters, and their families; country musicians also appeared on the scene, and by the light of the moon and stars an excellent supper was spread in the open air under the palm-trees.

Reconciliation, gratitude, love, hope, and friendship stirred every heart. They played, they sang, they danced. The tones of the instruments penetrated far and melodiously into the stillness of the evening, and allured the men and women from the more distant huts; so that with every hour the merry noises increased by the light of the blazing torches and lamps.

D'Aubant accidentally missed Augustine. She had withdrawn from the crowd. He found her not far from the dancing-ground, on a bank in the garden, concealed by wild, blossoming shrubs.

"May I share this solitude with you?" he asked.

"D'Aubant!" she said, softly. He sat down beside her. He would have spoken, but seized her hand, and, as he ventured to press this hand to his lips, forgot his promise.

Both were silent. The magic of the lovely evening, the recent occurrences, the music in the distance, all seemed to have a powerful influence over their hearts, and in each breast the sweet presentiment became more vivid — you will not live quite unloved.

Augustine, forgetful of all the past, gazed at the evening-world with dreamy looks. Every plant exhaled delicious perfumes. Shrubs, huts, and dancers,

all moved in the uncertain, magic moonlight; and the
red gleams of the tapers twinkled like stars in the
soft breath of the evening breeze which fluttered over
the country.

What she felt at this moment, seated at d'Aubant's
side, she believed never to have experienced before;
and how truly she loved him, she appeared never to
have known so clearly as at this instant. But these
moments were also the first in which he, who had
never before forgotten his deep respect for the beautiful Princess, broke through the bonds of respect. He
was silent, and trembled, and his lips were glowing on
her hand. His soul was in a tumult of rapture and
fear. His hardihood was bringing him to the threshold
of heaven, or to destruction; and these minutes were
to be decisive for him.

She wished to withdraw her hand from him, but
could not.

"D'Aubant!" said she timidly. He pressed her
hand to his heart, which heaved deeply with a sigh.
She was silent; she tried to repress the sigh which
responded to his. But he heard it, and in it the hope
of love in return.

A noise near them suddenly aroused both from
their reverie. Augustine, startled, drew away her
hand, too long the stolen spoil of the young man.
D'Aubant moved respectfully on one side. The old
governor stood before them elated with wine and happiness.

Both appeared to have wished for this surprise as
little as they had expected it. They could not speak
to him; and could not shake off the feelings in which,

as in a labyrinth, their hearts had for the last hour, or . perhaps more, been struggling and lost.

The governor looked at them for a while. "Here, then?" said he laughing. "And so silent! Oh you two cannot blind me: I have seen it a long time. Whether I have been obliged to-day to sanction one betrothal willingly or unwillingly, Chevalier, I must forthwith sanction a second; and when the missionary comes to-morrow or the day after, hold a double wedding." Without waiting further for a reply, he bent over them, threw his right arm round d'Aubant, his left round Augustine, and pressed them together so heartily, and so close that their lips were forced to meet.

D'Aubant's kiss glowed on Augustine's beautiful lips. Presence of mind, consciousness were lost. She felt in her astonishment that the warm lips of her lover were sealing hers, and involuntarily she answered by a kiss in return. And both sank trembling into the whirlpool of unknown joy, as though they saw themselves lifted by magic out of this mortal world into the immortality of Elysium, and were making their first entrance into it with timid doubt.

The governor laughed aloud at them, or at his own happy device; and with justice, went away triumphantly. His laugh recalled d'Aubant's senses. He feared, who had culpably violated the respect due to the Princess, to have deserved Augustine's displeasure; and yet love still kept him clasped to the heart of the wondrous lady. "D'Aubant!" she lisped tremblingly, and gently responded to the kiss which again sealed her lips. He threw his arm around her. He felt himself embraced by the most lovely, the noblest woman he had ever met in the world. He felt himself a god.

Merry sounds were heard through the shrubs, and the light of torches drew near. Hand in hand, the Chevalier and Augustine went to meet the approaching company. They received, as newly-betrothed, the congratulations of all, but could not stammer forth a reply, and had not yet confessed to themselves in words what they thought and felt.

Sleep fled from the Chevalier on this night: he turned about as if in a high fever. And when he awoke, all that had happened the day before seemed like a fairy tale.

Nervously he prepared to see Augustine — in order, if perchance she should repent of the sweet delirium — But what to do in that case was still quite uncertain to his mind.

She was alone, and simply dressed: but she had never looked lovelier. On d'Aubant's entrance into the apartment a soft blush suffused her face. She rose from her seat, but did not dare to look up at him. And yet her whole bearing announced, as did the calm gravity which pervaded her, that she had prepared herself to say some serious words to him about what had happened.

He flung himself at her feet; he could not falter a syllable of greeting. She motioned to him to rise. He rose, and sought with his eyes to read in hers mercy or his curse.

She gazed at him sadly, tenderly; and what was to have been spoken, became forgotten. Speechless, heart to heart, they forgot all the rest of the world; and only in trembling sighs, in tears of deeply-felt joy did their spirits converse with each other.

And as on the previous day, so on this occasion

the governor brought their ecstatic moments to a close. He came in, leading the Priest of Adayes, and with a joyous procession behind him: Agatha with her Desfontaines, and others from the colony who belonged to the retinue of the Governor.

Agatha clung sobbing to Augustine, kissed her with great feeling, and exclaimed: "A secret voice indeed whispered this to me, but I did not dare to believe it. You are happy, dear idolized recluse! I will crown you now with this myrtle crown; Christinen-thal is your kingdom; love, virtue, and happiness form the splendour of your court; — only do not in the arms of d'Aubant forget your Agatha."

And in very deed Madame Desfontaines fastened the myrtle crown on Augustine's head, and her hair fell from beneath it in charming confusion over her neck and shoulders.

The whole procession went to the nearest chapel, and the widowed Princess, married to her lover, became — Madame d'Aubant.

POSTSCRIPT.

AND a circle of happy months and years shed its blossoms over the richly-blessed pair in the solitudes of Louisiana. The birth of a lovely daughter increased the bliss of the princely mother. She brought up her child herself; and, as soon as it could lisp, instructed it in her mother tongue, German.

Thus did this exalted woman — where a victory over the prejudices of the world was involved, pro-

tected only by her own virtue — bend stern fate to
her will. Creator, in unknown regions, of her own
sphere, the heiress presumptive to the greatest empire
in the world formed her Elysium amid the huts of innocent settlers, and found here, amid tribes of savages,
a happier lot than had ever fallen to her share in the
imperial palace of Petersburg.

Thus passed the brightest and most important period
of her life.

D'Aubant's plantations increased every year. He
was master of abundant wealth. But two circumstances combined later on to induce these happy people
to change their abode — an illness of d'Aubant which,
failing advice from a skilful physician, threatened to
become dangerous in its consequences; and the false
and gold-greedy policy of the new governor of New
Orleans.

They sold their plantations at a great advantage,
and both travelled back to France. The Princess
thought herself long since forgotten in Europe. They
came to Paris, d'Aubant resigned himself to the physicians, and was quickly advancing towards recovery.

One day Augustine and her daughter were wandering for amusement through the gardens of the Tuileries.
They were conversing together in German. Count
Moritz, Marshal of Saxony, was standing near, and
remarked the ladies. As they were speaking his native
tongue, he did not wish to lose the opportunity of
forming an acquaintance with his amiable country-
women. He advanced towards them, and recognized
the Princess von Wolfenbüttel, whom his mother, the
Countess von Königsmark, had assisted many years
before in her flight from St. Petersburg. In vain did

the astonished lady endeavour to disguise herself from him. She was at once identified, and the Marshal entreated the single favour of being allowed to inform the king of her presence in Paris. All the representations the Princess made in opposition of this were fruitless. She at last resigned herself to his pressing requests: but with the condition that he would preserve the secret just for three months. He promised to do so, and then received permission occasionally to pay his respects to the Princess.

The Chevalier had in the meantime become perfectly restored to health. And when at the end of the prescribed quarter of a year, the Marshal went again to visit the Princess before he should make the important disclosure to the king, she had disappeared, together with her husband and her daughter. But he learned that she had embarked for the East Indies, and had selected the Isle of Bourbon as her place of residence.

Count Moritz hastened to the King. The latter, no less amazed at the discovery, sent orders immediately, through his minister, to the Governor of the island to treat the Chevalier d'Aubant and his wife with the most marked respect, and to anticipate all their wishes. And, not content with this, the king wrote a letter with his own hand to the queen of Hungary, although he was at war with her, and informed her of the extraordinary fate of her aunt, so long lost and mourned as dead.

The Queen's answer contained, besides the expression of her thanks, an enclosed letter to Madame d'Aubant. The Queen begged her to come to her court; the king of France would provide munificently for her husband and for her daughter, the offspring of their marriage. But the Princess replied in a manner worthy of her high mind, and with proud appreciation of her happiness. She declined all offers, and remained in her seclusion. She was still in the Island of Bourbon in the year 1754.

After the death of her husband and of her daughter, she repaired again to Europe.

Many maintain that she withdrew to Montmartre, where she is said to have been seen in the year 1760.

Others assure us that she spent the evening of her virtuous life in Brussels, where a handsome pension was bestowed on her by the House of Brunswick. Here she became the consoler of the poor; every unfortunate person, when forsaken by the world, found a helper in her. An unbroken, quiet cheerfulness played over her features, like a reflection from the inward peace of her mind. When approaching seventy years of age, she still preserved traces of her former beauty; and the throng of pure and sacred emotions amid which she had delighted to wander in the days of her youth, remained faithful to her in the winter of life.

And it is related of her, that when she saw the blessed hour arrive in which her spirit should be reunited with the friend of her heart who had preceded her, with d'Aubant, and with her children — and when all eyes were weeping around her dying bed, she turned towards the mourners with a peaceful smile, and said:

"I have dreamed a sweet dream — now let me awake to life!"

A NEW YEAR'S EVE ADVENTURE.

A NEW YEAR'S EVE ADVENTURE.

I.

MOTHER KATE, the old watchman's wife, pushed back her little lattice on New Year's Eve, and stretched out her head into the night-air. The snow, reddened by the glow from the window, fell in large, quiet flakes down on the streets of the royal borough. For a long time she watched the coming and going of the cheery people who were still making purchases of New Year's gifts in the brightly-lighted shops and warehouses of the various tradesmen; or who poured to and fro from the coffee-houses and taverns, clubs and dancing saloons, uniting the Old and New Year with joy and gaiety. But when two large flakes of snow descended upon her nose she drew back her head, shut the little window, and said to her husband, "Gottlieb, stay at home, and let Philip go out for you to-night. For it is snowing as fast as possible; and, as you know, snow does no good to your old bones. The streets will be lively all night. It seems as though there were dancing and feasting in every house. Truly our Philip will have no dull time of it."

Old Gottlieb shook his head, and said, "I am well enough pleased that it should be so. My barometer, the gunshot wound over my knee, has warned me these three days since that the weather would change. It is fair enough that he should now help me in the employment he will one day inherit from me."

It is as well to mention here that old Gottlieb had, in former times, been a sergeant in one of the King's regiments; and remained so until, at the storming of an enemy's fort which he, (ever foremost in the fray) scaled in the name of his fatherland, he was shot down, and became a cripple. His captain, who only entered the fort after it was scaled, received for his heroic act the cross of merit on the battle-field, and promotion. The poor sergeant must needs be content to come off with life, and a broken leg. A situation as schoolmaster was given to him out of compassion; for he was an intelligent man, wrote a good hand, and was fond of books. But, on the amendment of the school system, the situation of master was taken from him; because there was on the part of the school committee a wish to provide for a young man (who could neither read, write, nor cipher so well) on the ground that one of the committee was his godfather. The deposed Gottlieb was promoted to be watchman, and an assistant was given him in his son Philip, who had really learned gardening.

By these means, the little household earned their scanty subsistence. For Mother Kate was a good housekeeper, and very thrifty: whilst old Gottlieb was a true philosopher, who could be happy on even a little. Philip earned sufficient food in the house of the gardener whom he worked for; and whenever he took flowers for which orders had been given to the houses of the gentry, they always gave him a liberal present. He was a fine young fellow, about twenty-six years of age. His good looks often earned for him from the ladies a larger present than would have been given to others who had not so good a countenance.

Mother Kate had just thrown on her little cloak that she might call her son from the gardener's house, when he came into the room.

"Father," said Philip, as he gave his hand to his father and mother, "it snows. Snowy weather does not agree with you. I will take the watch for you tonight, if you will let me. Lie you down, and sleep."

"You are a good boy," replied old Gottlieb.

"Besides I was thinking that to-morrow will be New Year's Day, and I can dine with you, and enjoy myself. Mother, maybe you have no meat in the pantry?"

"None truly," answered Dame Kate, "there is only the other half of the pound of beef with greens, and rice and bay-leaves for supper. And for drinking, only a couple of bottles of beer. But do you come, Philip, and we will feast well to-morrow. Next week brings round the New Year's money for the watchmen, when they divide it; and then we can feast right well."

"Good! So much the better for you. And have you paid the rent?" asked Philip.

Old Gottlieb shrugged his shoulders. Philip put some money on the table, and said; "Here are twenty two gulden that I have saved. I can very well spare them. Take them as a New Year's gift. Then we shall all three be able to begin the New Year merrily, and without anxiety. God grant we may live through it in health and gladness! Heaven will provide even beyond it for you and for me."

14*

Dame Kate's eyes were filled with tears as she kissed him. Old Gottlieb answered, "Philip, you are indeed the staff and joy of our old age. God will reward you for it. Continue to be honest, and to love your parents. I tell you, the blessing then will not forsake you. I can wish you nothing better for the New Year than that you may preserve your heart still good and pious: this is in your own power. You will then be rich enough, and may look forward to Heaven."

Thus spoke old Gottlieb; and then he wrote down the sum of twenty two gulden in the large account-book; and said; "All that you cost me when a child you have paid off. We have now from your savings already received and enjoyed the use of three hundred and seventeen gulden."

"Three hundred and seventeen gulden!" cried Dame Kate in great astonishment: and then she turned pitifully to Philip, and said in a tender voice; "Child of my love, you grieve me; yes, you grieve me very much. Had you been able to save this sum to put by for yourself you might now buy a piece of land, carry on gardening on your own account, and be able to marry good little Rose. That cannot be now. But take comfort. We are old; you will not have to support us much longer."

"Mother," said Philip, slightly knitting his brow; "what are you saying? It is true that Rose is as dear to me as my life; but I would give up a hundred Roses for you and my father. In this world I can never have any parents but you; and if truth must be told not many Roses either, since among ten thousand I have yet loved none but Rose Bittner."

"You are right, Philip," said the old man. "Love and marriage can claim no merit: but it is both a duty and a merit to honor and support one's poor old parents. To sacrifice yourself, your affections and wishes for the happiness of your parents is true filial gratitude. It will make your heart rich, and earn for you a reward from Heaven."

"If only," replied Dame Kate, "that the time be not too long for the maiden, and that she should become inconstant. For little Rose is a pretty girl, that one must say. Though she is poor, she will not lack wooers; for she is a modest damsel, and understands how to take care of a house."

"Have no fears; mother," answered Philip, "Rose has solemnly vowed to me that she will have no husband but myself, and that is enough. Her aged mother has nothing to say against me; and if I could begin some trade on my own account to-day, and could support a wife, I might lead Rose to the altar to-morrow: this I know. It is only vexing that old Dame Bittner forbids us to see one another so often as we should like. She says it does no good. But I find, and Rose finds too, that it does us both a great deal of good. And we have agreed to meet at twelve o'clock this evening at the great door of St. Gregory's Church; for Rose is spending New Year's Eve with one of her friends. I shall then take her home."

Whilst they were talking thus, the three-quarters chimed from the neighbouring tower. Philip took his father's watchman's-coat from the warm stove on which his mother had laid it carefully for him, threw it around him, found the horn and staff, wished his parents good-night, and betook him to his post.

II.

PHILIP strode proudly along the snow-covered streets
of the royal borough, through which crowds were walking as though it were day; carriages were passing back
and forwards; all was light and brightness in the houses.
Our watchman enjoyed the lively gaiety: he called
ten o'clock, and chanted his tune on his beat most
joyfully, and with many thoughts of the house not far
from St. Gregory's Church where he knew that Rose
was with her friend. "Now," he thought, "she hears
me; now she is thinking of me, and is forgetting alike
conversation and game. If only she fail not to be at
the Church at twelve o'clock!"

And when he had completed his round, he returned
in front of the loved house and looked in the well-
lighted windows belonging to Rose's friend. Sometimes he saw female forms flitting across the window:
then his heart beat more quickly; he fancied he could
distinguish Rose. When the forms disappeared he
studied their lengthening shadows on the walls and
ceiling, trying to recognize Rose's shadow and guess
what she was doing. Certainly it was not very enviable
work to stand meditating in the frost and snow. But
what signify frost and snow to a lover! And watchmen
now-a-days love as romantically as did the knights of
old in romances and ballads.

He first felt the cold when the clock struck eleven,
and he had to begin his rounds again. His teeth
chattered with cold. He could scarcely call the hour,
or chant his tune; and he would willingly have turned
into a tavern to warm himself.

As he turned down a lonely alley, a strange form met him; a man with a black mask over his face, wrapped in a scarlet silk cloak, with a round hat stuck sideways on his head, and fantastically adorned with several tall waving plumes. Philip wished to avoid the mask; but it stepped before him in the way, and said: "You are a very good fellow; do you like my appearance also? Where are you going? tell me.".

Philip answered. "To Mary-street, where I must call the hour."

"Good!" cried the mask. "I should like to hear it. I will accompany you. One cannot have the chance every day. Come along, foolish fellow, and make your voice heard: but show yourself a good performer, or I shall not be pleased. Can you sing a merry tune?"

Philip perceived that the gentleman was a little excited by wine, but of high birth; and he replied: "Better over a glass of wine, Sir, in a warm room than out in cold like this, which chills the very heart within one." He then pursued his way to Mary-street, where he chanted his tune, and called the hour.

The mask followed him there, and now said:

"That is no great performance: I can do as well as that, you stupid fellow! You would laugh heartily if you heard me."

At the next station Philip acceded to the request of the mask, and allowed him to call the hour and sing. They went on in order, and the same took place for a second, third, and fourth time. The mask was not tired of being proxy for the watchman, and was unwearied in extolling his own skill. Philip laughed at the extraordinary whims of the merry gentleman, who came probably from a jovial party or a ball, and whom a glass of wine had elated above his usual every-day spirits.

"What do you think, old fellow? I have a great mind to keep watch for a couple of hours. If I do not now, I shall gain no credit. Give me your cloak and broad-brimmed hat, and I will give you my domino. Go into a public-house and drink a score on my account: when you have finished, come back and return me my mask. Here are a couple of thalers for you. What say you, old fellow?"

The watchman had no liking for this. But the mask would not relax his entreaties, and, as they turned together into a dark alley, he conquered. Philip was perished with cold; a warm room would be very welcome to him, and a good glass no less so. He therefore agreed with the young gentleman that he should act substitute for half an hour: that he should then come to the great gate of St. Gregory's Church, and exchange back horn and staff for the long red silk cloak, mask, and plumed hat. He named four streets to him in which it was his duty to call the hour.

"Best of friends!" cried the mask in delight. "I could hug you if you did not look so grimy. Well, you shall not repent. Make your appearance at the church at twelve o'clock, and earn wherewith to pay for something eatable as well as drinkable. Hurrah! I am watchman!"

The dresses were exchanged. The mask attired himself in the watchman's suit. Philip put on the mask; placed the plumed hat, adorned with a dark tassel, on his head; and wrapped himself in the scarlet silk cloak. As he turned away from his substitute, his heart sank a little. The young gentleman might perhaps in fun do something derogatory to a watchman. He turned back and said: "I hope you will not abuse my good nature, and play any pranks. This might bring me into trouble, and deprive me of my situation."

"What do you think I am, blockhead?" cried the substitute. "Do you suppose I do not understand my office. Leave me to take care of it; I am a Christian as well as you. Off with you, or I will cudgel you with your own staff. Be at St. Gregory's Church at twelve o'clock without fail, and return me my dress. Adieu, this is great fun for me."

The new watchman went on his way with an air of defiance. Philip hastened towards a public-house hard by.

III.

As he turned round the corner by the palace he felt himself touched by a mask who had alighted from a carriage in front of the palace. Philip stopped; and asked in a low, gentle voice after the approved manner of masks, "What are your commands?"

"Good, my Lord, in your reverie you have passed the door," replied the mask. "Will not your Royal Highness" —

"What Royal Highness?" said Philip, laughing. "I am no Royal Highness. What fancy has taken you?"

The mask bowed respectfully, and looked at the glittering diamond loop in Philip's plumed hat.

"I pray to be excused if I have exceeded the freedom allowed to a mask: but in whatever dress it may
please you to conceal yourself, your royal figure will
ever betray you. Will it please you to enter? Shall
you dance, if I may venture to ask?"

"I dance? No, you see I have boots on," replied
Philip.

"Then play?" inquired the mask again.

"Still less. I have no money with me," answered
the assistant-watchman.

"Good heavens! make use of my purse; of everything I am and have," cried the mask, and he offered
a well-filled purse to the amazed Philip.

"But do you know who I am?" inquired the latter,
and he waved back the purse with his hand.

The mask with a graceful reverence whispered:
"His Royal Highness Prince Julian."

At this moment Philip heard his substitute calling
the hour loudly and distinctly in a neighbouring
street. Now for the first time he bethought him of
the exchange. Prince Julian, famous in the town as
an amiable, clever, wild young man, had then taken
a fancy for changing characters with him.

"Well," thought Philip, "he plays the watchman
to perfection; and I will not disgrace him in my character of prince: but will shew that for half an hour I
can be a prince indeed. It is his fault if, by chance,
I make blunders."

He wrapped the scarlet cloak more closely round
him, took the purse, put it in his pocket, and said:
"Give me your name, mask; I will return your money
in the morning."

"I am the Chamberlain Pilzow."

"Very good. Go in first. I will follow you."

The Chamberlain obeyed, and strode up the marble steps. Philip followed him lightly. They entered a large saloon, lighted by a thousand wax-lights, whose brilliance was reflected in a multitude of mirrors on the walls, and in a chandelier hanging from the ceiling. A motley crowd of masks was moving back and forwards. Sultans, Tyrolese maidens, satyrs, knights in armour, nuns, jewellers, cupids, monks, ladies, Jews, Persians, and Medes. Philip was for a moment quite dazzled and stupified. Such a scene he had never beheld in his life. In the middle of the saloon a hundred dancers floated gracefully to the strains of harmonious music. Philip, to whom the genial warmth he here inhaled was very grateful, was so staggered with astonishment that he scarcely made even the acknowledgment of a bow when from among the moving mass several masks came to greet him, now rallyingly, now respectfully, now familiarly.

"Is it your pleasure to go to the card-table?" whispered the Chamberlain who, seen in the light, appeared as a Brahmin.

"Allow me first to thaw myself," said Philip; "I am desperately cold."

"Take a glass of hot punch," replied the Brahmin, and conducted him to a side-room.

The pseudo-prince did not wait to be pressed. One glass after another was emptied. The punch was excellent, and its warmth speedily glowed through Philip's veins.

"How is it, Brahmin, that you do not dance to-night?" he inquired of the Chamberlain when they

returned to the saloon.   The Brahmin sighed, and
shrugged his shoulders.

"Play and dance are alike over for me. Laughter
I have done with.   The only person whom I would
care to ask to dance — Countess Bonau — I thought
she loved me — think of my despair — our families
were on friendly terms.   Suddenly she broke off with
me entirely."

"Ha! this is the first I have heard of it," cried
Philip.

"What! did you not know it?   It is the talk of
the whole town," answered the Chamberlain.   "A
fortnight ago we broke with each other.   She has not
granted me one opportunity of clearing myself.   Three
letters she returned to me unopened.   She is a sworn
enemy of the Baroness Reizenthal.   I had promised
to avoid all intercourse with her.   Think of my ill-
luck.   When the Queen Dowager went to Freudenwald
on a hunting expedition, she appointed me as cavalier
to the Baroness.   What could I do?   Could I object?
On the very birthday of my adored Bonau I was compelled unexpectedly to depart.   She heard of it all.
She misunderstood me."

"Well, Brahmin, take advantage of this opportunity.   Occasions of public rejoicings justify everything.
Is not the Countess here?"

"Do not you see her yonder on the left?   The
Carmelite nun near the three black masks.   She has
taken off her mask.   Oh! my prince, your gracious
intercession with her —"

Philip, whom the punch had inspirited, thought,
"Now there is a kindness to be done:" and, without
ceremony, he crossed over to the Carmelite nun.   The

Countess Bonau looked at him earnestly for a moment, and blushed as he seated himself·by her side. She was a pretty girl; but Philip soon discovered that his little Rose was ten thousand times prettier.

"My Lady Countess," he faltered; and stopped, embarrassed, as she turned her keen, eager glance upon him.

"Prince," said the Countess, an hour ago you carried joking almost too far."

"Lovely Countess, for that reason I am now so much the more in earnest."

"All the better! then now I need not fly from you, Prince."

"Beautiful Countess, permit me to ask you one question. Are you in this nun's garb to do well-merited penance for your sins?"

"I have none to do penance for."

"But think, Countess, of your cruelty, your injustice towards the good Brahmin who stands yonder, forsaken by every one."

The lovely Carmelite cast down her eyes, and became a little uneasy.

"And do you also know, fair Countess, that the Chamberlain is as innocent in the Freudenwald affair as myself?"

"As you, Prince?" said the Countess, frowning. "What did you tell me only an hour ago?"

"You are right, dear Countess. I carried my joke too far. You said so yourself. I swear to you that the Chamberlain was compelled by command of the Queen Dowager to go to Freudenwald; was forced to go, against his will; was obliged continually to play cavalier to the, to him, odious Reizenthal."

"Odious to him!" laughed the Countess with scornful bitterness.

"Yes. He dislikes and despises the Baroness. Believe me, he has overstepped almost all the limits of good breeding towards her; and has by his behaviour drawn upon him much ill-will. I know this to be true, and he did all for your sake. He loves only you, adores you alone; yet you could reject him!"

"How is it, Prince, that you interest yourself thus warmly for Pilzow? Once on a time it was not so."

"That was, Countess, because I did not know him formerly; still less did I know the sad condition to which you have brought him. I swear that he is innocent. Indeed you have nothing to forgive in him, but he has much to forgive in you."

"Hush!" whispered the Carmelite, with brightened look. "People are watching us, come away from here."

She put on her mask, stood up, and took the arm of the supposed Prince. They passed together through the saloon, and into the empty side-room. Here she poured forth bitter complaints against the Chamberlain; but they were only the complainings of jealous love. She dried a tear — at this moment the tender-hearted Brahmin entered timidly. A dead silence ensued. Philip knew of nothing better to do than to lead the Chamberlain towards the Carmelite, place their hands within each other silently, and leave them to their fate. He himself went back to the saloon.

IV.

HERE a Mameluke joined him, and said hurriedly; "It is lucky, Domino, that I have found you. Is the Flower-girl in the side-room?"

The Mameluke stepped within, but returned in an instant. "A word alone with you, Domino;" and he conducted Philip to a distant part of the saloon, near the window.

"What are your wishes?" demanded Philip.

"I conjure you," said the Mameluke in a low voice; "tell me where is the Flower-girl?"

"What business have I with the Flower-girl?"

"But I very much," replied the Mameluke, whose suppressed voice and uneasy movement betrayed the terrible emotion stirring his breast: "Very much. She is my wife; she wished to make me uneasy. Prince, I conjure you do not drive me to distraction; conduct me to her."

"With all my heart," answered Philip drily. "How does your wife concern me?"

"Oh Prince! Prince!" cried the Mameluke, "I am resolved to go all lengths, should even my life be the forfeit. Do not attempt concealment any longer. I have discovered everything. See here! here is the note that that deceitful woman gave into your hand, and you, without reading it, have dropped it in the crowd."

Philip took the paper. On it was written in pencil, in a woman's hand; "Change your mask. Every one knows you. My husband is watching you. Me, he does not recognize. If you are prudent, I will reward you."

"Hm!" growled Philip; "so surely as I live that never was written to me. I trouble myself very little about your wife."

"For Heaven's sake, Prince, do not put me in a passion. Do you know who it is stands before you. I am the Marshal Blankenschwerd. That you follow my wife about has been no secret from me ever since the last court-masquerade."

"Nay, my Lord Marshal," replied Philip; "do not be angry with me; jealousy misleads you. If you knew me rightly you would not think such absurd folly of me. I give you my word of honor your wife need not trouble herself about me."

"Are you in earnest, Prince?"

"Decidedly."

"Give me a proof."

"What proof do you desire?"

"Hitherto, I know, you have prevented her from going with me to see her relatives in Poland. Persuade her that she agree to go."

"With all my heart, if it will do you any service."

"The utmost, utmost service, Your Royal Highness. You will by this means avert fearful, and otherwise inevitable, unhappiness."

The Mameluke continued to talk for some time; now entreating, now threatening, until the kind-hearted Philip began to fear that the man might, in his folly, force a quarrel upon him publicly. This would have been very inconvenient to him. He was delighted to get away. Scarcely had he mixed among the crowd when a female mask, attired in deep mourning and crape, took his arm familiarly, and whispered:

"Butterfly, whither go you? Have you no compassion for a forlorn widow?"

Philip replied courteously; "Lovely widows find only too many consolers. Permit me to number myself as one on your list."

"Why were you so disobedient, and would not change your mask?" said the Widow; as she turned to walk beside him, so as to enter more easily into conversation with him; "Can you then suppose, Prince, that you are not recognized by every one here?"

"People," answered Philip, "are doubtful, and are mistaken in me."

"Truly not, Prince, and if you do not dress yourself differently at once, I will desert you for the entire evening. For I do not wish to give my husband any excuse for making a scene."

Philip now discovered with whom he was talking. "You were the beautiful flower-girl: have the roses faded so quickly?"

"What does not fade away quickly? The constancy of man especially so! I saw how you slipped away with the Carmelite. Confess your inconstancy. You cannot deny it."

"Hm!" replied Philip, drily. "Do not accuse me, lest I should accuse you in return."

"As for instance, gay Butterfly."

"As for instance, then; there breathes no truer man than the Marshal."

"Truly none. And I have been wrong, very wrong, in listening to your fair words for so long. I reproach myself very much. He has unfortunately discovered our friendship."

"Ever since the last court masquerade, fair Widow."

"When you, bright Butterfly, were too imprudent and unguarded."

"Let us make all right again. Let us part. I esteem the Marshal, I would not wish to see him unhappy on my account."

The Widow gazed at him for a moment, speechless.

"If," continued Philip, "you have really any regard for me, you will go with the Marshal to Poland to visit your relations. It is better that we should not see too much of each other. A lovely woman is a lovely object: but a true-hearted, virtuous woman is even more lovely."

"Prince," cried the astonished lady; "did you ever love me, or care for me?"

"Do you see," said Philip, "I am an experimentalist after my own fashion. I seek virtue and truth; and so rarely find them. The truest and most virtuous can alone enthral me: therefore none has enthralled me. But no! Let me not tell a falsehood. One has enchained me completely. It only grieves me, fair lady, to say that that one is not yourself."

"You are in an odious temper, Prince," said the Widow; whilst the tremulousness of her voice, and the heaving of her breast, betrayed the emotion that was thrilling within.

"No," replied Philip; "upon my life, I am in the best humour possible. I would willingly repair the mischief caused by a foolish jest. I told your husband so."

"What!" cried the Widow in alarm. "You told all to the Marshal?"

"Not quite all, only what I myself knew."

The Widow rocked to and fro in great excitement.

She wrung her hands. At last she inquired, "Where is my husband?"

Philip pointed to the Mameluke, who was at the moment approaching with dispirited step.

"Prince," said the Widow in a tone of indescribable indignation. "Prince, may Heaven forgive you, I never can. I could not have believed the heart of man capable of such atrocity. You are a traitor. My husband is a noble in the garb of a Mameluke: but you are a Mameluke in the dress of a noble. You shall never see me again in this world."

With these words she turned from him quickly and proudly, and advanced towards the Mameluke: and whilst conversing together earnestly, Philip lost sight of them in the crowd.

Philip laughed to himself, and thought; "I should like to see how my substitute the watchman is getting on. I am not playing my part in his name so badly. If only he will carry on to-morrow what I begin to-night."

He moved towards the dancers, and was pleased to see among them the beautiful Carmelite by the side of her overjoyed Brahmin. The latter no sooner perceived the scarlet domino than he waved his hand to him, and in pantomime expressed the height of his felicity.

Philip thought to himself, "What a pity that I am not a Prince for life! Every one would soon be charmed with me. Nothing in the world is easier than to be a prince. He can do more by a single word than the best advocate by a long speech. He is privileged to go straight to the point, and speak openly.

15*

Ah!' but if I were a prince my little Rose would be
lost to me. No, I would not wish to be a prince."

He looked at the clock; it was only half-past
eleven. The Mameluke now came up hastily to him;
drew him on one side, and gave him a paper.

"Prince," cried he. "I would fain fall at your
feet, and thank you, bowing to the dust. I am reconciled to my wife. You have broken her spirit:
it is well that it is so. She wishes to start this very
night. She wishes to remain on our property in Poland.
Farewell. I am ready to obey your summons whenever you may call me, even though it should be to
lay down my life for your Royal Highness. My
thanks are eternal. Farewell."

"Stop!" cried Philip, as the Marshal was hurrying
away. "What am I to do with this paper?"

"It is my play-debt for several weeks," replied
the Marshal, "which I had almost forgotten, and which
I would not wish to have left unpaid before we depart.
I have endorsed the note of hand to Your Royal Highness."

So saying, the Marshal disappeared.

V.

Philip looked at the paper, read in it something
about five thousand gulden, put it in his pocket, and
said to himself; "What a pity I am not the Prince!"

At this moment some one whispered; "Your Royal
Highness, we are both betrayed. I shall blow out my
brains."

Philip looked round astonished, and perceived a
Moor.

"What do you want, Mask?" said Philip with composure.

"I am Colonel Kalt," answered the Moor in a whisper. The Marshal's spiteful wife has tattled everything to Duke Herman, and he is breathing fire and flame against you and against me."

"At me!" replied Philip.

"And the king has heard everything!" sighed the Moor disconsolately. "Perhaps this very night I shall be arrested; and to-morrow taken to the fortress. I would rather hang myself."

"You have no occasion to do that," said Philip.

"Shall I pay the penalty of life-long shame? I am lost. The Duke will require satisfaction to the death. No doubt he is still black and blue with the blows I gave him. I am lost; and the baker's girl besides. I will jump from the bridge, and drown myself this very night."

"Heaven forbid!" said Philip. "What have either you or the baker's girl to do with this affair?"

"Your Royal Highness jests whilst I am in despair. I humbly pray you to grant me an interview of two minutes."

Philip followed the Moor into a side-room in which a few tapers shed a dim light. The Moor threw himself on a sofa as if paralysed, and sighed aloud. Philip found some refreshments and excellent wine on the table, and began to partake of them.

"I cannot understand how your Royal Highness can be so composed over this confounded affair. Would that that villain, the Neapolitan Salmoni were here, who played necromancer. The fellow was full of tricks from top to toe, and might perchance be able to help us by some stratagem. But he has made off."

"So much the better," answered Philip, filling his glass again. "You can now throw all the blame on him. He is absent."

"How throw it on him? The Duke knows now that you, I, the Marshal's wife, and the baker's girl, were all in the plot to take advantage of his superstition. He knows that you bribed Salmoni to play conjurer, that I instructed the baker's girl, with whom he was smitten, to decoy him; that I was the ghost who threw him down and gave him a drubbing. Would that I had not carried the joke so far! but I wanted to beat out of him his fancy for my sweetheart. It is an ugly affair. I will take poison."

"You had better take a glass of wine," said Philip; and, with renewed appetite, he helped himself again to a tart. "Besides," he continued, "I must tell you fairly, my good Colonel, that you are a very weak-minded man for a Colonel, if, like a fool in a story-book, you would at one and the same time be shot, drowned, hung and poisoned. One of these would be more than enough. I must tell you again that with your chattering of one kind and another I shall presently lose my wits."

"I beg for pardon from your Royal Highness; I know not which way to turn. The Duke's gentleman of the bedchamber — he is an old friend of mine — confided to me only a moment since that the Marshal's wife, prompted by some demon, went to the Duke a few minutes ago, and said to him: 'Prince Julian was the originator of the farce played upon you in the baker's house, grudging you his sister. The witch

you saw, was myself, deputy of the Princess, as witness of your credulity. Prince Julian has the list of
your debts which you threw into the vault from whence
you were to raise the treasure, as well as the agreement with the baker's girl to continue to be friendly
with her after your marriage with the Princess, and
to have her ennobled. And the ghost who cudgelled
you was Colonel Kalt, the Prince's henchman. This
is the reason why your marriage has been delayed.
Hope for it no longer; you will wait in vain.' This
is what the Marshal's wife said to the Duke, and
vanished immediately."

Philip shook his head, and muttered, "This is a
sad affair. Among the common orders any one would
be ashamed of such a trick. What wicked follies, and
no end to them!"

"No," cried the Colonel; "in revenge and vul-
garity none can excel the Marshal's wife. The woman
must be a fury. Good Prince, save me."

"Where then is the Duke?" inquired Philip.

"His gentleman of the bedchamber said that he
rose quickly, and almost shrieked: 'I will go to the
King!' Only think, Prince, if he should go to the
King, and give his own version of the story."

"Is the King here?"

"Certainly. He is playing at cards in the adjoining room with the Archbishop and the Minister of
Police, l'Hombre."

Philip strode up and down the room. Wise counsel was of the utmost importance.

"Save me, your Royal Highness," said the Moor.
"Your own honor is at stake. It will be easy for
you to arrange. However I am prepared now for

everything, and with the first breath of mischief I am
over the frontier. I will pack up. To-morrow I will
look for your final commands as to my movements."

With these words the Moor disappeared.

VI.

"It is high time that you became watchman again,
Philip," said he to himself. You are entangling yourself and your substitute in godless affairs from which
neither his prudence nor yours will be able to extri-
cate him and yourself. Besides there is a wide differ-
ence between a watchman and a prince. I have no
talent for this. Good Heavens! how many follies go
on among the gods of earth in the paradise of a court
of which we with our watchmen's horns, our looms,
our spades, and our lasts have never dreamed! We
imagine that these exalted beings lead a life like the
angels, sinless and sorrowless. Pretty doings! Here
in one quarter of an hour I have had more knaveries
to repair than I ever heard of in the whole course of
my life before."

"So pensive, my Prince," whispered a voice behind him. "I deem myself fortunate to find your
Royal Highness alone for a moment."

Philip looked round. It was a man in the dress of
a miner adorned with gold, silver, and precious stones.

"What would you of me?" asked Philip.

"Only a gracious audience for a moment," replied
the miner. "My business is urgent; the result perhaps
important to yourself."

"And who are you, mask, if I may ask?"

"Count Bodenlos, the Minister of Finance, at your

Royal Highness' commands," replied the miner; and he lifted his mask and disclosed a face that with its little eyes and large copper-coloured nose might have itself passed for a mask.

"Well, my Lord Count, what are your wishes?" inquired Philip again.

"May I speak candidly? I have already sent in my name three times to your Royal Highness without having obtained the privilege of admission; and yet no one at court takes a more lively interest than myself in your Royal Highness' joys and sorrows."

"I am obliged to you, my Lord Count!" answered Philip. "But what would you now? Make your story short."

"May I venture to speak of the mercantile firm of Abraham Levi?" asked the miner.

"As much as you please."

"They have applied to me respecting the fifty thousand gulden that your Royal Highness is indebted to them. They threaten to apply to the King. And you know what promise you made to the King when he ordered your last debts to be paid."

"Cannot these people wait?" asked Philip.

"As little as the brothers Goldsmid will wait, who dun you for the seventy-five thousand gulden."

"It is all the same to me. If the people will not wait, then I must — "

"No despairing resolves, gracious Prince. I am in a position to put all straight again, if — "

"If — what then?"

"If you will accord me your favour, if you will deign to listen to me for a moment. I hope to settle all your debts without difficulty. The house of

Abraham Levi has arranged for immense purchases of corn on speculation, so that it has risen very much in price. A prohibition on the exportation of corn to the neighbouring states will quickly raise the price again to double or treble. Then special licenses will be granted to Abraham Levi, and all will be right. The house will cancel the debt, and undertake the payment of the seventy-five thousand gulden for you, and I will hand over the receipts to you. But all hangs on this condition, that I shall remain for some years longer at the head of the finance department. Should Baron Greisensack succeed in dislodging me from the cabinet, I shall be powerless to act for you, as it would be my greatest desire to do. It remains with your Royal Highness to quit the Greisensack party; and then our game is won. To myself it is the same thing whether I remain in the cabinet or not: but as regards your Royal Highness, I am not so indifferent. If I cannot shuffle the cards as I wish, I lose."

Philip knew not for a moment what to reply. Whilst the Minister of Finance waiting for an answer drew out a jewelled snuff-box, and took a pinch of snuff, Philip at last said, "If I understand you rightly, my Lord Count, you propose to famish the country somewhat in order to pay my debts. Do you consider how much mischief you will do? and will the King consent?"

"If I remain in office, let that be my care, gracious Prince. As soon as the price of food rises, the King will himself think at once of an embargo on the exportation of corn, and impose heavy duties upon it. Permission will then be granted to the firm of Abraham

Levi for the export of ten sacks, and he will export a hundred. Nothing easier than that. But, as I said, if Greisensack should be at the head of affairs, none of this can take place. Years will go by before he will well have mastered the duties of his office. From sheer necessity he will have to play the honest man, if only to be able afterwards to cheat the King and country the better. He must first feel his ground. There breathes not a more arrant Jew than Greisensack. His avarice is disgusting."

"Grand prospects!" said Philip. "How long do you think a Minister of Finance should hold his appointment before he is competent to fleece the people for the benefit of himself and those belonging to him?"

"Hm! if he have a good head he may manage it in a year."

"Then one ought to advise the King to appoint a new Minister of Finance every year if he wishes to be served faithfully."

"I trust, gracious Prince, that since I have conducted the affairs of the finance department nothing has been lost by the King and court."

"I believe that, Count; but so much the worse for the unfortunate people. They hardly know how to pay the multitude of taxes and imposts. You ought to treat us with a little more compassion."

"Treat *us!* Do I not do all in my power for the court?"

"No, I mean that you should deal more compassionately with the people."

"My Prince, I know the respect I should pay to your words. The King and his illustrious family are

the nation whom I serve. They who are commonly
called the nation are not to be thought of in comparison. The country is the King's property. Its
inhabitants are only to be considered so far as they,
like cyphers which follow a cardinal number, increase
its wealth. But this is not a moment in which to
renew the threadbare discourse as to the value of the
mob. I entreat your gracious decision as to whether
I shall have the honor of settling your debts in the
manner I have proposed."

"My decision! No; no, now and for ever, not to
the cost of a hundred thousand and more poor families."

"Your Royal Highness, it but regards the account
of the house of Abraham Levi. And what if I press
the firm to add fifty thousand gulden to the acquittance
of the debts? I think this might be done. This
house will gain by this transaction alone so much,
that —"

"Probably also a little douceur for yourself is to
be provided, my Lord Count?"

"Your Royal Highness is pleased to be jocular.
I can gain nothing by it. I only burn with anxiety
to regain your favour."

"You are very good."

"Then may I hope, Sir?"

"My Lord Count, I will do what is just: do you
perform your duty."

"My duty is to serve you. To-morrow I will send
for Levi, settle the affair with him, and have the honor
of handing over to your Royal Highness the aforenamed
acquittances with a bill of exchange for fifty thousand
gulden."

"Begone! I will listen to nothing of the kind."

"And, your Royal Highness will then receive me into your favour again? For unless I remain in the cabinet I cannot possibly settle with Abraham Levi—"

"I wish you, and your cabinet, and your Abraham Levi were all on the top of Blocksberg together. This I tell you, should an embargo on the export of corn be issued, even though an increase in the price of the necessaries of life should not immediately follow, yet if your traitor house does not forthwith sell the stored-up grain at the purchase price, I will go straight to the King, tell him of all your villanies, and give a helping hand towards chasing you and Abraham Levi out of the country together."

Philip turned away, went back into the dancing saloon, and left the Minister of Finance standing petrified.

VII.

"WHEN is it your Royal Highness' pleasure that the carriage should come round?" whispered a voice, as he passed down the saloon through the crowd of masks. It was a stout Dutch merchant with a bob wig who addressed him.

"I am not going to drive."

"It is past half-past eleven, Prince. The beautiful songstress is expecting you. She will be tired of waiting."

"Then she can sing to herself."

"What, Prince, have you changed your mind? Would you forsake the charming Rollina? Lose the golden opportunity for which you have sighed for these two months? Your note that you sent by me this morning to Signora Rollina with the watch set in brilliants has obtained it for you. The haughty prude relents. You were so delighted at noon, and now have you all at once become icily indifferent. What has happened to you? I cannot understand the change."

"That does not signify to me."

"But you ordered me to attend you at half-past eleven. Perhaps you have some other engagements?"

"Certainly I have."

"A supper perhaps with the Countess Born. She has not appeared at the ball; at least among all the masks here she has not been discovered. I should know her among a thousand by her walk, and by the peculiar manner in which she carries her pretty little head. Is it so, Prince?"

"Supposing it were, am I obliged to tell you?"

"Ah! I understand, and will say nothing. But will you not at least send a message to the Signora Rollina that you are not coming?"

"As she left me to sigh for two months for a meeting with her, she may now sigh for two months for one with me. I am not going."

"Then the beautiful necklace that you intended as a New Year's gift for her will probably now come to nothing."

"If it depends on me."

"Would you then break with her entirely, honored Prince?"

"I have not yet made any engagement with her."

"Well then, Prince; now I may venture to be candid. Now I may venture to tell you the truth which however you perhaps know already. At least I conclude so from your sudden change of mind. It was only your infatuation for Rollina that deterred me from telling you sooner. You are deceived."

"By whom?"

"By the artful opera-singer. She is flirting with a Jew at the same time that she coquettes with you."

"With a Jew?"

"Yes indeed; with the son of the wealthy Abraham Levi."

"Is that rogue everywhere?"

"You do not then know it? I tell you the perfect truth. If your Royal Highness had not come between them, the Jew would have openly acknowledged the engagement with the mercenary beauty. I am vexed about the watch."

"I am not."

"The little flirt deserves the rod."

"There are many people in the world who do not get their deserts."

"Only too true, your Royal Highness. For instance, I saw a little girl the other day; ah Prince! the whole town, the whole kingdom cannot show a prettier or one more fascinating. Yet very few know of the existence of this lovely being. Rollina is not to be compared to her. An old witch! But this girl is slender and graceful as a reed: with a colour, a complexion, like sunset glow on a snow-drift: a pair of eyes like stars, a profusion of thick, golden hair: in short, in all my life I never beheld any one more beautiful. But who is worthy of such a Venus? She is a goddess in the garb of a common citizen's daughter. You must try to see her."

"Is she then a citizen's daughter?"

"Certainly, only a poor girl: but indeed you must

see her. Of what good are my praises and descriptions! Whatever you have pictured in dreams of most beautiful and fascinating is here embodied in Nature; and with it all, the most winning, gentle, unsullied innocence! She is but seldom to be seen. She seldom leaves her mother. But I know her seat in church, and the Sunday walk that she generally takes with her mother by the Ulmen-gate. Also I have already discovered that a gardener, a handsome young fellow, is paying his addresses to her. But he cannot marry because he is poor, and she has nothing either. The mother is the widow of a linen-weaver who died of consumption."

"What is the mother's name?"

"Widow Bittner of Milk-street; and her daughter, lovely as a rose, is named, what she truly is, Rose."

Honest Philip became hot and cold by turns at this name. He had the greatest longing to give the speaker a cuff over the head with his fist. "Are you an evil spirit?" he cried.

"Truly!" said the Dutchman. "I have played the spy well. But you must see the pretty creature. Or, what, my Prince, if your quick eye should already have discovered the costly pearl. Do you know her?"

"I know her very well."

"So much the better. Have I praised her too highly? Do not you agree? We must not lose sight of her. We can go together to the mother. You can play the part of philanthropist. The widow's poverty has come to your ears. You cannot bear to see the sufferings of want. Sympathizingly you make inquiries as to the circumstances of the good woman, leave a present with her, repeat the visit, continue your charity, and become acquainted with little Rose. The rest is plain. The gardener lubber is quickly settled with; it would contribute thereto perhaps to give him a dozen good thalers in his hand."

Philip hardly knew how to speak for rage. "May thunderbolts crush —" he cried.

"If that clown the gardener should make any difficulties;" interrupted the Dutchman. "Oh leave me to take care of that. I will make a conscript of the gardener and send him to the army. There he can strike for his fatherland. In the meantime you will be left master of the field: for I think the girl will cling to him with something of the obstinacy of her class. It will not altogether be easy to drive out of her head the prejudices which are current among the citizens. But I will take her in hand."

"I will break your neck if you do."

"You are too good. Only your good offices with the King, and —"

"My Lord, I wish I could put you in the place —"

"O do not flatter me, gracious Prince. You know every moment of my life is devoted to your service. Had I imagined that you were already acquainted with this lovely being, that you were not indifferent —"

"Not a word more on the subject," replied Philip angrily; as angrily as in the lowered tone needful in order not to betray himself in this place, and in the neighbourhood of the dancing, moving, listening, and humorous masks, he could venture to exclaim; "Not a word more!"

"No, deeds!" replied the Dutchman cheerily. "The trenches for the siege shall be opened to-morrow.

Then you may advance. You are accustomed to win.
We are ready with the outposts, I will take the gardener in hand: the mother will yield to your golden
standard. Then, quick march!"

Philip could scarcely contain himself any longer.
He seized the arm of the Dutchman, and said, "Sir, if
you dare —"

"For Heaven's sake, my Lord, control your joy.
I shall be obliged to cry out. You are squeezing my
arm to pieces."

"If you dare," continued Philip, "to lay snares
for this innocent girl, I will, as true as I live, squeeze
every bone in your body in pieces."

"Well! well!" sighed the Dutchman in great pain;
"only be pleased to leave me alone now."

"If I ever find you looking about for her, or even
in the neighbourhood of Milk-street, you shall die by
my hand. Now act accordingly."

The Dutchman stood stupified. "Your Royal Highness," said he trembling, "I could not be aware that
you were so seriously attached to this lovely maiden,
as you appear to be."

"So seriously that I will confess it before the world."

"And are loved in return?"

"What concern is that of yours? Never speak of
her to me again. Never think of her again. Your
very thoughts insult her. Now you know my mind.
Leave me!"

With these words Philip turned his back upon the
Dutchman who went away rubbing his ear.

VIII.

IN the meanwhile Philip's substitute was also playing his part as watchman in the streets. It is indeed hardly necessary to say, what all must have found out, for themselves, that he was none other than Prince Julian, who, elated by wine, had taken the fancy of making himself watchman for the nonce. As soon as he left Philip, he began to call the hour and to sing with hearty good will from corner to corner of the streets: he made all sorts of comic additions to his songs, and troubled himself very little about the prescribed district within which it was his duty to sing and call the hour.

Whilst he was bethinking himself of a new verse, the door of a house beside him opened; and a nicely-dressed little girl stepped out, and looked up and down with a timid "Pst! Pst!" She then drew back within the shadow of the passage. The Prince resigned the verse to its fate, and followed the lovely apparition. In the darkness a gentle hand seized his, and a soft voice whispered, "Good evening, dear Philip! Speak low, that no one may hear us. I have only slipped away for a moment from the company just to speak to you as you passed. Are you pleased?"

"Pleased as if I were in Paradise, my angel;" said Julian. "Who could be gloomy near you?"

"Philip, I have some good news to tell you. You are to sup with us to-morrow evening. Mother has given leave. Will you come?"

"Every evening, any evening," cried Julian; "and for as long as you please. I wish you could be always with me, or I with you, till the end of the world. That would be a life worth something."

"Listen, Philip; in half an hour I shall be at St. Gregory's Church. I shall expect you there. Do not fail me. Do not let me have long to wait. Then we can take a walk through the town. Now go, that no one may catch us."

She was going, but Julian drew her back.

"Would you part so coldly from me?" he asked, and pressed his lips to hers.

Rose did not know what to say to Philip's audacity. For Philip had always been so modest and retiring, that at most he had only ventured to kiss her hand, and that once when her mother had forbidden all and every intercourse between them. Thus in her mind feelings of deepest tenderness and deepest pain had grown from that first kiss, which had never been repeated. Little Rose resisted; but the supposed Philip was so obstinate that, to avoid making a noise which must betray them, she was obliged to yield. She returned the kiss, and said: "Now, Philip, go!"

But he did not go, only said: "Then I should be a fool indeed. Do you suppose I love my watchman's hour better than I love you? By no means, sweetheart."

"Ah!" sighed Rose; "but this is not right."

"Why not, little goose? Is a kiss forbidden in the ten commandments?"

"Well," said Rose, "if we always lived together it would be a different thing."

"Live together! If that is all, you may be with me any day you like."

"Oh, Philip! how strangely you talk to-day! We dare not even think of that yet."

"But indeed I think very seriously about it, if only it is your wish."

"Philip, have you been drinking? If I wish it! Go away, you insult me. — But listen, Philip; I dreamed of you last night."

"What did you dream, my beauty?"

"That you had won in the lottery, Philip. We were both delighted. You had bought a lovely garden for yourself: there was not a prettier either within the town or near it. We had everything in profusion; flowers upon flowers, like a paradise, and beautiful beds full of the finest vegetables; and the trees were covered with fruit. I felt very sorrowful when I awoke, and found it only a tantalizing dream. Tell me, Philip, did you put into the lottery? To-day was the drawing."

"When I have won such a grand prize as you, sweet little one, who knows what may not happen? How much must I have won now to please you?"

"If you were but so fortunate as to have won a thousand gulden, then you might buy a beautiful garden."

"A thousand gulden! Suppose it were more."

"Oh, Philip! What do you mean? Can it be true? Nay, do not deceive me as my dream did. You did put in; you have won. Confess!"

"As much as you could wish."

"Joy! joy!" cried little Rose; and in a paroxysm of delight, she threw her arms round his neck and kissed him affectionately. "More than a thousand gulden! and will the people really give you so much money?"

Her embrace made the prince forget to reply. It seemed to him quite wonderful to be clasping to his heart this tender, noble-hearted girl, whose caresses were not intended for him, though he would willingly have received them on his own account.

"Answer, answer," cried Rose impatiently. "Will they really give you all this quantity of money?"

"I have it already; and if it will increase your pleasure, will give it to you now."

"What, Philip! Have you brought it with you?"

The Prince drew out his purse, heavy with gold, which he had put into his pocket, intending to turn into a gaming-house.

"Take it and weigh it, little one;" said he. And, kissing the soft little lips, he put it into Rose's hand. "Will you be kind to me for this?"

"No, Philip; certainly not for your money, if you were not my own Philip."

"But how would it be if I gave you twice as much, and yet were not your Philip?"

"I would throw all your treasures at your feet, and make you a distant curtsy," said Rose.

At this moment a door opened: the voices and laughter of young girls were heard; the gleam of a light fell on the steps from above. Rose became frightened, and whispered, "In half an hour, at St. Gregory's Church;" and then she sprang away up the steps. The prince stood alone again in the dark. He walked about outside the house, watching the building and the well-lighted windows. The sudden separation he naturally felt to be very inopportune. It is certain that he did not trouble himself much about the purse of gold with which the maiden had flown off; but he did feel vexed that he had not seen the features of the unknown beauty in the light, that he had not found out her name, and that he had even less notion whether she would in good earnest fulfil her threat of throwing his money at his feet if he should appear before her in his true character. However he consoled himself with the prospect of the meeting at St. Gregory's Church. This was also the place that the watchman had named to him. Julian readily perceived that to the latter, though unintentionally, he owed his adventure.

IX.

WHETHER owing to the excitement of the wine being increased by the cold of New Year's Eve, or to Rose's mistake, so it was that the waggery of the royal watchman became even greater than before. He remained standing at the corner of a street in the midst of a crowd of passengers, and blew his horn so energetically that all the ladies started back screaming: and the men stood still with astonishment. Julian then called the hour, and sang;

> "Traffic in our much-loved town,
> Is rudely smitten dead;
> For e'en our maidens, fair or brown,
> No man now seeks to wed:
> Deck the sweet goods fine as you may,
> No lover sues for bridal day."

"This is too insolent!" cried several women's voices from the crowd. "Compare us to goods!" But several of the men laughed heartily. "Encore," cried some jovial young fellows. "Bravo, watchman!" shouted others. "How dare you insult our ladies in the open streets, you snob?" growled a young lieutenant who had a pretty girl leaning on his arm.

"Sir Lieutenant, what the watchman sings is unfortunately true," replied a miller. "That very young lady on your arm is a proof of its truth. Ah! young lady, do you recognize me? do you know who I am? Eh? Is it becoming in a betrothed bride to be walking about at night with young men? I will tell your mother of you to-morrow. I will have no more to say to you."

The girl hid her face, and pulled the officer's arm to make him come away.

But the lieutenant, who was a great fire-eater, would not so easily fly from the miller: but honourably maintained his ground. He poured forth a volley of oaths; and when this had no effect, he brandished his cane. Suddenly two stout Spanish cudgels, wielded by some of the citizens, were raised menacingly over him. "Sir," cried a broad-shouldered brewer to the man of war, "begin no brawls here on account of a faithless girl. I know the miller: he is a good fellow: and, upon my life, the watchman is right. An honest tradesman or citizen can, and will, hardly marry a single girl in our town. The women all seek to raise themselves above their station: instead of knitting stockings they read novels: instead of looking after their kitchen and store-room they run to plays and concerts. In their own homes, all is slovenly; whilst in the streets they go about decked out like princesses. They bring to a man no dowry but a couple of handsome gowns, some laces, ribbons, flirtations, romances, and untidiness. Sir, I speak from experience. If our citizens' daughters were not so spoilt, I would myself have married long ago."

· The bystanders raised a shrill laugh. The lieutenant extended his cane slowly in the direction of the Spanish cudgels, and said peevishly: "One does not come here to listen to a pack of townspeople preaching."

"How now! a pack of townspeople!" cried a nailsmith, who was the owner of one of the cudgels. "You idle gentlemen who fatten upon our contributions and taxation — will you call us a pack of townspeople? Your disorderly ways are to blame for all the misery in our homes. There would not be half so many respectable girls unmarried if you had learned to work and to say your prayers."

Several more officers now sprang to the front; but tradespeople, both masters and men, collected also. Boys, intent on their share of the fun made snowballs, and sent them flying into the midst of the crowd. The first snowball hit the lieutenant on the nose. This he supposed to be an assault from the town-pack, and again raised his stick. The fight began. The prince had only heard the beginning of the altercation, having long since gone away into another street, merry and laughing, and quite unconcerned as to the consequences of his ditty. He reached the mansion of the Minister of Finance, Bodenlos. With this gentleman he was not on the best of terms, as Philip had already discovered.

Julian saw that all the windows were lighted up: the Minister's wife had a large party. Julian in his poetic-satiric mood, planted himself directly opposite the house, and blew his horn lustily. Several gentlemen and ladies opened the window, perhaps because they had nothing better to do, curious to hear the watchman.

"Watchman!" one of the gentlemen called to him; "Sing us a pretty New Year's song." This request attracted still more of the company to the window.

Julian, after calling the hour according to custom sang very distinctly and loudly:

> "All ye who sigh with weight of debt,
> Bankrupts for lack of ready wit;
> Pray Heaven to make you for the nonce
> Right Hon'rable Minister of Finance,
> With private hoards to fill a church
> But leave the country in the lurch."

"That is outrageous!" said the Minister's wife, who had just come to one of the windows; "who is the mean creature that has the impudence to sing this?"

"Your Ladyship," replied Julian in a disguised voice, and assuming the Jewish accent, "I wished to give you some little pleasure. I am the Court Jew, Abraham Levi, at your commands. Your Ladyship knows me very well."

"Heyday!" cried a voice from the window above, "Vile rascal! how can you be Abraham Levi? am not I Abraham Levi myself? You are an impostor."

"Call the watch," exclaimed the wife of the Minister. "Have the man arrested."

At these words the guests all left the window as quickly as they could, neither did the prince linger: but in double quick time took a road that led down some small cross streets. A swarm of servants, accompanied by some of the Secretaries of the Finance Department, poured forth from the mansion, and hunted all about to find the libeller. Suddenly several shouted,

"We have him." The others hastened at the cry.
They had, in good truth, found the watchman of the
district, who was making his rounds in perfect innocence. He was surrounded, overpowered, and much
as he struggled, was dragged off to the main-guard,
on account of his sarcastic imagination. The officer
on duty shook his head with astonishment, and said:
"One watchman has already been brought here who
has, by some verses that he made upon the girls of
the town, occasioned a fatal brawl between some of the
officers and citizens."

The newly-brought prisoner would confess nothing,
and complained bitterly that a party of young people,
who had apparently been drinking too freely, should
interrupt him in the discharge of the duty entrusted
to him. One of the secretaries repeated the verse
which had excited the natural indignation of the
Minister's wife and of her guests. The soldiers shook
with laughter, but the honest watchman swore, with
tears in his eyes, that he had never even thought of
such words. While they were still occupied with the
investigation, the watchman maintaining his innocence,
and throwing on the young gentlemen the responsi-
bility of all the consequences that might result from
their conduct, so that the secretaries began really to
doubt whether they had seized upon the right man,
the sentry outside called, "To your arms!"

The soldiers sprang up; the secretaries continued
to ply the watchman with questions. In the meantime,
the Field-Marshal entered the guard-room, accompanied by the captain on duty.

"Confine this fellow," cried the Field-Marshal, and
pointed with his finger to some one behind. Two

officers entered, bringing with them a disarmed watch-man.

"Are the watchmen all gone mad?" exclaimed the captain on duty, quite amazed.

"To-morrow I will pay the fellow off for his in-famous verses," cried the Field-Marshal.

"Your Excellency," replied the ·newly-brought watchman in a trembling and imploring voice, "Heaven knows I have made no verses; never made one in my life."

"Silence, ruffian!" roared the Field-Marshal in a portentous tone. "You shall be sent to the fort, or to the gallows; and if you mutter a mutinous word, I will strike you down like a cabbage-stalk."

The captain on duty observed respectfully to the Field-Marshal, that a poetic epidemic appeared to have broken out among the watchmen of the city, for that he had already received three of · these protectors of the public to be taken into his charge within a quarter of an hour.

"Gentlemen," said the Field-Marshal to the officers who accompanied him, "as the fellow will not confess by any means that he has sung these verses, recal to your minds the lampoon before you forget it. Write it down. To-morrow we will make him acknowledge it. I will not waste time now from the ball. Who can remember it?"

The officers thought for a while: one helped the other. The officer on duty wrote, and the following was the result:

"By busby covering addled brains,
By pigtail greased with care and pains,
By pinched-in waist and padded breast,
Of military air possest;

By dancing, and fiddling, and acting, you see,
And kissing, you may a Field-Marshal be."

"Will you still deny it, rascal?" shouted the Field-Marshal with renewed vehemence at the terrified watchman; "will you still deny that you sang this as I came out at the door of my house?"

"Let whoever may have sung it, I know nothing of it," said the watchman.

"Why then did you run away when you saw me come out?" asked the Field-Marshal.

"I did not run away."

"What!" cried both the officers. "You did not run away? Were you not quite out of breath when at last we stopped you at the market?"

"Yes. I was frightened out of my senses at being seized upon so violently by gentlemen. My limbs are shaking still."

"Lock up the obstinate mule," cried the Field-Marshal to the officer on duty. "He will have time enough to recollect himself before morning."

With these words the Field-Marshal hastened away.

The noise in the streets, and the satires of the watchmen, had set all the police in motion. Within that quarter of an hour three other watchmen, and certainly none of them the right one, were seized and brought to the main-guard. One had sung a libellous song at the Minister of Foreign Affairs, to the effect that he was nowhere more abroad than in his own office. Another was accused of having sung before the Bishop's palace that there was no lack of lights in the Church, but that they shed more smoke and confusion through the land than brightness.

The Prince, who was playing so mischievous a game among the watchmen of the city by his whimsicalities, escaped unharmed, and grew bolder as he went from street to street. The affair made a great commotion. It was even reported to the Minister of Police, who was sitting at the card-table with the King, that there was a poetical insurrection among the formerly peaceful watchmen, and one of the lampoons was brought in writing as a specimen. The King listened to the verses which happened to be levelled at the police themselves, accusing them of poking their noses into every family-secret in the city, yet of finding out nothing in any single house unless rewarded for doing so. The King laughed heartily, and ordered that one of the watchman-poets should be caught and brought to him. He got up from the card-table: for he saw that the Minister of Police had lost his temper.

X.

WHILST in the dancing-saloon near the supper-room, the watchman-prince perceived by his watch that the time had come for him to make his appearance at St. Gregory's Church. He was delighted to give back the scarlet robe and plumed hat to his substitute, for the princely disguise was not at all to his taste. As he was seeking the door in order to slip away, a negro stepped up to him, and whispered, "Your Royal Highness, Duke Herman is seeking everywhere for you." Philip shook his head angrily and went out, followed by the negro. As they entered the ante-room, the negro whispered, "Here comes the Duke;" and with these words he hurried back into the saloon. A tall mask strode with quick strides towards Philip, and cried: "Wait a moment. I have a word to say with you. I have been seeking you this long time."

"Only be quick," replied Philip. "I have no time to lose."

"I wish I had lost none in finding you. I have sought you long enough. You owe me satisfaction. You have given me mortal offence."

"I was not aware of it."

"You do not know me?" cried the Duke, pulling off his mask. "Now you see who I am, and your guilty conscience will tell you the rest. I demand satisfaction. You and the vile Salmoni have deceived me."

"I know nothing of it," said Philip.

"You planned the scandalous scene in the baker's cellar. It was at your instigation that Colonel Kalt seized upon me."

"That is not true."

"What! not true? Do you deny it? The wife of Marshal Blankenschwerd disclosed all to me only a few minutes ago. She was witness of the ghost-farce that you played on me."

"She has imposed upon your Grace with a made-up story. I had no hand in that treatment of you. If you allowed ghost-farces to be played on you, that was your own fault."

"I ask you, whether you will give me satisfaction' If not, I will make a stir about it. Follow me at once to the King. Either fight, or come to the King."

"Your Grace," stammered Philip in embarrassment.

"I have no intention of either fighting with you, or going to the King."

This was Philip's full determination, for he was afraid of being obliged to pull off his mask, and of falling into serious disgrace on account of the part which, contrary to his wishes, he had had to play. He therefore made all sorts of evasions to the Duke: and continually glanced towards the door, that he might seize some opportunity of springing out at it. The Duke, on his side, noticed the anxiety of the supposed Prince, and was rather pleased at it. At last he took the unfortunate Philip by the arm, wishing to conduct him back to the saloon. "What do you want with me?" Philip exclaimed in despair, and shook himself free of the Duke.

"To go to the King," replied the Duke in a rage. "He shall learn the insulting treatment that a princely guest receives at his court."

"Very good," answered Philip, who could think of no better way to save himself than by maintaining the character of Prince; "Come then. I am ready. Fortunately I have with me the note in which with your own hand you gave the baker's girl the assurance —"

"Nonsense! a trick!" replied the Duke. "That was merely one of the jests that one carries on with a silly citizen's daughter. Show it to the King. I will, on that very account, present myself before him."

At the same time, the Duke did not appear to be very much in earnest in this proposal. Matters went no further as regarded going with Philip to the King, and this was so far agreeable for Philip: but all the more vehemently did the Duke persist that they should both get into a carriage and drive, no one knew where, to settle the affair of honour with pistols or sabres. This was not at all convenient to the annoyed Philip.   He represented to the Duke the evil consequences of such a step; but the latter, in his fury, would not allow himself to be turned from his purpose: and assured Philip that he had already taken all precautions against every contingency, and would depart that very night on the termination of the affair.

"If," continued the Duke, "you are not the most cowardly man in your dominions, Prince, you will follow me to the carriage."

"I am no Prince," answered Philip, who saw himself pushed to extremities.

"You are.   Every one at the ball has recognized you. I know you by your hat. You cannot deceive me."

Philip took off his mask, turned his face towards the Duke, and said, "Now! am I the Prince?"

When Duke Herman saw the strange countenance, he started back, and then stood motionless as if petrified.   To have betrayed his most private affairs to an unknown person increased his dismay and confusion. Ere he could collect his thoughts, Philip had laid his hand already on the door, and had gone out.

XI.

IMMEDIATELY that Philip found himself free, he took off the plumed hat and silk mantle as quick as lightning, rolled up the former in the latter; and, with both on his arm, bounded along the streets to St. Gregory's Church.   There stood little Rose all ready and waiting for him in a corner near the great door.

"Oh Philip! dear Philip!" she said, as soon as she recognized him, and had pressed his hand. "What joy you have given me! Oh, how lucky we are! I had no peace any longer at my friend's house. Thank Heaven, you are come. I have been standing here shivering for nearly a quarter of an hour. But I can hardly think of the cold for joy."

"And I, dear Rose, thank Heaven, too, that I am once more here with you. To the winds with the tittle-tattle of the great! Well, I will tell you another time of the foolish scenes I have been witnessing. Tell me, sweetheart, how do things fare with you? Do you still love me a little?"

"Ah! you have become a grand gentleman, Philip, and it is rather for me to ask whether you still love me a little."

"Holloa! How did you know already that I was a grand gentleman?"

"Because you told me so yourself. Philip, Philip, suppose you should grow proud now that you are so immensely rich. I am but a poor girl, and now certainly not good enough for you. But, Philip, I have already been thinking that if it were possible you could forsake me now, I would much rather you had continued to be a poor gardener. I should break my heart if you were to desert me."

"Tell me, little Rose, what are you talking about? I have been a prince for half an hour, but it was only a joke; yet for the rest of my life, I never again will join in such a joke. Now I am once more a watchman again, and as poor as ever. True, I have about me five thousand gulden that I received from a Mameluke; but, though that would raise us from poverty, unfortunately it does not belong to me."

"You talk strangely, Philip," said little Rose, and she handed to him the heavy purse she had received from the prince. "Here! take the money again. It is almost too heavy for me in this knitted bag."

"What am I to do with all this money? Where did you get it, Rose?"

"It is what you won in the lottery, Philip."

"What! have I won? They told me at the town-hall that my numbers were not drawn. You see, I have hoped and fancied that they might win a dower for us. But Gardener Rothman said to me when I arrived at the town-hall this afternoon too late for the drawing. 'Poor Philip, no ticket!' Hurrah! I have won! Now I will buy a large garden, and you shall be my wife. How much is it?"

"Philip, have you taken a glass too much this New Year's Eve? You must know better than I do how much there is. I only at my friend's house peeped secretly under the table into the purse, and was quite startled when I saw one piece of gold shining through after another. I thought then, 'I do not wonder now that Philip was so uncontrollable.' Ah! you were very rude. But, indeed, you were not to blame. I could myself have fallen in your arms and have cried for joy."

"If you like to do so, Rose, I shall be very well pleased. But there is some misunderstanding. Who brought the gold to you? and who told you that it was my lottery prize? I have my ticket still in the chest at home, and no one has asked me for it."

"Philip, do not jest with me. You told me of it

17*

yourself only half an hour ago, and yourself gave me the money."

"Think what you say, Rose. This morning I saw you on your way from mass when we settled together about our meeting for this evening. But since then we have not met until now."

"Except half an hour ago, when I heard you blow the horn, and called you for a moment into the Steinman's house. But what are you carrying in that little bundle under your arm? Why do you come out on this cold night without a hat? Philip, Philip, take care of yourself. This money is turning your head. You have surely been sitting in some public-house, and have taken more than is good for you. Is it not so! What is in that little bundle? Oh! it is indeed a bundle of beautiful silken clothes, like ladies' dresses. Philip, Philip, where have you been?"

"Certainly not any where near you during the last half hour. I think you are trying to make yourself merry at my expense. Answer me, where did you get that money?"

"Answer me first, Philip: where did you get those ladies' clothes?"

As each grew impatient for a reply and yet neither did reply, they began at last to grow distrustful of each other, and to quarrel.

XII.

What generally happens in cases of a dispute between a pair of lovers happened now. As soon as little Rose took out her white pocket-handkerchief, rubbed her eyes, turned away her head, and that one sigh after another burst from the very depths of her breast, it became quite evident that she was in the right, and equally plain that he was in the wrong. And whilst he consoled her, he owned his injustice, and confessed that he had been at a masked ball, and that what he carried under his arm was not ladies' clothes; but a silk cloak, a mask, and plumed hat.

Yet after this penitent confession he was subjected to a strict examination. A masked ball is, as every girl in a large city knows, a dangerous maze and combat ground for an unwary heart. One plunges there into a very ocean of pleasing perils, and generally sinks unless one is a good swimmer. And Rose did not hold her friend Philip to be the best of swimmers: it is hard to say why. Therefore first he must tell whether he had danced; on his denial, she inquired whether any of his adventures had been with female masks. This could not be denied. He confessed all, but added every time, that the ladies were of good family, and had mistaken him for another person. It is certain that Rose felt a little dubious: however she suppressed her misgivings. But when, to her question for whom had they taken him? and from whom had he borrowed his mask? he named Prince Julian, she shook her incredulous head: whilst Philip's story that the Prince had undertaken the watchman's duty during his absence at the ball seemed to her still more improbable.

But Philip allayed all her doubts by the assurance that the Prince (for such he deemed his substitute) would, according to appointment, appear at St. Gregory's Church in a few minutes, and exchange the watchman's cloak for the beautiful mask.

A new light now shone upon the frightened Rose with regard to her adventures in the dark passage. Now it occurred to her that there had been something incongruous in the appearance of the supposed Philip. When it came to her turn to confess everything minutely, and how she came by the money for the lottery ticket, she stammered and hesitated for words until Philip grew uneasy.

At last she related everything: yet when it came to the kiss and the return kiss, she again stammered.

"It is not true!" cried Philip. "I never gave you a kiss, nor received one from you."

"It passed for yours," said Rose softly and coaxingly.

Philip twisted his hair into a mass of tangles: he almost fancied it would stand on end.

"Listen, Philip;" said Rose, vexed: "if it were not you, then, as I believe all the improbabilities that you have told me, it was Prince Julian dressed in your clothes."

Philip had already long been suspecting this; and he cried out, "The knave! I understand now, it was for this he gave me his mask; it was for this he wished to be me for half an hour."

He renewed his questions more minutely: and asked whether a gentleman or any one had come to her mother, and had offered her money to break off their engagement. Rose's reply was altogether so reassuring, and bore so fully the impress of perfect truth that Philip's heart grew light again. He warned Rose against all flatteries; and felt himself entitled to claim the caress which had been designed for him, but which he had not received.

At this moment the pair were disturbed by a strange apparition. A man came running towards them at full speed until he stood breathless beside them. By the cloak, staff, hat, and horn, Philip recognized his man immediately. The latter on his part looked for the mask. Philip handed the hat, and silk cloak to him, and said, "Most noble Sir, here is your dress. We will not exchange characters any more as long as we live. I had the worst of it."

The Prince cried, "Quick! quick!" He threw off the watchman's costume on the snow, put on the mask and cloak, and placed the hat on his head. Rose sprang back in alarm. Philip dressed himself in his old felt hat and cloak, and took the staff and horn.

"I promised you a present, comrade," said the Prince: "but, as true as I stand here, I have not my purse with me."

"I have it," replied Philip, holding the purse to him. "You gave it to my betrothed: but, my Lord, we decline any present of the kind."

"Keep what you have, comrade, and go off quickly. You are not safe here!" cried the Prince hurriedly: and he was going away also.

Philip caught his cloak, and said, "Gracious Prince, there is yet something to settle between us."

"Fly, Watchman, I tell you; fly. They are after you."

"I have no occasion to fly, my Lord. And I have here your purse —"

"Keep it! keep it! run off whilst you may."

"And note of hand for five thousand gulden to give you from the Marshal Blankenschwerd."

"How on earth came you and Marshal Blanken-schwerd to meet, Watchman?"

"He said it was a gaming debt that he owed to you. He and his wife are leaving to-night for their estates in Poland."

"Are you mad? How did you hear this? When did he tell you of my affairs with him?"

"Good my Lord, the Minister of Finance Bodenlos, will also settle all your debts with Abraham Levi, if you will intercede for him with the King that he shall remain in the cabinet."

"Watchman, you are possessed with a demon of second sight."

"I refused him in your Royal Highness' name."

"The Minister!"

"Yes, my Lord; on the other hand I have effected a complete reconciliation between the Countess Bonau and Chamberlain Pilzow."

"Which of us two is the fool?"

"Yet once again. The singer, Rollina, is worthless, my Lord. I know the history of her flirtations. You are deceived. Therefore I deemed it derog tory to your Royal Highness to visit at her house, and have refused the invitation to supper for this evening, in your name."

"Rollina! How did you meet her?"

"Again. Duke Herman is fearfully incensed against you on account of the story of the cellar. He intended to complain of you to the king."

"The Duke! who told you all this?"

"He himself. You are not yet safe. However he will not go to the king, for I threatened him with the note he gave to the baker's girl. Therefore now he is determined to fight with you in mortal combat. Have a care of him."

"Tell me one thing. Are you aware whether the Duke knows that I —"

"He knows all, from the wife of Marshal Blanken-schwerd; she has blabbed all to him, and how she was the witch in the farce."

The Prince took Philip by the arm and said, "Jester, you are not a watchman really." He turned Philip towards the light of one of the lamps that gleamed from the distance, and was alarmed when he saw before him an entirely strange face.

"Are you possessed? or — who are you?" asked Julian, now completely sobered by alarm.

"I am Philip Stark, the gardener: son of the watchman, Gottlieb Stark," replied Philip quietly.

XIII.

"Ha! indeed!" here are those we seek. "Stop, fellow!" cried several voices: and Philip, Rose, and the Prince, found themselves suddenly surrounded by six stout servants of the worthy police. Rose uttered a scream; Philip took the hand of the affrighted girl, and said, "Do not be afraid." The Prince tapped Philip on the shoulder and said, "This is a sorry joke. It was not for nothing that I bade you take advantage of the opportunity. But do not be alarmed. Nothing shall happen to you."

"That remains to be proved hereafter," answered one of the men. "In the meantime he will come with us."

"Whither?" asked Philip. "I am at my duty. I am the watchman."

"So we have already heard; it is for that very reason you are to come with us."

"Let him go, good people," said Julian: and he searched his pocket for money. As he found none, he whispered to Philip to give them some from the purse. But the policemen pushed them asunder, and exclaimed, "Forward! No more making agreements here. The mask is suspected also, and must come with us."

"Not he!" said Philip. "You want the watchman. I am he. If you can justify yourselves for removing me from my duty, then take me where you will. But let this gentleman go."

"It is not your business to teach us who we are to look on as suspected people," replied one of the policemen. "March all of you with us!"

"The lady also?" inquired Philip. "I hope not."

"No, the young lady may go. We have no orders about her. But we must know her appearance and name in case of need, and also her place of residence."

"She is the daughter of Widow Bittner, of Milk-street," said Philip: and he was not a little annoyed when the churls turned the weeping Rose to face the light of the street-lamps and stared at her.

"Go home, Rose;" added Philip. "Go home, do not be frightened about me. I have a clear conscience."

But Rose sobbed so loudly as to excite the compassion of the policemen. The Prince would fain have availed himself of this opportunity to escape by a bound. But among the police was one even more active than he, who with one spring stood in the road before him, and said; "Holloa! this one has a guilty conscience, he must come with us. Forward! March!"

"Where to?" inquired the Prince.

"Direct and straight to his Excellency the Minister of Police."

"Listen, good people," said the Prince very gravely, yet affably, for this episode was not much to his taste, as he did not wish to disclose his play at watchman. "Listen, good fellows, I only came up accidentally to this watchman a moment ago: you have no business with me. I belong to the Court. If you persist in compelling me to go with you, you will repent of your mistake, and will find yourselves in prison to-morrow on bread and water."

"For goodness' sake, let the gentleman go, good Sirs," cried Philip. "I assure you, on my honor, he is a great gentleman who has power to make you rue your doings. He is" —

"Silence!" cried Julian. "No one must ever learn from you who I am, if by chance you have really discovered it. Do you understand, *no one!* No one, I say, let come what will. Do you understand?"

"We are doing our duty," replied a policeman, "and therefore no one can send us to prison. That may chance to befall the gentleman in the mask himself in the end. We have often heard threats like these before, and are not afraid of them. Forward! March!"

"Listen to reason, good gentlemen," cried Philip. "He is a gentleman of high rank at Court."

"And if he were the king himself he must still come with us. It is our duty. He is suspected," returned one of them for answer.

"Oh yes!" exclaimed another. "A likely story that a great Court-gentleman should have secret business with a watchman, and the like of you, whispering in your ear as he did just now."

Whilst this dispute about the Prince was going on, a carriage with eight horses, and burning torches preceding it, drove past to the church.

"Stop!" cried a voice from within the carriage when it reached the group of policemen who surrounded the Prince.

The carriage stopped. The door opened, a gentleman in a frock-coat with a star gleaming on its breast, sprang out and went up to the party. He pushed aside the policemen, stared at the Prince from head to foot, and said; "Folly! did I not then discover the bird in the distance by his feathers. Who are you, Mask?"

Julian did not know whither to turn in his embarrassment, for he recognized Duke Herman.

"Answer me!" cried the Duke in a voice of thunder. Julian shook his head, and signed to the Duke to go away. But the latter only became still more bent upon finding out with whom he had been talking at the ball. He asked the policemen. They stood with uncovered heads round the Duke and said, "they had orders to take the watchman immediately to the Minister of Police: the watchman had sung scurrilous verses as they had heard with their own ears; but he had fled from them down cross streets and alleys; till here at the church they had apprehended him whilst in confidential conversation with the Mask, who appeared to them to be almost as worthy of suspicion as the watchman. The Mask had wished to pass himself off as a grand gentleman from the court, but that was plainly humbug. They had therefore deemed it their duty to arrest the Mask."

"The man does not belong to the Court," replied the Duke, "that you may be assured. I give you my word for it. He glided into the Ball in an unlawful manner, and made every one believe he was Prince Julian. At last he was forced to unmask himself to me, for he deceived me also, and then escaped from me. He is an unknown man, an adventurer. I have warned the Lord Steward of it. Good people, bring him to the royal palace, you have made a great capture."

With these words the Duke turned away, got into the carriage, called out once more, "Do not let him escape," and drove off.

The Prince saw that he was lost. He thought it unseemly to show his features to the policemen; his pranks had become well known by all of them throughout the town. He should run less risk if he unmasked himself before the Steward of the Household, or the Minister of Police. So he said resolutely, "On my own account, now! Come on!"

He and Philip went away. Rose looked after them, weeping.

XIV.

PHILIP could almost have believed in witchcraft, or that he was dreaming. For on this night everything happened in a more strange and confused manner than he had ever met with in all his life. He had nothing to reproach himself with, except that he had changed clothes with the Prince; and then, against his will, had had to play the character of the Prince at the ball. But probably the Prince might not have acted the part of watchman according to rule — but why must he be imprisoned as the watchman? — he hoped in this to obtain pardon.

The palace reached, poor Philip's heart beat faster. His horn, cloak, and staff were taken from him. The Prince said a few words to a gentleman of rank.

The policemen were immediately sent away: the Prince went up the steps, and Philip was obliged to follow. "Do not be afraid!" said Julian, and he quitted him. Philip was conducted to a small ante-room, where he remained alone for a considerable time. At last one of the royal retainers entered, and said, "Follow me; the King would see you."

Philip was almost beside himself with alarm. His knees felt weak. He was conducted into a beautiful apartment. The old King sat laughing at a little table. Near him stood Prince Julian without his mask. No one else was in the room. The King looked attentively at the young man for some time, and apparently with some approbation.

"Relate accurately to me every thing that you have done during the evening," said the King to him.

The encouraging manner of the revered monarch restored Philip's self-possession, and he confessed minutely all that he had seen and done from beginning to end. But he was discreet and modest enough to keep silence regarding all he had heard from the courtiers in his disguise of prince by which Julian might have been placed in an embarrassing position.

The King laughed aloud several times during the narration; he then made a few inquiries respecting Philip's family and occupation, took a couple of pieces of gold from the table, gave them to him, and said; "Now go, my boy, and await your summons. No harm shall happen to you. But disclose to no one what you have heard and seen in the course of this evening. This I strictly enjoin you. Now you may go."

Philip threw himself at the King's feet, and kissed his hand, as he stammered forth his thanks. When he again rose to depart, Prince Julian said; "I humbly request that your Majesty will be pleased to allow this young man to wait outside. I still have something to settle with him on account of the annoyance to which I have this evening subjected him."

The King nodded and smiled. Philip withdrew.

"Prince!" said the King, and he raised his finger in a warning manner; "it is fortunate for you that you told me the truth. Yet this once more I will forgive your wild, foolish, pranks. They have deserved punishment. If you perpetrate such outrageous jokes again, I shall be inexorable. Nothing then shall be held to excuse you. I must learn more about this story of Duke Herman. Well and good, if he choose to go away. I do not like him. As regards that which is alleged against the Minister of Finance, I likewise expect proof. Go now, and give the young gardener your present. He behaved with more discretion beneath your mask than you beneath his."

The Prince quitted the King. In a neighbouring room he took off his ball-dress, put on a frock-coat,

ordered Philip to be summoned, and commanded him
to attend him to his palace. Here Philip was desired
to relate, word for word, all that he had heard and
said at the ball whilst Julian's substitute. Philip
obeyed. Julian tapped him on the shoulder, and said,
"Listen, Philip, you are a discreet fellow. I can
make you useful. I am pleased with you. All that
you have done in my name regarding the Chamberlain
Pilzow, the Countess Bonau, the Marshal and his
wife, Colonel Kalt, and the Minister of Finance, I consider very sensible; and I will respect and abide by it
as though I had said it all myself. In return you
must take the blame of the verses which I have sung
in your name as watchman. You will as a punishment be dismissed from your office of watchman: but
submit to that. I will then make you my gardener
at the castle. I will give you the charge of my
gardens at both castles, Heimleben and Quellenthal.
The money that I have given to your betrothed shall
stand as her dowry, and I will now cash the bill of
Marshal Blankenschwerd for you for the five thousand
gulden. Now go. Serve me faithfully and conduct
yourself well.

XV.

WHO happier now than Philip! He flew at full
speed to Rose's house. Rose was not yet gone to bed,
she was sitting at the table with her mother, and crying. He threw the well-filled purse on the table, and
said breathlessly; "Rose, this is your dower; and here
are five thousand gulden for mine. I have committed

an error as watchman, and therefore I lose the rever-
sion of my father's situation; and the day after to-
morrow I am to go to Heimleben as castle-gardener to
Prince Julian. And you, mother, and Rose must
come with me to Heimleben. My father and mother
must also come with me. I can now easily maintain
you all. Hurrah! Heaven send all the world as happy
a New Year!"

Dame Bittner did not know whether to trust her
ears as she listened to Philip's news, or her eyes at
the sight of so much money. But when Philip had
related everything, and how all had happened, yet
withal only just so much as it was necessary that she
should know, she rose sobbing, embraced him with
delight and placed her daughter in his arms. Then
the overjoyed woman ran and danced bout the room,
and asked, "Do your father and mother yet know all
about this?" and when Philip said No, she cried;
"Rose, make up the fire, put on water to boil, and
make some good coffee for us five!" took her woollen
cloak, wrapped herself up in it, and went to their
house.

But on Philip's breast Rose forgot fire and water
both. They still stood locked in a close embrace
when Dame Bittner returned, accompanied by old
Gottlieb and Dame Kate. They circled round their
children and blessed them. Dame Bittner, if she would
have coffee, must make it herself.

That Philip lost the office of watchman; that little
Rose became his wife in a fortnight after; that both,
with their parents, went to Heimleben; none of this
belongs to the New Year's Eve's adventure which did

so great injury to no one as to the Minister of Finance, Bodenlos.

Since this time nothing has been heard of Prince Julian having perpetrated any such absurd tricks.

————————

THE INN AT CRANSAC.

THE INN AT CRANSAC.

"WHAT place is that before us?" I inquired of the post-boy.

"Cransac, Captain."

"Cransac? Can one remain there comfortably for the night?"

"I believe you. It is the best of inns; none better to be found, far or near."

This was pleasant hearing, for I was very tired. It is no trifle, when only half recovered from an illness, to be obliged to start off and take a journey of several hundred miles. My regiment was quartered in Perpignan, and I was coming from Nantes. A good long distance! And from Perpignan a very agreeable pilgrimage at the head of my company awaited me through that odious Catalonia in which so many a brave Frenchman had already found a grave.

We drove into the little place which is situated very pleasantly at the foot of a copse-covered hill. We stopped in front of a pretty house. Thomas, my servant, sprang down, and let me out of the carriage. The landlord, a prepossessing man, conducted me into an apartment so soon as he had given orders to his people about my luggage. Within the room, which was very cheerful, spacious, and clean, every part was full of little girls. Some sat on the table, some under

the table, some had clambered up to the window, some
of the smallest sat and played on the floor.   A well-
grown girl of sixteen held a child of a year old in
her arms, and was dancing about with it among the
others.   In one corner sat a young man who, his head
leaning on his breast, seemed to be deep in thought,
and troubled himself very little about the noise of the
children or the grace of the dancer.

"Quiet there!" cried the landlord, as he entered
the room with me.   "Annette, take the noisy troop
out of doors! and you, Fanny, prepare a room for this
strange gentleman; number eight.   He will remain for
the night."

At this order Annette, a pretty damsel of about
fourteen, led the whole swarm of little ones outside.
Fanny, the dancer, only made an easy, graceful
curtsey by way of greeting, danced up to the medi-
tative young man, and said: "Good Mr. Philosopher,
condescend to amuse my youngest sister for a little
while.   I trust you will prove yourself gallant."   And
with these words she seated the child, whom she had
till now held in her arms, on his lap.   This did not
appear to be a very acceptable charge, but he undertook it.

"You are richly blessed, mine host," said I; and I
pointed to the joyous troop of little ones.   "Are they
all yours?"

"I should be well enough pleased, if only for the
curiosity of the thing," replied M. Albret, for such
was the landlord's name.   "But only about half of
them belong to me; the other half are playmates who
have come to spend the birthday of my third daughter."

"And how many children have you, M. Albret?"

"Six girls, no more."

"Heaven help you! All girls! Six girls!"

"Thank Heaven! you should rather say, Captain. A father could desire no happier fate, if the girls be pretty. For some portion of their brilliancy is reflected upon him. Every one courts him, because every one is thinking of the girls. I have already observed that my Fanny wins this for me. When she shall have taken wing, they will play the agreeable for Annette. When Annette has flown, then for Juliette; she gone, for Kate; then for Celestine, then for Lisette, then for whoever may follow."

"But confess, M. Albret, that the prospect is not a pleasant one of being obliged to give them all up, one after another, to husbands; and of losing them from the house."

"Nay, I look at it in quite a different light from what you do. When I give away a daughter I put out my capital to interest. I shall become a grandfather. That is a fresh enjoyment of life."

"You try to console yourself, M. Albret. But six handsome boys, instead of girls, would have made you very proud."

"Boys! Heaven forbid! The wild fellows would make me grey-headed before my time with their romps and lubber-tricks; whilst with my daughters I grow young again. When my boys grew up one would become shrivelled up over accounts as a merchant; another become crippled for his country; a third even be killed; a fourth travel over land and sea; a fifth become a jovial spendthrift; a sixth would be sharper than his father. That would not answer."

Fanny now came dancing in, curtseyed prettily to

me, and said: "Your room is arranged, you have only to take possession of it." The landlord was called away at the moment. I took up my hat to go to my room.

"If you will allow me," said Fanny, "I will do myself the honor of showing it to you." Then with two bounds she stood before the man to whom she had given the child: "Mr. Philosopher, you are very impolite to your little lady. See how Lisette is smiling at you. Kiss her hand directly, and beg her pardon." So saying, she took hold of the little hand of the child, and put it to his lips. The man smiled gloomily, and scarcely looked up.

She then skipped back to me, and said: "I have the honor." And she flew up the staircase before me. She then opened the door of a small, cheerful room. But she had some time to wait before I came up with her. I excused myself for the delay. I was only half recovered from an illness.

"You will soon be completely restored here," said she. "The baths at Cransac work wonders, as you know."

"I never heard a word of them, fair Fanny," said I. "Then you have medicinal waters here, have you?"

"The most celebrated in the whole world. People come here even from Toulouse and Montpellier. No one ever leaves us without being thoroughly cured and pleased."

"But who could be pleased to leave you, pretty Fanny?"

"Leave me to settle that, if need be, Captain. I understand how to tease people till they are glad to be rid of me."

"Oh! I beg, do me the honor of teasing me a little."

"That may happen. But now I must go and take my little sister away from the philosopher downstairs."

"If I may venture to ask, who is the gentleman that you call the philosopher?"

"An extremely amiable, clever, agreeable young man, whose only fault is that he cannot laugh; seldom speaks; and when he does speak, is pleased with nothing. His name is Herr von Orny; he is a visitor to the baths, and wishes them where he should not, because they smell of sulphur."

With these words she dropped a curtsey, and disappeared.

I confess the little girl was charming enough to tease any man. I resolved to remain in Cransac for the following day, and to try the baths. Where could I find better company or better entertainment? I was in need also of recreation.

But in the solitude of my room I became weary. I went out that I might at least see the pretty ladybird, Fanny. She was flitting about, goodness knows where. No one remained to amuse me but Herr von Orny, who was drumming a march with his fingers on the window-pane. I inquired of him the nature of the waters. He said, "They have a strong smell, like rotten eggs." I said that I had not come exactly for the sake of the baths. "So much the better for you," he replied. I observed that the country round seemed to be pretty. He answered, "What does that signify? the people are so much the more disagreeble."

"Yet one might well endure a Fanny," I added.

"As well as a hornet that buzzes around one's head."

As I turned from him, Herr von Orny uttered a loud cry. I started in alarm. I would have sprung to him. There stood Fanny beside him with affectionate, yet threatening, gestures: in her extended hand, a pin which she had stuck into the back of his shoulder. "Are you then aware, Sir, that we hornets can sting? This is the smallest of my punishments; tremble at thoughts of the greatest."

"You would then pierce his heart," said I.

"Oh! one could pierce none with Herr von Orny," she replied, and went away quickly.

The young man grumbled something, and left the room. A strange scene indeed to me. Never before had I beheld a man of his age, endowed by nature with birth, breeding, and a pleasing exterior, so insensible to the fun of a pretty girl.

Alone I would not remain. I went out of doors, examined the premises round the house from very ennui, and went into the garden adjoining it, where Fanny's youngest sister, Annette, was watering flowers. I watched the young girl's industry with pleasure. I deemed the father blessed. This angelic being, on the verge of quitting childhood, retained all its harmlessness and innocence even while already budding into the beauty of womanhood; whilst flitting about among her flowers, she would have formed for Leonardo da Vinci's picture of the Virgin at the Sepulchre, a model more attractive, more ideal, than are any of his figures.

"Who is it?" she said, when she heard my step, but without turning round.

"A thief," said I.

"What would he steal?" asked she laughing, still without looking at me.

"Annette's prettiest flower."

She now put down her pot, and came towards me half timidly, and said: "I would like to see it myself then."

I cast my eyes around, and perceived a half-blown moss-rose. "May I break it off?" I asked.

"A thief should not ask," was her reply; and she reached a small pair of scissors for cutting it.

"I do not steal it for myself," said I.

"To whom then do you wish to give the rose?" she asked.

"To the prettiest girl in Cransac."

"Well, Sir, I must give leave for that. But do you then know the girls in Cransac already? You have hardly been here an hour yet."

"I only know her who is the prettiest of all."

"You make me very curious, Sir; will you allow me to accompany you?"

"I will only ask you to remain still for a moment," replied I; and I hastily placed the rose in the ribbon round her head which confined her luxuriant brown tresses.

"You are wrong! you are wrong! My sister Fanny is the prettiest of all."

"How can you contradict me, lovely Annette? Can you be allowed to be judge in your own cause? If I choose to declare that you are the beauty of beauties in Cransac, what can you say against it?"

"Nothing but that you must show me who is in your opinion the next prettiest."

Thus the dispute went on. But she was forced to keep the rose. She then led me round to see all her flowery treasures. We became friends in a short time. Before evening I was so with the whole family. Madame Albret, the mother of the six children, was a graceful little woman; chatty, full of spirits, and lively like the rest. That morose fellow, Orny, alone took no part in the jokes, amid all our laughter.

The one day at Cransac became eight. I packed up every evening for the following morning, and as punctually unpacked again in the morning. Fanny kept her word faithfully, and teased me even more cruelly than her philosopher, who remained indifferent to all her raillery. Never was I more painfully, nor more pleasantly teased. How could I see the pretty, gentle, graceful, merry sylph play off her little tricks on me unnoticed? I felt how dangerous she was becoming to my peace of mind, and armed myself in vain. She herself, only entering on her sixteenth year, perceived nothing of this. She trifled with Cupid's arrows not knowing how formidable they were. To all the witching grace of a young woman she united the light-hearted nature of a child. Whatever of tenderest one might say to her, her mischief turned the serious into comic.

I often fancied that an interest in me had been aroused within her; when she was silent, when her glance rested on me with satisfaction, or when a smile full of unutterable pathos beaming from her eyes

seemed to say, "Understand me, Doubter!" But by
no means. This was only kindness; a certain true-
heartedness which, with her want of knowledge of the
world, arose from delicacy of mind. She remained
the same; and felt no more warmly towards me than
she did towards others to whom she wished well. Over
anxious to please she was not, nor had she any occasion to be. For she pleased every one and won all
hearts, and knew that she did so. This did not make
her vain: but only excited within her a grateful kindliness towards every one, such as children feel with
whom every one is ready to have a game of play. And
the womanly tenderness of feeling, the maidenly nobility of soul, which are ever wont to be united with
innocence of heart, gave even to her playfulness a
dignity which allowed no one to forget that he could
never venture to overstep the bounds of strict propriety
without for ever forfeiting her esteem.

Sometimes it seemed as though the young man-
hater von Orny had a stronger claim upon her than
any one else. I must own that he was a man whose
exterior might well attract. Even his gloomy mood
gave him something of interest. Though nothing went
right with him, he always did what was right; and
though he was continually grumbling, he was the best-
hearted fellow in the world. I once went into the
room when Fanny, pushing back his hair from his
forehead, tried with her hand to smooth the wrinkles
on his brow, whilst he sat with folded arms and would
not even look at her. I confess that the sight of this
familiarity excited in me something of jealous vexation.
She however thought so little harm that, when her
parents entered at almost the same moment as myself,

she did not even change her position in the least, but carried on her amusement, at which we could not help laughing. When his departure became the subject of conversation, she was so indifferent that, with her own peculiar sort of comic-earnest, she gave him this advice; "Go with the Captain to Spain. That is the real paradise of misanthropes. They kill each other wherever they meet; and, Herr von Orny, you will certainly, in one way or another, get quit of your fellowmen there."

Her sister Annette had the same undisturbed cheerfulness, the same liveliness, and the same gracefulness of mind: but she was even more childlike. She evinced therefore greater warmth of feeling than Fanny. There was a surprising dignity about this innocent child. Her features were regular. One might say that she was prettier than Fanny; but it would be impossible to say which of the two was the more loveable.

It gave me great pleasure to watch the differences and the peculiarities of these two young creatures. Annette attached herself more to me. Herr von Orny was less pleasing to her on account of his sometimes strange moods. "They are contrary to my taste," said she. "I like the sky to be ever blue and cloudless." With childlike confidence she imparted all her little secrets to me, and asked for my advice about everything she told me. I must even give my opinion as to her dress, and what was most becoming to her.

The child fascinated me greatly; and when at last on the eighth day of my stay at Cransac, I signified my unalterable intention to take my departure, Annette knew how to entreat so prettily, and so earnestly, that I found myself compelled to yield to her; provided that Orny, who had resolved on making the journey to Perpignan with me, and who pressed forward our departure more than I did, would concede two days longer.

I was astonished when Orny himself came and begged of me a respite of some few days. "Have you allowed yourself to be persuaded by Annette?" I asked. "I should not have expected it from your iron nature."

"Ah!" said he, and he passed his hand across his face as though to wipe away a faint smile that gleamed upon it. "I could not refuse the poor child when my denial at last brought her tears. I was obliged then to enter on terms of capitulation with the little witch, and she coaxed me out of another eight days, under promise that she would not then utter a syllable of opposition. When at last I had consented, — and how was anything else possible? — she threw her arms round my neck with insane delight, and gave me a kiss forthwith. She was quite beside herself."

"Ah!" said I, "for such a price one might well dispose of oneself, or of a fellow-traveller either."

"It remains with you, Captain, to go if you wish it. My promise binds me. Still it would be a great pleasure to me to accompany you on your journey to Perpignan."

I assured him that the gratification of his society was too great for me not to be willing to delay a week longer; not to mention that the quiet had a beneficial effect on my yet scarcely restored health.

When soon afterwards I again saw Annette, she skipped and danced towards me with an air of triumph.

"Well, Sir, so one of us girls can tame even a half-wild creature like Herr von Orny!" she said laughing.

"I can easily believe it: by means of the powerful weapons with which you laid siege to him you would have made an easy conquest of me also. Yet I envy him a little for the way in which you brought him to capitulate, as also for the thanks that you accorded him." She smiled silently and thoughtfully at me, with an air of indescribable loveliness.

"At least," continued I, "without any injustice I deem myself entitled to implore as sweet a recompense as was bestowed upon him unasked."

She gazed at me earnestly with a strange, penetrating look, whilst a delicate blush overspread her angelic countenance. Suddenly she turned away, and went off dancing, and warbling a popular melody. I did not receive the reward. Now, first I suspected that, with her as with her elder sister Fanny, I had been like the good-natured fool in the play, taking to my own credit what had been simply the result of interest in Orny. I composed my mind.

The eight days passed quickly away. I often repented afterwards of having prolonged the time of my stay in Cransac with this charming family. For these kindly hearts entwined themselves daily more and more closely round my own. Fanny's beauty made the liveliest impression upon me. I loved the little girl with ever-increasing fervency; and was all the more unhappy because I convinced myself that she had not the slightest idea what the passion of love was. She was not reserved, nor yet cordial as she had been on the first day. She appeared rather to keep more closely to the melancholy Orny, and to behave to him something as young girls are wont to behave, without giving it a thought, in their intercourse with old people. Yet in truth, Orny was no older than myself, nor was I younger than he.

I acknowledge that, until now, I had amused myself with women without understanding myself. But Fanny was my first real love. I had need of all my self-control, not to make myself ridiculous. Meanwhile the time for parting came; and indeed I was glad that it should come, however bitter it might be to my own heart.

M. and Madame Albret were as friendly in their leave-taking as they had been in their greeting. Orny, as distant and cold as anywhere one could be when leaving an inn to continue a journey. Fanny, who never showed herself more attractive than at this moment in which I was about to take leave of her for ever, appeared in quite a new character. She wished each of us a prosperous journey with equal kindliness, volunteered several notions of her own respecting it, and seemed determined to soften as far as possible the disagreeables of leave-taking, unavoidable when persons are separating who have been living in the same house for several happy days, and even weeks.

But little Annette betrayed more emotion and agitation. She held my hand for a considerable time, then went hastily away. When, after a short absence, she returned, she brought a newly-blown moss-rose, and gave it to me with one hand, whilst, with the other, she showed me a faded rose which I instantly recognized as that which I had given to her on the day of my arrival. She did not utter a word. Her countenance was full of melancholy. When I kissed her hand in adieu she threw her arms around my neck, kissed me, sobbed deeply, and hurried away.

Now I also, for the first time, noticed tears in Fanny's eyes, and in those of her mother.

We got into the carriage; it drove off.

For the first hour we talked but very little. Herr von Orny sat sullen in one corner of the carriage, I in the other. I was glad of it. I was also glad that in his presence I was forced to control myself; for I felt that I could have wept like a child. Fanny, with her tearful face, seemed to me to be hovering about the carriage.

Things were already brighter with me on the next day. We stopped at Toulouse, and at ill-built Carcassonne. My travelling companion, in addition to not being talkative, never opened his lips but when he found something to grumble at. "People only torment each other with their follies and misdeeds," said he. "It is so alike in palaces and cottages. I am perhaps a torment to others; but I am so, because they are torments to me."

"Yet the lovely little Fanny did not seem to be a torment to you," I replied. "Or were you barbarous enough to be unjust even to the most harmless being under heaven?"

"I do not deny," answered he, "that children are to our world as angels of light to souls in torment. And Fanny is a perfect child. I avoided the little girl, because I never in my life have seen one more deserving of good training. I would have staid longer in Cransac; for the retirement of the little place suited me, as did a sort of heavy manner in the people, who are at least ignorant how to varnish over their follies and tricks. But I did not stay, because Fanny was there."

"What a contradiction!" said I.

"Not at all," he replied. "The little girl would perhaps only have become an apt pupil that she might destroy all the fruit of my painfully earned knowledge of the world, and of myself; that she might make a fool of me, or double my misery."

He spoke thus; then stopped short. I tried in vain to beguile him into further talk of the Albret family, with whom he had lived for nearly three months. He either would not answer at all; or only did so by a nod of the head, or shrug of the shoulders.

As he had already said at Cransac, his intention was to travel with me to Perpignan in order to leave me there. His business I did not know. At the second stage after Carcassonne he found in the posting-house a map of the country hanging on the wall. He stood before it for a long time; rubbed his forehead, then wrote something in his pocket-book, came up to me, and said: "It is best so. I will go to Marseilles, and from thence to Italy."

Yet he again seated himself by my side in the carriage. We drove on, till deep into the night. The moon shone brightly. There was something solemnly beautiful in traversing the line of mountains whose forests and peaks rose in sharp outline of mass and point against the clear sky.

Suddenly Herr von Orny, who had appeared until

19*

now to be asleep, turned towards the door of the carriage to look at the country.

"What is that ruin yonder on the hill?" he called
to the post-boy.

"The Castle Loubre," replied he.

"Good!" said Herr von Orny. "Then beyond is
the road to Siegean?"

"Exactly so," returned the post-boy. "It is scarcely
a month yet, since one bright moonlight night like
this a coach full of travellers was attacked by robbers
on that road. My brother-in-law, Matthew, who drove
it, was murdered."

"And are we not further from Belloc?" –interrupted Orny.

"A short half league," replied the post-boy.

Orny threw himself back into his corner of the
carriage again, and said no more.

I gazed attentively at the gloomy, gigantic, tower-
ing ruins of the old castle. Rising amid the still,
wild solitude, and illumined weirdly by the moonlight,
they presented a truly fearful appearance. Indeed I
have never beheld similar ruins without experiencing a
peculiar sensation of mingled awe and melancholy.
For I reflect involuntarily on the long tale of years,
and on the days of trial, of those who once wept and
laughed, were born and died within their walls, from
grandfather to grandson. And the vast contemplation
of the transitory nature of all that is earthly closes
at last with a view of the decay even of their very
home.

"But this castle does not seem to me to have been
standing empty very long," said I to the post-boy.

"So far as I know, it is about eight or twelve

years since it was burnt down, with all in it," answered he.

"How dreadful! And through what accident did such a calamity happen?" I inquired further.

He returned, "How? The country people had flocked together at the outbreak of the revolution. The lady was hated because of her harshness and austerity. The castle was stormed, and everything burnt. It was to a rich Countess that the castle belonged. She also was burnt."

"False!" cried Orny suddenly, close beside me.

"Well, Sir," replied the man, "I know it from the lips of trustworthy people who related the tale to me. A young man also who was born in the castle, and was said to be the son of the Countess, only she would not acknowledge him, was burnt with her. This has been told to me by very reliable persons who had every means of knowing the truth."

"They told lies!" exclaimed Herr von Orny.

"Upon my word, if you do not choose to believe me, or if you know better than I do, what do you ask me questions for?" muttered the post-boy, angrily; he then turned round to his horses, gave them a cut with the whip, and gallopped them on with a jerk.

"Then are you acquainted with the ruin?" said I to Herr von Orny.

"Very well," he replied; "since I am myself the son who is said to have been burnt there."

"What! You yourself re the son and grandson of the old inhabitants of that castle!" I cried in astonishment.

The story, and this incident, made a deep impression on me.

"I am no one's son!" he murmured.

"But you said just now that you were —"

"Ah, yes!" he replied; "there is no contradiction in it."

He seemed to observe my curiosity; and, which pleased me very much, gratified it by the following narration, without waiting to be pressed.

Until my fifteenth year I was educated by the clergyman of that village the lights of which we saw about half an hour ago gleaming on our right amid the darkness. I supposed him to be a near relative, or indeed my father: for he had no occasion to add to his duties. I was wrong. I discovered afterwards that I was the child of totally different persons: that I had been brought to him when in my fourth year: that he had received regularly a handsome sum of money for me; that he was even under engagement to give me the best of educations.

When I questioned him about my parents, he usually only replied; "My child, you ask too much. Your parents died long since. I never knew them. You were given in charge to me. A considerable salary is paid to me for you. Therefore I imagine that you will possess a good property. But of what value, and where, you will only learn when you are older."

I loved the venerable man very much. My young heart felt the need of attaching itself to another. It was not good for me that I had no parents, no creature to whom I was nearly related. I envied the poor children in the village their good fortune in being able to feel themselves kissed by a mother's lips, embraced in a mother's arms.

The pious old gentleman gave me a very good education after his fashion. He instructed me in languages and in the sciences. When I was fifteen, he took me to Montpellier, a year afterwards to Toulouse, in order to complete my intellectual training. After this, I beheld him no more. He died. I then regularly received a fixed sum of money quarterly from a banker to whom the clergyman had given me references. I believed for a long time that I was indebted for this to my venerable foster-father. But I learned from the banker that sometimes one, and sometimes another Paris house sent orders to my credit.

I was happy. Who would not be so at that age? My passions were just awakening. I had a fervid imagination. I was a poet. The world lay before me bathed in rosy light. I revelled in exquisite illusions. I knew nothing of my fellowmen. I loved them all with the unreserved ardour of my soul. I had more money than I wanted. I could live comfortably myself, and help others also. I had a friend to whom I was attached with all my heart: and, what was even more, I had for the first time attained the happiness of loving, and of being loved. All the delights of existence were then opening before me. Truly now I seem to myself to have been a madman.

A few weeks destroyed my paradise, and brought me to my senses. I had entered on my nineteenth year. My beloved one (whom I, no not loved, but adored) was of very good birth; but, with her mother, (the widow of a Major,) in limited circumstances. I resolved to seek for an appointment; and, so soon as

I should have obtained one to entreat the hand of my beloved, that my happiness might be complete. She had been able, since I had made their acquaintance, to live very comfortably and without anxiety, with her mother: for, without her being aware of it, I had bestowed the greater portion of my income upon her. For this purpose I employed my friend and confidant. He was to find ways and means to give the family assistance in such a manner as that my name should remain concealed. For I did not desire gratitude, but love. I feared to injure the delicate relations between us, if I appeared before my beloved as a benefactor.

Meanwhile I was ignorant that my bosom friend maintained both mother and daughter, in every sense, with my money: that he made use of their poverty and my wealth to obtain the daughter for himself; that whilst I, in all humility, reverenced her for her innocence and piety, she was deceiving me: that I was designed, as being a simple fool, to become her husband should her scandalous flirtations prove too notorious. All this I discovered quite unexpectedly, and quite accidentally, on the very morning of her birthday, when I was on the point of giving her a birthday present. I fled with horror. I was in despair. I was seized with a violent fever. After my recovery I learned from other people, with whom I had not previously been intimate, the history of my wrongs. Both the traitors made efforts to renew the intimacy with me. I repulsed both. From that day this Judas became my most bitter foe. He insulted me publicly. We fought. I shot him through the arm. Whilst still bleeding, he vowed death and destruction to me.

At this time I received a visit which removed me

from Toulouse. One day a traveller came to me. When I had proved to him that I was really the person whom he sought (in order to do so I was obliged to go with him to the banker from whom I was in the habit of receiving my income), he gained confidence.

"Herr von Orny," said he, "I am deputed to hand over to you this sealed packet. You will be so kind as to give me an acknowledgment of the receipt of it."

I took the packet, and gave the acknowledgment. He then said; "Herr von Orny, you will do well to betake yourself at once to the Countess von Loubre, and to make her acknowledge your rights as her son. The Countess is your mother. The proofs thereof, from the hand of your father who died lately in Scotland, are in this packet. They cannot be gainsaid. The payments hitherto made to you will cease from this time: it is your mother's business to provide for you in the future." This is what he said.

"Where is my mother? Where shall I find my mother?" I exclaimed in joyful surprise and astonishment. Heaven alone knows what I felt. The traveller told me that she certainly had lived in Paris for eighteen years: and now, after a long absence, had on account of domestic affairs gone for the first time to Languedoc, to her family seat, Castle Loubre, where she would only remain for a few months.

In vain did I teaze the traveller with questions about my father, my mother, and their relatives. He knew nothing of any of them, had not even met them personally. He was but executing a commission, probably from the family of my deceased father. The messenger himself was not French, but English. He had fulfilled his commission, and he left me.

Neither did the packet, which I broke open with trembling hands, give me any information as to the circumstances of my parents, nor as to why they had so long delayed acknowledging me as their son. I found in it explanations in the handwriting of my father; letters concerning me in the handwriting of the Countess; certificates of baptism; depositions of my nurse; of a farmer's family unknown to me, but with whom I had probably been boarded until my fourth year; certificates from my venerable foster-father, the clergyman; and other papers which indisputably proved if not the legitimacy, yet the authentic facts, of my birth.

Oh! how joyfully I quitted that, to me, hateful Toulouse! I had lost my friend and my love, but had now found a mother. I remembered sometimes in my boyhood, when I was living with the old clergyman to have heard of the Countess at the Castle Loubre. At that time it was only known that she had been as beautiful as unfortunate. Now I could plainly see that I myself might have been more or less the cause of her unhappiness.

I arrived. I betook myself tremblingly to the Castle. I sent in my name to the Countess. During the whole of my journey I had been rehearsing the part I would act before sinking on my mother's breast as her newly-found son. I dreaded lest surprise and rapture should break my mother's heart.

I was conducted to her apartment. The Countess entered: a dignified figure inspiring me with awe; and still retaining so much of youthful beauty that I could scarcely believe her the being to whom I owed my existence. She was not yet thirty-nine years of age, and looked like a person who had scarcely reached thirty.

I advanced towards her. My heart was full of anxiety. I wished to gaze at her; but tears of joy dimmed my eyes. I would have spoken, but my voice failed from excess of emotion. I faltered forth my name. I told her from whence I came. I asked whether she had mourned a lost son. I sank on my knees beside her, stammering the name of mother.

She appeared to be alarmed, and said; "Young man, compose yourself. What do you want? Who is it you wish to see? Why do you weep?" I related my history, and called her my mother.

"Young man," replied she calmly, "you are mistaken. It is true that I am the Countess whom you seek; but I was never married, and am not so now; still less have I ever had a son, consequently have never lost one. No doubt some person has taken leave to play off an unseemly joke on your credulity, or has wished to make use of you as a tool to insult me. Rise."

I stood up, but was quite confounded by her words. I had some difficulty in regaining my self-possession. I saw that she was perturbed, and full of thought; but in her mien there was none of the disquietude of a mother on the point of embracing a long-lost son, only the uneasiness of despair and of mortally-wounded pride. She treated me as one who had been hoaxed, or who was really perhaps half a fool. This annoyed me. But I attributed it to my own conduct, to my over-haste, my embarrassment, that the Countess had assumed such a tone. I then calmly and quietly explained my circumstances to her; I showed her some of her own letters among my papers; different certificates; her own written declaration that she would undertake to provide for me when I should come of age, and would, during her lifetime, insure me a good share of her property, so that I might not one day be deprived of my inheritance by her family. I then showed her a deed in my favour, formally signed by herself, for an annual income of fifteen thousand livres which, by the desire of my father, she had for nearly ten years sent to him for me. But in the deed I did not appear as her son; this point was only made clear by her letters, and by some of the accompanying depositions. I then requested to know what were her wishes.

She was indescribably perplexed. "Young man," she at last said, "I never was married. You will see that I cannot pronounce you my son, and expose myself in my old age to public scorn and disgrace. You are in possession of papers which — you must perceive it is necessary that I should first satisfy myself thoroughly as to the nature of these documents, as also of your identity. Leave your papers with me for a short time for my examination. In the meanwhile I will provide accommodation for you in the Castle."

She spoke thus. Now I first plainly perceived that she could not disclaim me, but that she might look on me as a blot upon her life, and renounce me: that it was important to her to get these documents, my only legal proof, into her power.

I put the papers into my pocket; expressed to her my astonishment that no emotion within her own breast should plead for me: told her that I would not give up the papers except before a court of justice;

that I gave her eight days for reflection; that I would await her summons at Siegean, and would then assert my claim if she did not allow the natural feelings of a mother to overrule her agitation respecting her previous life.

She stood speechless. I left her with a troubled mind. As I was going down the castle steps, I heard her calling names of every kind after me, and giving orders: "Hold that man fast! Do not let him out of the castle! Arrest him! Pursue him!" Servant-maids stared at me in terror, and called to the porter to shut the gate. I threw the old fellow down as I led out my horse. I mounted, and gallopped off. A shot was fired after me. I looked round. At the castle-gate I saw servants and gamekeepers; at the window above, the Countess, my wicked mother.

I had to wait in the miserable inn at Siegean for the appointed eight days. On the third night I was awakened from my sleep by a confused noise. There were men in my room, probably thieves. A gleam of light shone on the ceiling. It came from a dark lantern. I flew like a madman from the bed, seized the table, swung it round, and struck out on all sides. The lantern fell to the ground with its bearer. Another man uttered a smothered cry. I fought with fury for a long time, until I became out of breath, and thought that I must now be left alone. I took up the lantern, and lighted my candles. All the people in the inn were still in their first sleep. On the ground lay a strange man. I took him for dead. I resolved to give the alarm, and began to dress myself hastily. Whilst doing so, I noticed that the stranger began to move. He had only been stunned by a heavy blow.

I threw myself upon him, and searched him. He had about his person a pocket-pistol loaded, and a long knife. I bound him hand and foot with the cord of my trunk, so that he could not escape me. By this time he had come completely to himself. He groaned when he perceived his position. With the knife at his breast, I compelled him to confess what he wanted in my room. Not my money, not my life, but my papers were what he sought by order of the Countess. They had hoped to seize upon me unawares in my sleep, and terrify me.

On the ground lay a mask.

To spare the Countess, I gave no alarm. The fellow remained my prisoner and hostage. I wrote to the Countess by a messenger that she must within twenty-four hours appear herself here at Siegean in person, and redeem the prisoner by a reconciliation with me. A man invested with full powers came in her stead. An agreement was entered into. In the presence of notaries and witnesses I received in due form a surrender of the deed by which I came into possession of an income of fifteen thousand livres yearly. But, on the other hand, I was obliged to leave all my papers sealed in the hands of the Countess.

Thus we parted. I now stood more alone in the world than ever. The only friend of my youth had deceived me. My love had been false to me. My mother had despised and disowned me.

All this happened in the first year of the revolution. Since then I have travelled much about the world, and have found wickedness everywhere. In Paris I with difficulty escaped death. Judas was there, my former friend at Toulouse, now become a vehement apostle of liberty, and denouncer of the aristocracy. I took service with the Republican army. I made some expeditions with it, and was engaged on the Rhine against the Condés. In one of the encounters with *Émigrés*, I perceived Judas among them. He recognized me. "Have I got you at last?" cried he in a fury, and threw himself on me, I on him. Whilst we fought together, a soldier of my company coming to my rescue, shot him down.

Now you have my history.

During this narrative we had reached the post-house of a small town. We resolved to enjoy some hours' rest here, and to proceed with early morning. This unhappy man had become endeared to me by his misfortunes.

Whilst we were sitting at breakfast on the following day, he began suddenly: "It is settled. I will go to Marseilles, and from thence into Italy. I am about to leave you."

I felt sorry to be obliged to forego his society, but did not urge him to accompany me further. "Herr von Orny," said I, "you have inspired me with feelings of profound sympathy by your friendly confidence. I wish I were in a position to render you any service at all in proportion to my regard for you. But alas! I have nothing better to offer than a word of good advice."

"What is it?" he asked gloomily.

"You are unhappy, very unhappy, since with all your excellent qualities you have become the most unjust of men, only because once as a young man you

were deceived in some persons who accidentally became intimate with you. It commonly happens that
he who begins by trusting too implicitly and too
blindly, afterwards trusts and believes too little. One
must not despise the whole world for the sake of
some few contemptible men in it. How many a noble
heart that would gladly have formed a friendship for
you since then, may you not have coldly repulsed!
Do not go to Marseilles, do not go to Italy, you will
not enjoy yourself. Go to Cransac. You will find
healing there with the Albret family. . They know
you there. There they show forbearance to your
weaknesses, there they honor your virtues. And you
too know the family. Tell me, which member of it
has any worse disposition than yourself? If then the
worthy people at Cransac are as good as yourself, why
do you struggle against the conviction that they, at
least, are deserving of esteem?"

I spoke this in purest friendship. He was not
offended. He only murmured a word or two to himself, and then went out to order horses. He accompanied me to the carriage. We embraced each other
like old friends. He appeared to be affected. I pressed
him once again to my heart, and said softly: "Your
healing is in Cransac." Then I left him.

Arrived in Perpignan, I learned from the General
that my regiment had left for Catalonia six days before. At the same time he gave me a pleasant surprise in a step of rank. The Emperor had promoted
me to be Major. I hurried after the regiment and
entered forthwith on my duties with it.

For two years we fought with the Spaniards, with
varied success. I will not here give an account of our

campaigns. They are well-known, and in the immense crowd of grand events the exploits of individuals become forgotten. This only will I say, and because I speak from experience, that people do by far too much honor to the Spaniards when they laud their heroism to the skies; and especially to the Catalonians, against whom we were chiefly opposed. To possess courage is no great merit in a man, and not worth making a wonderment of. The Catalonians, and indeed the Spaniards generally, are not endowed with any greater courage and steadiness than other nations. But the great mass of them, especially in the villages, are bred up in poverty and want, in immorality and idleness, in ignorance and prejudice. Such people are but little concerned when their wretched huts are burnt down. For they can quickly rebuild them. If they have a couple of onions and a crust of bread, they are happy for the day. Consequently they fear no enemy; and have no longing for peace, because they have nothing to lose.

In civilized countries all is quite different.

The common class of Spaniard can in a war live at the cost of foreigners, plunder, take booty. Thus he has more than a time of peace can afford him. In wealthy countries, in the course of a war even the victors lose something of their wealth. For this reason the Spaniard is always more persevering in war than other nations. It is not the result of his heroism, his great courage, his patriotism. He scarce knows what these mean. He is born a slave to his superiors, to his priest. They lead him as they will by means of money, or by the influence of the place of torment, of purgatory, and of indulgences. His whole Christianity hangs on the tie of a rose-wreath.   There are among the Spaniards lofty, noble, and generous spirits, but their number is exceedingly small.   I pity these true-hearted men for being compelled to dwell among such compatriots.

We had severe service; almost daily marches and skirmishes. Both the soil and the climate of the country were against us.   The happiest moments I passed were those in which I was alone, and could dream.   And of what did I dream?   Of Cransac and of Fanny. Her image was so enshrined in my memory, that times without number I cut out her likeness with the scissors in paper, and it was always a good one.

Moreover, even amid the tedium of a garrison I lived in Spain a very secluded life.   My comrades called me the Misanthrope.   In truth I had almost become the very character from which I had wished to preserve Herr von Orny.   But I had arrived at my mood by a very different road from his.   I had become indifferent to society (yes, even avoided it as much as I could); not because I had been deceived, but because I had no hope of ever again meeting with such amiable people as the Albret family.   He who has luxuriated in what is most costly, no longer seeks what is common.   The death of my father, who left me a comfortable property, and the impossibility of withdrawing myself from the army, both tended to increase my present mood.

I remained in this uncomfortable condition for two years.   They were fertile in events and achievements which, however, deserve rather to be forgotten than talked of.   A bullet terminated my military career under the walls of Tarragona.   Shortly before, I had received the order of the Legion of Honour; soon after, I obtained the rank of Lieutenant-Colonel. The fortifications of Tarragona were stormed; I was at the head of my battalion, when a musket-ball which struck my foot, threw me to the ground. Those around had so much compassion for me as to carry me out of the action. My soldiers were attached to me. I lost much blood, and lay senseless for a considerable time. I was taken to Barcelona. At first it was a question whether the injured portion of my foot should be amputated. It was all the same to me. If they had told me I must die, I should have expressed no dissatisfaction. The thought of being obliged to hobble about on crutches a cripple for life had certainly nothing very enlivening in it.

Things changed. A young surgeon took a fancy to me, and boldly opposed his superiors, who wished to amputate my foot. The young man had more sense than his elders, not uncommon in this world. The gentlemen disputed for a long time. The head-surgeon maintained that I must lose either my foot or my life: mortification would be inevitable. The young assistant-surgeon protested that both might be saved: only that the wounded foot would remain stiff, and render me unfit for military service. At last they gave me the choice. I determined, even at the threatened peril of my life, to trust myself to the young surgeon. And I did well in this decision. I preserved both my foot and my life.

Meanwhile I received an honorable *retraite* with a pension. I was dragged from Barcelona to the baths, from the baths to Figueras and Perpignan. With the help of a crutch I could once more walk without pain,

20*

without being forced to limp. My foot only continued extremely weak. But this, together with a certain degree of stiffness, was wearing off by degrees.

I was advised to continue the use of mineral baths.
I had determined on going home to take possession of
my paternal inheritance. But as my property was well
taken care of under the superintendence of a relative,
I thought, not without some throbbings of the heart,
of the baths at Cransac. I had already thought of
them only too often. Yet many anxious reflections
deterred me from going there. No doubt Fanny was
already married. Doubtless the Albret family had
changed very much in the lapse of four or five years.
And even if Fanny were still free, what had I to hope
from her? I had once loved her, but she had never
loved me. I should again stake my contentment and
peace of mind for a long time. Besides, Fanny might
be dead. My heart trembled at the thought. Better
for me to remain in ignorance. I was now as happy,
as free from care, as with a stiff foot one well could
be. No violent emotions disturbed me. The storm
of first love had passed over. I was independent, and
the world lay open before me.

I struggled with myself a long while: and at last,
against the warnings of my judgment, determined to
go whither my heart led me — to Cransac.

In a comfortable carriage which I found an opportunity of purchasing at Perpignan, and attended by
my faithful Thomas, I travelled to Cransac. When
at the end of a few days I at last saw the little place,
which had so often occupied my thoughts, lying be-

fore me in the distance, an unusual thrill of anxiety
disturbed me. I wished I were further off; and but
little was wanting to make me give the post-boy orders
to turn back again. It seemed a presentiment that
it was not well for me to go there, that some misfortune awaited me. In vain did I seek to overcome
my superstitious fears. I drove through the village,
and stopped in front of the but too familiar inn with
a beating heart.

It was a lovely Sunday in spring. The whole
Albret family had gone to church, except ——. She
came to meet me as I entered. Whose heart would
not have throbbed then? It was Fanny. No, it was
not Fanny, it was an etherealized resemblance of
Fanny. I had always pictured the maiden of scarce
sixteen summers to my imagination; but what changes
will not four years make! This was a perfect woman
in grace, in softness, in dignity. I cannot describe the
impression that this apparition made on me. I bowed
silently, and stood speechless before her. She greeted
me in her friendly manner, with her own peculiarly
innocent, bewitching smile.

"Goodness! how lovely you have grown!" I said
at last. "But you do not remember me."

She had in truth recognized me as quickly as I
her. Her blush, the joyous gleam in her eye betrayed
her. "Do you take us for persons of such short
memories?" said she: "only yesterday evening we
were talking about you. We thought you were dead
and lost, at least to us. What miracle has brought
you back to us?"

"How can you ask?" said I, as I pressed her
hand to my lips. "What miracle could it be, but the

greatest miracle of beauty in the world? you yourself. Had I even fallen in Spain you could have summoned my spirit back to this upper world."

"If that had been in my power," said she laughing mischievously, "I would have been well on my guard against summoning you too quickly from purgatory, before you were purified from all love of flattering and had become as true as truth itself."

"Ah!" cried I, whilst we entered the room in which everything still remained in the well-remembered arrangement of olden times; "Let Spain do duty for purgatory, and let me find my heaven for ever here again; for I have had no peace since I left you."

"Then you are one of the fallen angels who left heaven for ambition's sake," she replied. "Who can engage that you will not again set a rebellion on foot, and exchange the tedium of heaven for the more exciting regions of Spain?"

"For that I can give no surety save the lovely queen of paradise herself: if she will look graciously on me, I will prove the most grateful of her subjects."

She held up her finger menacingly at me, and said, "You have indeed still much of the fallen angel left in you, and are come back even worse than when you left."

"Then reform me by your kindness. My return surely proves to you that I long to become better. If you do not thrust me out of paradise, I will never leave it again. Would you thrust me out?"

She blushed and did not reply.

"Would you thrust me out?" I asked, and I gazed inquiringly at her.

She resumed her lively mood, and replied; "According as you behave well. We shall see. But I fear you have not learned much that is good in the school of the lovely Spanish ladies."

Whilst we were talking thus, the door opened. M. Albret, with his wife and some of his little daughters (all like little Graces) came into the room. M. Albret and his wife embraced me, as I did them, with affectionate cordiality and emotion. I was forced to relate to them how I came hither, what had befallen me. They stood around me, their faces beaming with joy. I could see how welcome I was to these kind people. The timid little girls drew nearer; but in vain did I seek among them for the sweet Annette. I scarce durst ask for her. I feared a reply which, even in my present mood, I would fain avoid. I feared lest her gentle spirit, too lovely, too pure, for this world should have winged its flight to a better; and yet I looked round on all sides in quest of her.

"You are seeking, Colonel —?" said M. Albret.

"One is wanting," I said, and checked myself.

"You are right," cried Madame Albret. "Fly, Juliette, and tell Fanny she must come directly; the friend of whom we were talking yesterday is with us." Juliette bounded away. "Goodness! how pleased Fanny will be," added Madame Albret.

I listened to these words with incredulous embarrassment. It must then have been Annette whom I had taken for Fanny. Yet surely I ought to have been able to calculate that after the lapse of four years Annette could no longer still be a little girl of fourteen, but must now be a young lady of eighteen. I do not know how I looked in my surprise. But they all observed my perplexity. I fixed my eye askance on her whom I had taken for Fanny. It was indeed Annette herself: but at this moment she became so grave, so pale, that I was frightened.

"Are you not well?" said I, and moved towards her. She passed her hand over her face, and forced a laugh. Her mother looked anxiously at her, and bade her go into the air. "You have startled the little girl," said M. Albret, "by your sudden appearance. It might have the same effect on Fanny. We must prepare her for it. The start might do her harm. I hope in a few months to be again gladdened by the arrival of a grandchild."

"What! Fanny is married?" I exclaimed.

"Have none of us yet told you that she has been married to Orny these two or three years?"

"To the Misanthrope?"

"Exactly so," replied M. Albret. "But she has worked a complete change in the queer fellow: no one could now be more agreeable. He is quite an altered man. He lives in Cransac, has purchased the most splendid villa we have in the place, and has taken up his residence here permanently. For I will not allow any of my daughters to leave Cransac; and the girls know it."

"M. Albret," said I in a low tone to him, and led him towards the window. "A word with you! May not a second pretty house perhaps be found for sale in Cransac?"

He laughed heartily at the question, looked at me for a moment, and then answered; "Only during the last few days people have been talking of the new house with a garden that you drove past on the great road before you came to the barrier. It was reported that that would be sold. But ask Annette; she knows more about it than I do."

Whilst I was renewing my acquaintance with the little girls, or rather making it, for they had all grown and altered during my absence, my old misanthrope Orny approached; on his arm a handsome young woman who carried a cherub of a year and a half old in her arms. It was — now indeed I recognized her — it was Fanny. We greeted each other affectionately, like intimate friends.

"I am largely your debtor," said Herr von Orny to me. "I hope you will at least give me the pleasure of showing my gratitude to you, and of welcoming you to my house as a guest. I have followed the advice you gave me at parting, and with great success. Do you recollect that you recommended me instead of going to Italy to come to Cransac; that I should here find medicine to cure me? I went to Italy, but did not find it there. In Florence your words recurred to me. I came to Cransac, and found the medicine; and took it; and it was not on the whole so very bad to take." With these words he kissed the glowing cheek of his lovely wife.

"Do not believe him altogether!" cried Fanny. "He still sometimes makes wry faces, and complains that the medicine is rather bitter."

"Because it was and is medicine," he answered laughing.

They were a happy young couple. Orny invited me to dine with him. The Albret family usually went to his house every Sunday. He told me that he had become reconciled to his mother, and had brought her to his house. In the years of the Revolution she had lost the greater part of her property. This impelled him, immediately after his marriage with Fanny, and indeed at Fanny's request, to write to her and offer her a home with him. I became acquainted with her. She was an intellectual woman, in intercourse with whom one could trace the tone of the great world and also a certain pride of station; but under her many misfortunes, she had attained a gentleness of spirit, a patient resignation to the trials appointed for her, a religious view of life which made her all the more interesting.

At table a friendly strife was begun among the most amiable people in the world respecting me. Orny and Fanny insisted that, so long as I should remain in Cransac I must stay with them. M. and Madame Albret maintained, with much eloquence, the force of their old claims. Even Juliette, Kate, and Celestine, the younger children of the Albret family, with whom I had soon become intimate, joined with childish vivacity in the war of words. She alone to whom I would most gladly have listened, whose word would at once have decided me, Annette alone was silent. I looked inquiringly towards her, as though I wished to receive her orders. But she appeared so indifferent that I was pained. She only amused herself with the dispute as a listener who was in no way interested in it. And when the young Frau von Orny appealed to her for help on her side, Annette answered laughingly; "You humble-minded little Fanny, why do you doubt your success? When did you ever need the aid of your sister to give you victory?" But jokingly and merrily as she said these words, there seemed to me, if I did not very greatly deceive myself, to be a little bitterness — no, hardly bitterness, a slight expression of pain hovering around her lovely mouth, which I ought to have interpreted to my own advantage.

I foresaw that in the end the difficult decision would be thrown upon myself. So I begged to be allowed to flit from Albret's house to Orny's and back, as often as my lame foot would permit. A few hundred paces would be to me no distance from any of the beloved ones to whom in Catalonia even I had ever been near in spirit.

This last assertion might be questioned. And now for the first time I received a torrent of reproaches because that during four years I had never sent one single little word across the Pyrenees to Cransac. All showered these reproaches on me, Annette alone excepted. She rather took my part, only very maliciously.

"It was exactly because the Colonel was present with us in spirit," said she, "that he did not write: one never writes to those from whom one is not separated."

Now this defence evidently was not valid. My silhouettes that I had cut out in Spain now occurred to my mind; and I told how it had been my favourite amusement to make the family continually present with me. At this point I told a little fib; and, in order to punish Annette for her malice, said that of all the silhouettes hers had always been the most successful. I immediately undertook to cut out her profile without looking at her. They took me at my word. Scissors and paper were brought. I reckoned on Annette's likeness to Fanny. I went to the window. In a few minutes the work was completed in which I had had very sufficient practice. I handed Annette's likeness to the pretty damsel herself.

She looked at it for a moment, shook her little head, and said: "That is Fanny."

The silhouette was passed from hand to hand, and every one said, "That is Fanny." I became embarrassed. Fanny made me a curtsey, and said, "That is me." Orny held up a threatening finger, and said; "I congratulate myself that I did not arrive too late." Madame Albret, in trying to make things better, made them worse. "Indeed," said she, "I see in it a strong likeness to Annette: only when Herr von Orny left us she was but a child of fourteen, and the silhouette rather resembles her at her present age. She did not wear her hair like that at that time, it was rather Fanny's style. But these are trifles."

"Important points," cried all. "Proof that he was only thinking of Fanny."

"No," replied I; "not so. Only proof that the image of the two, with their different characteristics of beauty, were blended into one in my memory; and if I were to open my trunk, I could still show you the carefully treasured rose that I took away as my single relic from Cransac, the rose that Miss Annette gave me on taking leave."

Annette's cheek glowed with consciousness. She cast a doubtful glance at me. Madame Albret said: "We have yours still in a frame and glass, wreathed round with pretty embroidery."

It pleased me that every one now was eager to

give proofs of uninterrupted friendship and remembrance. Thus I escaped from a painful dilemma.

For I had indeed formerly admired Annette as an ideal of childlike beauty: but Fanny I had loved, Fanny I had always thought of, and had sought for again at Cransac. At the moment of my arrival I simply saw Fanny in Annette: but I saw her possessed of far more attractions than I had ever seen in her before. I loved her from that moment with greater intensity. It was a strange feeling when I became conscious of my mistake: and convinced myself that Annette was the object that had fascinated me. I was in a state of painful, half-stupified expectation and tension until I saw the real Fanny again. But as soon as she appeared by the side of her husband, all was changed within me. Every feeling spoke for Annette alone. Fanny was still young, still pretty, still loveable; but by the side of Annette she seemed no longer to be Fanny. The spell was broken. Fanny was still to me as a dear friend; but I could not myself understand how I ever could have made an idol of her. And if she had been now unmarried, I should have loved Annette alone, not Fanny. Even at the time of my first stay I had conceived a strange, inexplicable interest in Annette, which I could neither account for nor describe. I loved Fanny as a pretty girl, Annette as an angelic being not created for this world, a being of a higher order, whom one could scarcely approach with earthly feelings.

Fanny was very happy with her husband. He was in paradise with her. The villa in which they lived was very pleasantly situated, surrounded by a large and pretty garden, roomy, cheerful, and built

in good taste.   Orny had also made many improvements in it.   I went there almost every day, and
walked among the shady paths in the garden when I
came from the bath.   I envied Orny his good fortune
when I saw him wandering arm in arm confidingly
with his young wife among the shrubs, or watched
him beside her on the green mossy bank before their
house, chatting with her.   Then too I pictured my
own happiness if I could but wander thus by the side
of the lovely Annette; yet day by day, with expiring
hope; for Annette loved me not.   I staid four weeks
in Cransac, but found no change in her intercourse
with me.   I remained four weeks longer, but could
seize no moment on any single occasion on which I
could see her alone.   Three months fled, and I lingered on, as though bound by some invisible spell,
yet ever further removed from her than on the first
day.

As had been the case in my intercourse four years
before with Fanny, so now with Annette.   Like the
former, the latter knew how to laugh off every serious
expression, and how to foil every attempt at an advance without appearing to do so purposely.   What
Fanny had often effected by means of her volatility,
in not hearing, or not understanding what she did not
choose to listen to, came much more easily to Annette
owing to her characteristic of truly childlike innocence,
and to a certain dignity, which, blending wondrously
with all that was lovely in her and in her ways, inspired those who approached her with irresistible
feelings of respect.   So great was the power she exer-
cised over me, that whenever I was in her presence I
could be nothing but what she would have me be:

that in the presence of the calm, pure, radiant angel of my love I blushed for my passion as for an unholy feeling, an insanity.

So much the more was my heart torn and distracted. With the appearance of autumn I gave up hope, and thought only of escaping from more intense suffering by flight. The peace of my life was destroyed.

I announced that the pressing invitations of my relatives summoned me to my paternal estate; and I prepared everything for my departure.

All bemoaned losing me, and Annette the same as the rest. They wished to make me promise that I would return again for some months to Cransac, at latest with the coming spring: but, in this, Annette did not join with the others. I was in doubt whether perhaps she loved me, or whether indeed she wished to be rid of me.

One morning I was walking with her and Fanny in Orny's garden. I stopped before a rose-bush, and said jestingly to her: "When I left Cransac the first time, you gave me a rose to take away with me. This time I shall not be able to receive one. The queen of flowers is gone. She has only left, like every joy when faded, the thorn behind."

Annette blushed and looked down embarrassed: but she quickly recovered herself, and answered with her own peculiarly winning smile: "It is my sister's turn this time." Fanny was on the point of replying, when a little girl coming up, interrupted her, and called her away. Annette seemed as though inclined to follow her sister. But the latter went away quickly, saying: "I will be with you again in a moment. Meanwhile come to an amicable decision on this knotty point."

"Then I am to leave this time without any remembrance from you?" said I.

"Do you need one?" returned she.

"Not to remind me of you. Alas! everything will remind me that I am far from Annette. Yet this something from your own hand would render you in some slight degree less absent. There might perhaps lie in it some little consolation for me."

She smiled with a sly glance at me, and said "Yet Annette who gave you the rose was not so present with you in Spain as Fanny who gave you nothing. Therefore I wish to exchange with Fanny You see I am selfish."

"And at the same time rather unjust, and very cruel. You know it, you feel it, and yet you can be so. So that I wish now that I had never come back to Cransac; for it has made me unhappy, and perhaps for ever. Therefore I never will visit Cransac any more."

"You frighten me, dear Colonel. Why do you blame me?"

"Because you drive me from the place which is to me the dearest spot on earth."

"Heavens! what are you dreaming of? I drive you! Heaven forbid! The whole family are lamenting, and I no less than the others, that you are obliged to go."

"Whilst it depends on yourself alone whether I shall stay. Not for Fanny, not for all your family, but for you alone, will I and can I remain. One sign from you decides it. You know that I live for you alone, love you alone. The world has in it nothing so dear. Shall I stay?"

Annette cast down her eyes and walked silently by the gap between the clipped beeches.

"Shall I stay?" I asked more earnestly; and I took her hand.

She looked at me with grave dignity, and said; "Colonel, do not deceive yourself or me. What use is there in that? Acknowledge this frankly to yourself. You forgot Annette whilst in Spain, and thought only of Fanny."

"No. I thought of Annette, and did not forget Fanny. Annette's rose has ever been my most sacred treasure, and shall go with me to the grave."

"But, Colonel, when you came back from Spain you took me for Fanny. Be honest with yourself."

"Yes, dear Annette, I did take you for Fanny: but I thought you lovelier than Fanny; more enchaining, more fascinating, than Fanny. I felt joy at the award of the rose that I had given to you four years before, in preference to your sister. Ah! Annette, I worshipped you in Spain not as an earthly being; but as an angel not belonging to this world. Believe me now, and at least pity me that my fate now divides me from you, that I never, never, can be worthy of you."

"Who said that?" asked she, turning her tearful eyes on me.

At this question, which sprang from the very depths of her heart, at these tears, I was filled with rapture. "Oh! Annette, shall I stay?"

"Do you ask again when I have been weak enough to betray my heart to you?" she asked; and she laid her head silently on my breast.

We were still locked in a close embrace when another pair of arms were thrown round us. Fanny had glided up; she flung her arms around us, and kissed first her sister, then me. "I hope, Annette," said she, "that you will not be angry if at last I give your timid swain a sisterly kiss."

Thus by common consent my departure came to nothing. Amid Fanny's merry, affectionate banterings we recovered from our deep emotion. We returned to Herr von Orny. He said, "Now the joy of my life is complete!" An exclamation for which naturally enough Fanny gave him a severe lecture. Whilst they were squabbling, I went away for a moment and flew near by to the possessor of the house mentioned to me by M. Albret as for sale. I had already visited it, and had looked through it several times. I should long ago have come to terms about it with the owner who asked a moderate price, if I had had Annette's decision. He was there, and the purchase was agreed on, and terms put in writing on the spot. Then I came back.

Annette extended her hand to me; and, astonished at my sudden and long-continued disappearance, inquired, "Where have you been?"

"I have with all speed," whispered I, "purchased a pretty house and a garden full of the loveliest roses. From to-day it is yours."

She blushed with joy, and exclaimed, "Only think! he has bought the Dinants' house for us."

We now returned with Orny to the inn in joyous procession. I related my purchase of a house to M. Albret and his wife. M. Albret looked keenly at Annette for a moment. She flew to her father, then to her mother's breast in happiness inexpressible.

From this day I date my days of heaven on earth. Annette is my wife. The inn at Cransac has made the happiness of Orny and myself. It may still make four other people happy.

THE END.

www.ingramcontent.com/pod-product-compliance
Lightning Source LLC
Chambersburg PA
CBHW060529030726
47498CB00004B/1128